I REMEMBER CHRISTINE

I Remember Christine

O S C A R   L E W I S

With a Foreword by Lawrence Clark Powell

University of Nevada Press
Reno & Las Vegas

Vintage West Series Editor
Robert E. Blesse

I Remember Christine by Oscar Lewis was originally published in 1942 by
Alfred A. Knopf, Inc., of New York. It was published simultaneously in
Canada by The Ryerson Press. The present volume reproduces the first
Knopf edition except for the following changes: the front matter has been
modified to reflect the new publisher, and Lawrence Clark Powell has
provided a foreword to the new edition.

The paper used in this book meets the requirements of American National
Standard for Information Services—Permanence of Paper for Printed
Library Materials,
ANSI Z39.48-1984.

Library of Congress Cataloging-in-Publication Data
Lewis, Oscar, 1893–
I remember Christine / Oscar Lewis ; with a foreword by Lawrence
Clark Powell.
   p.   cm. — (A Vintage West reprint) (Vintage West series)
   Reprint. Originally Published: New York : Knopf, 1942.
   ISBN 0-87417-151-2 (alk. paper)
   I. Title.   II. Series.   III. Series: Vintage West series.
   PS3523.E8754I16   1989   88-37037
   813'.52—dc19   CIP

University of Nevada Press, Reno, Nevada 89557 USA
Cover design by Richard Hendel
Printed in the United States of America

Foreword

WHEN my bibliography of thirty-two "best" novels about Southern California, from *Ramona* to *The Loved One*, brought an invitation to make a similar selection for San Francisco, I came up thirty short. That was because the north has never equalled the south in the field of fiction. Whereupon someone—was it Herb Caen?—remarked that it only went to prove that San Francisco is more real than Los Angeles.

More than four decades separated my choices of *Mc-Teague* and *I Remember Christine*, although greater differences than time lay between them. Frank Norris's grim story of the Polk Street dentist is surely the heaviest hand ever laid on that fair city. How different is the feather-light touch of Oscar Lewis, in his blend of Nob Hillites, academics, and ordinary folk, the whole lightly seasoned with satire and irony. The south has never had writers to match those two.

The origins of *McTeague* have been dug into by scholars. No such rough treatment has ever been inflicted on *I Remember Christine*, although we do know something of its origins. Toward the end of the 1930s Oscar Lewis wrote, "I had always thought the '70s and the '80s a particularly colorful period in San Francisco's history and had mapped out a novel to be laid on Nob Hill. As I read of the period, however, I grew fascinated by the careers of the Huntington and Stanford group, and the result was that I decided to try to do their biographies instead. So the Nob Hill story is still in the future."

That sidetracking of the novel led instead to a serial in the *Atlantic* during 1938, titled by the editor "Men Against Mountains." It was expanded next year into the book bearing Lewis's title, *The Big Four*, now regarded as a classic of its genre.

The prime mover in all this was the legendary publisher Alfred A. Knopf. In the beginning, with his keen nose for literature, he had come upon an early magazine story by Oscar Lewis and sensed that some good unwritten books were there. No publisher was ever more right.

Knopf did not warm, however, to the author's suggestion that the first book be the novel he was planning, and so Lewis continued to work on the Nob Hill moguls. The success of *The Big Four* led to a book on the Palace Hotel, *Bonanza Inn*, written in collaboration with Carroll Hall.

By then Oscar Lewis was so saturated with the lore of families and city that the novel needed only his creative imagination and sustained work to see it written.

Knopf's intention was to place this novel, too, as an *Atlantic* serial, but when the magazine wanted a year's delay, he persuaded Lewis that the book should not lose the momentum generated by his earlier success. Accordingly only the first chapter, called "Portrait of a Professor," appeared in the monthly journal.

There was suspicion that the satirical character Casebolt might prove libelous of Berkeley professor Herbert Eugene Bolton, whereas the truth was that Lewis had taken the name from Henry Casebolt, the early San Francisco builder of cable cars and business associate of his architect father.

Yet so worried were the *Atlantic*'s editors and lawyers that they changed the name to Casement!

If someone would like to investigate more deeply into the book's origins, here is evidence in a recent letter from the author: "The story is entirely imaginary," Lewis wrote me, "that is, not based on any actual person or event, though of course any fictional character has to derive in part from persons the author has known or observed. So I suppose it is true that Christine, Casebolt and the others are not completely fictional after all." Let the scholars go to it.

Knopf had no such fears. *I Remember Christine* made its debut in 1942, wearing an elegant Borzoi jacket and binding. The timing was bad for any book to appear, and good timing is essential to a book's fortune. "There is a tide in the affairs of men, which, taken at the flood, leads on to fortune . . ."

Despite a flood tide of reviews, on both coasts and in the *Manchester Guardian* (an English edition was also published), and sales which exhausted the first printings, wartime restrictions on metal, paper, and cloth forced Knopf to let the book go out of print. Alas, no copies were in the bookstores to meet the rising demand.

Thus was Oscar Lewis deprived of a growing audience. Imagine the fate of *The Grapes of Wrath* if it had been published in 1942 instead of 1939! Timing is indeed all.

That sadly aborted success led Knopf three years later to publish Lewis's second novel, although the timing was still bad, and *The Uncertain Journey* suffered even more from the restrictions now in full force. Whereas *Christine* had been manufactured from a stock of prewar materials, this next book was reduced to a drab format.

Although workmanlike, it is light years from its predecessor. Such is literary fate. Only once did everything come together for this writer, when setting, plot, and style were in perfect conjunction. When I queried Lewis about this gulf between the two novels, he replied with characteristic self deprecation: "I suppose it was because I hadn't hit on a theme that called for that first treatment. *The Uncertain Journey* was an attempt to make the commonplace interesting and significant, as so many writers are able to do. It's a very dull book and I hope you won't try to read it; I've tried a number of times and always bog down after a page or two."

The truth is it's not *that* bad! It can at least be read as valuable Bay Area sociology, as well as for a wry look back at Lewis's own journey to success as a freelance writer. When the depression of the 1890s curtailed the practice of Oscar's father, the family was forced to leave San Francisco for a Sonoma County ranch. After country grammar school, the boy went on to Berkeley High School. Remembrance of these moves enrich this novel.

This was Lewis's last move into fiction, except for *The Lost Years*, a charming fantasy of Lincoln's having survived the shooting, to vacation each year in the Mother Lode country, another landscape beloved to Lewis. Again he demonstrated his mastery of historical sources, especially pioneer diaries and memoirs.

Now for a look at this writer's long career and his present eminence as the state's venerable literary arbiter. In high school Oscar learned from his class assignments, and also from a teacher's encouragement, that he had a calling as a writer. This promise he proceeded to fulfill. Graduation in 1913 was followed by a summer session at the University of California, confirming his desire not to be a scholar. A sophisticated head of the English department, Professor Benjamin Lehman, agreed with him. He advised the youth not to return in the fall. He never did.

Instead Lewis rented a Shattuck Avenue office for $10 a month and was off and writing for the rest of his life. Now in his ninety-sixth year and author of the recently published history of the Book Club of California's first seventy-five years, he bids fair to go on doing it! In the beginning it did not take him long to have a small regular income from the sale of stories, scores of them, to boys' magazines. A bibliography of Lewis's lifetime output would run to many pages.

A break came with service overseas during World War I with the Army Ambulance Corps, followed by an idyllic time in a writer's paradise at Hyères on the French Riviera. Those two experiences were all it took to cure him of Continental fever.

Ten years passed before Lewis married, moved from his mother's home in Berkeley, and returned to stay for good in his natal city of San Francisco. There he settled in for twenty-five years as secretary of the flourishing Book Club of California, in charge of its publishing program, and also contributing to many volumes of Western Americana. He was now writing for more prestigious and profitable literary markets. The pages of *Smart Set* offered the lucrative opportunity to indulge a flair for stories of satire and irony.

Together with other writers and artists, present and past, Oscar Lewis was part of the bohemian world which made San Francisco a mecca. Nearly everyone, native and foreigner, grows to love this city—a passive feeling that fails to provoke a vital fiction. On the contrary, many dislike and some downright hate L.A., and from such strong emotions have come the novels of Nathanael West, Aldous Huxley, and Raymond Chandler.

I am glad to be able to report that I did not overlook Oscar Lewis and *Christine* in my years of writing for *Westways*, the Southern California monthly, although its editorial policy excluded reviews of novels. In 1947 I wrote, "Oscar Lewis's name on a book is assurance of good reading"; and two years later, in a review of his *Sea Routes to the Gold Fields*, this: "Readers of his subtle *I Remember Christine* will recognize the novelist's skill in the way he has sifted the stuff of a hundred diaries for their essential and revealing details."

Then in 1953, in recalling the Zamorano Club's trek north for its biennial meeting with the Roxburghe Club, I told of confessing to Oscar Lewis that no one loves San Francisco in the way an Angeleno does. "Then why don't you move up here for good?" he asked. "Oh no," I replied. "If I did, where would I have to visit?" Whereupon he teased me with a story of two little old ladies from somewhere in Texas who, on their annual pilgrimage to San Francisco via the Sunset Limited and a change to The Lark in Los Angeles, always remained between trains in the waiting room of the Union Station in order not to be unfaithful to their beloved northern city.

I Remember Christine has delighted readers during the nearly half century since it first appeared. In addition to muted irony and satire, there is frank love of life and relish of the parade which passed below the writer's bay window. Today, from his Olympian height, Oscar Lewis can look tolerantly back on the rise and fall of several movements, and on bubbles burst by changing literary fashions.

When I asked him if *Christine* had been hard to write, he did not remember that it had given him any trouble. "As I recall," he wrote me, "I had no fixed plan when I started. I let it develop as it went along, following whatever paths seemed attractive at the time. The result is that the book as it stands is no model of how a book should be constructed. That was recognized at the Knopf office; AAK sent me a copy of a reader's report that ended, 'I hope Lewis never, never, NEVER tries to write another novel.' Its construction also outraged Gertrude Atherton, whom K. had sent an advance copy. She said something nice about it for publication but pointed out that it was badly planned . . . that the main character, Christine, doesn't appear until page 55 or whatever that page be."

I should add that in *My San Francisco*, subtitled by her "A Wayward Biography," Mrs. Atherton devoted several generous pages to Oscar Lewis.

Alfred Knopf was too smart a publisher to be influenced by a pedantic reader. For teachers of creative writing in workshops and college courses, which have mushroomed in our time, this book is no model to follow. If it be a bad novel—which I do *not* concede—it is also a great book, a distinction not always recognized by those who profess this mysterious art.

In today's perverted literary market, when sexual wrestling matches are called romances, this book's single erotic episode, underwritten with skill and intensity, outweighs many shelves of bestsellers. When I reread *I Remember Christine* for the first time in a long while, how fresh and how good it seemed, seen now with eyes that look less and see more.

As for the heroine, whatever the page of her first appearance, what man could say no to this woman of common sense and serenity who, when in doubt, always says yes and then asks who was ever hanged for trying? She and her supporting cast are breathing composites, men and women of a century ago and also of today and tomorrow. Theirs is the lasting life of those in Restoration drama. That is why this book brings joy to succeeding generations.

Lawrence Clark Powell

I REMEMBER CHRISTINE

Chapter 1

I HAD been away for the week-end. When I got back to town on a Sunday night I found, along with some other mail on my desk, a package bearing the label of the fine old publishing house of Howison & Metcalfe. I guessed at once that Casebolt had sent me a copy of his *Life of James Horton.*

As I unfastened the wrappings I was aware of a considerable curiosity, for I knew that Casebolt had been engaged on this work for the better part of two years and that he had high hopes for it. I stood the book on my desk and looked at it. It was a very handsome volume. It was two inches thick and correspondingly tall and broad. I guessed it would sell for about six dollars a copy, and sell very well, too. Casebolt's books are popular in California.

It was generous of my old friend to make me so substantial a gift, yet I felt no intense gratitude and I was a little annoyed because I could not at once hit on a plausible reason why he had so honored me. Of course I recognized that in casting about for an ulterior motive I might have been doing Casebolt an injustice. He might merely have been feeling in a generous mood and so have yielded to an impulse to do a kindly act for a fellow writer. It was possible, but I doubted it. Casebolt has many excellent qualities; he is as widely admired as any literary man in the state, but acts of generosity to other authors are a bit out of his line. Surely, I told myself, he would hardly do a favor to a writer who cultivated somewhat the same field as he did. That would be expecting too much of human nature.

Casebolt has been writing so voluminously on California history, and so successfully, and over a period of so many years, that he has come to feel a sort of proprietary interest in the whole subject. It is perhaps an exaggeration to say that he regards the publication of a book on California by someone other than himself as a personal affront, but one often gets that impression. Because of his standing in academic circles and his wide popular following, his services as a reviewer are in demand both by the scholarly journals and the literary weeklies. Casebolt has reviewed almost every California book of importance, except his own, that has appeared during the past twenty years. His reviews are always models of impartiality. He goes into the subject in detail and with authority. He weighs the book's good and bad qualities, points out errors of fact and interpretation, and tells what field the author has attempted to cover and why he has failed. After reading one of these comprehensive analyses no one ever feels any desire to look into the book itself. Moreover, although Casebolt invariably finds that the volume under discussion is worthless, his reasons for reaching that conclusion are stated so fairly and with so engaging an air of detachment that no one (except, perhaps, the wretched author) ever thinks of accusing him of bias.

The fact that writers of books on California fail to gain Casebolt's approval is very largely their own fault. He has ideas on the subject and he has never hesitated to express them. I suppose he has delivered " The Winning of the Golden Empire " — the most popular of his lectures — at least five hundred times during the past twenty years. If there is a Chamber of Commerce, or a Rotary or Lions or Kiwanis club from Redding to El Centro that has not heard that spirited talk, it can only be because their managers lacked the enterprise to invite him. I once heard Casebolt lament the fact that his services as a lecturer were so much in demand, and I don't doubt that his constant traveling up and down the state is a drain on even his abundant energy. But when I asked him why, if lecturing was burdensome, he continued to do it, Casebolt confessed that he enjoyed it.

" I've never been an armchair historian," he added, " and I guess I'm too old to begin now. It's not that I don't envy you fellows who can retire to your studies and come out in a few weeks with a new book under your arm. It's just that I can't work that way — I often wish I could. I can't let myself get detached from my subject. I've got to get out where I can see it and touch it, where I can grapple with it at close quarters. You know what I mean, Walter? "

" No," I said.

" I suppose it *is* different with you fiction-writers," he acknowledged. " You don't have to worry about names or dates or the reliability of sources or the hundred other things that give us historians gray hairs. You invent your tales as you go along, and stir in a bit of love interest and a complication or two, and presto! you've got another novel. Another ' gripping romance of Old California '! "

I was well aware of the source of Casebolt's grievance against us fiction-writers who sometimes use California as the locale of our tales. The fact that every now and then one of these novels has a mild popularity and out-sells his own solid historical works doesn't alter his con-viction that all such books are trash. His chief complaint is that their authors haven't a proper knowledge of the periods of which they presume to write. If, in a review of one of these innocuous romances, he finds a historical error (he usually finds more than one), he drags it out and corrects it, citing chapter and verse to prove his point. But his attitude is more often one of sorrow than of anger; no fair-minded reader ever believes there is any rancor behind his judgments. He leaves one with the feeling that he would gladly have said something nice about the book if only its author had done one thing right and so have given him an opportunity to be gen-erous.

Anyone who has listened to Casebolt's " Golden Em-pire " lecture — and who has not? — will recall that tell-ing phrase of his: " When it comes to history, ladies and gentlemen, I'll take mine straight." That is a good exam-ple of his informal platform manner. He is not afraid to say that something he likes is " swell " (twenty-five years ago he would have said " bully ") or that something he doesn't like is " lousy." That puts his audiences at their ease and, as he says, takes the curse off his academic connection. Than Casebolt there is not in all California a more striking exemplification of the fact that a college professor can be, in another of his phrases, a good egg.

Of course, Casebolt's prestige here on the Coast is not based solely on such grounds. He has been writing industriously for a third of a century and he has produced more than a score of books. Besides that he has held a series of progressively more important jobs at his university, ending with a full professorship and the chairmanship of his department. There are those who think he is in line for even higher honors when old President Van Amberg retires, as he inevitably will soon. Casebolt has been a leading spirit in the Historical Association from its founding, and a director since 1926 of the First National Bank of his home town. And of course everyone recalls his venture into politics a few years ago, when he ran far ahead of his ticket and missed becoming lieutenant governor only because of the Democratic landslide that year.

But Casebolt's reputation is primarily based on his historical writings. Although I feel that his books make heavy going, I must add that this is a personal reaction and that many think otherwise. Besides, my belief that he is a bad writer does not prevent my recognizing that he is an influential one. It is well known that an inability to express oneself lucidly has never prevented a scholar from receiving the homage to which his other talents entitle him. At worst this is looked on as a minor blemish that throws one's other qualities into relief, like a well-placed mole on the cheek of a beauty.

◆◇◆◇◆◇◆◇◆◇◆◇◆◇◆◇◆◇◆

Casebolt's theories are not in the least complicated. I am not over-simplifying when I state that his entire professional career has been devoted to furthering the belief that from the early nineteenth century until about the year 1865 every man who entered California from the east coast underwent a remarkable transformation at the moment he set foot on our soil, and that everyone who came from any other place whatsoever suffered changes equally drastic, but for the worse. The convenience of such a belief is evident. Once Casebolt had established that point in mind he was relieved from the necessity of ever giving it another thought. In his subsequent writings his heroes and villains fell automatically into their proper categories and thereafter they gave him no further trouble. It is a great boon to a member of any of the learned professions to be able to do all one's thinking at the outset of one's career.

It has done a lot for Casebolt. While he was still at college he decided what was to be his life's work. He would teach California history and he would write about California history, and his field should be that period from the coming of the first Yankee until the close of the Civil War. Both his theory and his method are well exemplified in the work that first established his reputation, his two-volume *Conquest of California*, published in 1916. Many thousands of sets have been sold; one sees the stout red volumes on the shelves of every California library that amounts to anything, and I don't doubt that most of their owners have made conscientious attempts to read them. That the *Conquest* is not easy going Casebolt himself candidly admits. " You won't find the nuggets lying on the surface," he tells his students in History B–1, the most popular of his lecture courses. "You've got to dig for them." Six generations of college students have heard that warning — Casebolt never hesitates to make his own books required reading in his courses — and it must be admitted that those who dig industriously enough often feel that they are rewarded.

Those who believe that California was conquered and annexed and settled by a race of idealists who acted on all occasions out of motives of pure benevolence will find in Casebolt's books much to admire. On the other hand, anyone who suspects that the rough shirts of the Yankee trappers and traders and miners did not invariably conceal hearts of pure gold are likely to regard much of Casebolt's writings as pernicious nonsense.

I felt no pressing urge to read his life of Jim Horton.

ii

In the next morning's mail I found a note from Casebolt.

He was, he stated, asking his publisher to send me a copy of his book, and he hoped that I, who had known the Hortons well, would enjoy glancing through it. He added that he didn't know how well he had done the job — the old man had been a devilishly difficult subject — but he had done his best and he knew his friends would look leniently on its shortcomings. Then followed this paragraph, which I read with particular interest:

" I'm not afraid of what the public will think, or the

critics. I'm reasonably sure, too, of the old-timers who knew Horton, and of Horton's daughter, although it's hard to know what the reaction will be in that quarter. It's not important, really, but if you chance to see Aunt Julie, I hope you'll sound her out. I am sending her a copy too. It will be interesting to have her reaction, don't you think? As I recall, she is always ready to state her opinions, and they are always worth listening to. Please give her my warm regards."

I was not deceived by this offhand reference to Aunt Julie. Casebolt is an old hand at writing biography (for years it has been a sort of by-product of his work as a historian) and he must surely have had a wide experience with the granddaughters and nephews and cousins of those of whom he has written. For no one has so large an acquaintance among the descendants of an illustrious figure as the man who has just written his biography. Before his book has been out a month he is likely to have met, either personally or over the telephone or through the mail, positively everyone who has any claim to relationship with his subject. And let no one suppose that these strangers look him up in order to congratulate him on the excellence of his characterization, or to thank him for rescuing a forebear from the obscurity into which his memory has fallen (and so enhancing their own importance), or to commend his discretion in soft-pedaling that deal in C. P. & R. bonds, or for failing to mention the lawsuit filed in 1868 by that Marysville waitress. Not at all. They seek him out so they can set him right on any errors that may have slipped into his narrative, and to chide him for his blindness for failing to get in touch with them before he committed his half-baked notions to print.

But these matters never bother Casebolt. He really enjoys such visitors and he knows exactly how to handle them. When some tottering grandson of a pioneer looks him up, Casebolt is seldom at a loss to know how to smooth his ruffled feelings. If the caller charges that Casebolt has erred in a date or omitted a middle initial, he acknowledges the fault with manly frankness, gratefully thanks his caller for setting him right, and promises to correct the slip in the next printing.

The visitor usually ends by staying to lunch. Afterwards they walk across the campus together and Casebolt drops in at the office of the college daily and introduces his new friend all around. The result is often an entertaining story in the next morning's issue, in which Casebolt's book is praised for its accuracy and general excellence by a descendant of the man about whom it was written. Casebolt keeps on the best of terms with the staff of the college paper. When he has a chance to throw a story that way he is delighted to do it. But he makes it clear that his only aim is to help the boys get out a lively sheet. If, as often happens, the San Francisco papers pick up and elaborate such stories, Casebolt is annoyed, but in a perfectly good-natured way. " It's all right to print such trifles in the *Maroon*," he says, " where it's all in the family. But when the outside papers get hold of them, that's another matter. You never know where the thing will end. You may recall the time the *Maroon* quoted from my lecture on the Vigilance Committee of '56 — the part where I drew a rough parallel between conditions then and now — the city papers got my remarks rather badly garbled. What's worse, the news services sent the story all over the country. I got clippings from the most surprising places. The newspapers have got me in a lot of hot water."

" Why don't you forbid the *Maroon* to quote you? " I asked.

" Well, since that Vigilance business I make them submit their stories to me before they print them. But one can't shut down on them entirely. It wouldn't be fair to the boys. Many of them are campus correspondents for the state papers and they work on space rates. It's their livelihood."

" Besides," I pointed out, " when they graduate, some of them get jobs on papers up and down the Coast."

Casebolt nodded. " You'd be surprised to know how many of our old *Maroon* boys are working on the state press. Many of them have quite responsible positions. I've kept in touch with most of them. It never hurts a writer to have some friends in the newspaper game."

" Or a politician? " I suggested.

" I suppose you're referring to that lieutenant-governor business," he laughed. " As a matter of fact, the newspaper boys were most helpful. At least they saved me from disgracing myself completely."

" Well," I said, " keep your fences in repair. You never know."

Casebolt shook his head. " No, Walter, I've learned my lesson. I'm a historian, not a politician. When it comes to practical politics I'm a babe in arms."

iii

That Casebolt was anxious to know what Aunt Julie might think of his biography of her father did not surprise me.

It is hard to explain the position Juliet Horton occupies in San Francisco. Rightly or not, our town has acquired over the years a reputation for tolerance. It is said than anyone who refrains from making a nuisance of himself may be, or say, or do, very much what he pleases. For a long time now it has been the custom to cite the case of Aunt Julie as the most conspicuous example of our collective broad-mindedness. I think there has not been in the past forty years any worth-while movement for civic betterment launched locally that Aunt Julie has not fought tooth and nail. She has a sharp tongue, an unstable temper, and a pretty talent for vituperation. The one sure way to get in her good graces is to scold her for being a hard and selfish old woman with no more sense of her duty toward society than a Digger Indian. She boasts that she has led a thoroughly frivolous life and that she has enjoyed every minute of it. She claims to be eighty, but that is a mild exaggeration. I happen to know that she was born in 1863. She is worth about four million dollars.

Because she is a very wealthy woman and because her manners are so bad, San Franciscans have long esteemed it a privilege to know her. Since the death of her brother Clifford in 1932 she has been James Horton's only surviving child. Aunt Julie, too, will inevitably die some day, but I don't think it will be soon. She takes excellent care of herself and, except for a slight limp, she is as active as she was two decades ago.

The manner in which she acquired a limp is illuminating. Several years ago she entertained an old friend at tea. The friend brought her daughter-in-law, and the daughter-in-law brought her dog. The dog, according to Aunt Julie's version, was a decrepit and bad-tempered beast that curled up on a rug and alternately snored and yawned during the entire visit. Aunt Julie took a dislike to it. When her callers were leaving the dog got up and Aunt Julie, out of the corner of her eye, saw him lift a hind leg against one of her Victorian sofas. She accompanied her guests to the door of her upstairs sitting-room.

" Your dog has left a memento of his visit and I think I should return the compliment," she said. Thereupon she drew back an ancient leg and gave the animal a resounding kick in the rump. The blow did far more damage to Aunt Julie than to the dog. She had forgotten she was wearing bedroom slippers. Several bones in her foot were fractured and she was on crutches for three months.

No one is fooled by Aunt Julie's pretense that she is a shallow woman without a serious thought in her head. She has a keen eye for business and she has always managed her property with shrewdness. I am sorry to say that her reputation for business ethics is not good; some of her transactions have been definitely on the shady side. Indeed, there was one period of several months when her friends thought it likely that she would be committed to the old Ingleside jail for bribing a city official.

That story is worth recalling. When James Horton died, his estate was divided, share and share alike, between Clifford and Juliet. It included, as everyone knows, large holdings in San Francisco real estate. One of the parcels was a block of land in North Beach, on the western slope of Telegraph Hill, in what was then, and still is, the poorer Italian section. After the 1906 fire there was a shortage of cheap living-quarters in town, and during the next two years James Horton rebuilt his North Beach block, and some others elsewhere in town, with three-story flats. San Francisco has long enjoyed the distinction of having the worst domestic architecture on the continent, and Horton's flats helped maintain its pre-eminence in that respect. They were narrow frame structures, cheap and barren, built in long, identical rows, with many small rooms and not a great deal of light or air. Casebolt makes a passing reference to them in his biography, in the chapter dealing with Horton's part in the rebuilding of the city.

In the distribution of the estate this block was divided down the middle and each heir took half. Clifford, whose sense of *noblesse oblige* was already well developed, went around a few days after the funeral and looked over the flats. He was shocked at the smells and squalor, the rickety stairs and halls and the crowded, airless rooms. He hurried home and told his sister that the property must be cleaned up at once. Juliet refused to listen. She too had been to see the place and she professed to find nothing wrong. The truth was that she did not want to spend the considerable sum it would cost to remodel her slum, but she chose to put her objection on a higher

ground. The flats, she insisted, were quaint and picturesque. They had a charm all their own. To be sure, they
were dirty, but so were the people who lived in them.
These Italians throve on squalor. It was their normal environment. They were happy there, playing their accor-
dions and breeding children and making wine each fall
on the sidewalks. Why disturb them?

The sanitary arrangements had especially offended
Clifford's sense of what was fitting. For reasons of economy the elder Horton had placed the toilet of each flat
in a little shed on the back porch. One who stood in the
court below could, by looking to the left and right, see
perhaps a hundred of these identical sheds ranged verti-
cally in groups of three. Clifford insisted that in all decency they should be moved inside and put in the bathrooms he planned to install. Aunt Julie was unconvinced.
"Your tenants will move," she warned him. "I know
the Italian temperament. They're a gregarious race and
they get sullen and depressed when they're alone. They
don't like being cooped up in bathrooms. I know what
I'm talking about."

What had happened is that Aunt Julie had visited
North Beach one evening during the sociable post-dinner
hour. What she had seen and heard had delighted her.
The rear court was filled with a din of voices as news and
gossip were relayed from neighbor to neighbor. There
were shouts of laughter and occasional bursts of song.
No one was visible. It was some minutes before Aunt
Julie discovered that the voices were coming from the
open doors of the toilets. Could anything be more de-
lightfully naïve? Clifford was impossibly prim.

Aunt Julie did nothing to her property and for fifteen years it earned a satisfactory sum each month. Clifford thoroughly modernized his half of the block. A conscientious landlord, he kept the flats in excellent repair as long as he lived. His net loss amounted to perhaps five hundred dollars a month, which he could well afford, and he had the satisfaction of knowing that no tenants of his lacked the conveniences and privacy he considered essential to the development of good Americans. He must have been secretly pleased — although he was also pained — when the city finally condemned Aunt Julie's property as a menace to the public health. The old lady was, of course, outraged. Many will recall the fight she put up to prevent the order being put into effect. It was as a result of that lawsuit, which she lost, that the county grand jury indicted her on the charge that she had bribed an inspector of the health department. Aunt Julie was unbowed. " Let them throw me into jail," she cried. " The city can afford to support me for a few months. At least I'd get some return from the thieving taxes I've had to pay all these years."

The charges were eventually dismissed and Aunt Julie — to her regret, I've always thought — escaped incarceration in the county jail.

iv

I have always had a high regard for that reprehensible old lady. On the other hand I have never felt any really warm enthusiasm for her brother Cliff, who was unlike her in all ways. I am not alone in this, and it is hard to explain why. When Cliff Horton died, everyone of importance in the city attended his funeral. The officiating clergyman stated that by his death San Francisco had lost its most valuable and generous and public-spirited citizen, and no fair-minded person in the crowded church could possibly have objected. Yet on looking about I failed to see on any of the hundreds of solemn faces an expression that could be said to reflect genuine regret. Who can explain why it is that when we part from the good and the just we are able to keep our emotions under such admirable control, whereas tear-filled eyes and the grief-stricken blowing of noses form an invariable accompaniment to the funerals of scoundrels?

Cliff Horton died about midway in his fifty-ninth year, at half past two o'clock on a Monday afternoon. His passing was unexpected, for he had been in the best of health — the Hortons are a long-lived family — and there was reason to hope that San Francisco would continue to have the benefit of his sound advice and open purse for at least another decade. The cause was acute indigestion brought on, it was said, by over-indulgence in California shrimps, a delicacy for which he had long had a weakness. Some professed to see a note of irony in the fact that the career of this great benefactor of our city had been prematurely terminated by a food so typically San Franciscan as a plate of shrimp Louis. Next day both our morning papers had his picture on their front pages and each devoted a column to an outline of his life and good deeds.

The list of his benefactions was a long one: the James Horton Scholarship Fund for Research in San Francisco

History (administered by his friend Dr. Casebolt); the admirably equipped playground, Horton Field, in the Potrero; the Music Bowl in Golden Gate Park, one of the most charming open-air theaters in the country, attractively placed on a wooded, but chilly, hillside near Stow Lake; the North Beach Boys' Club; the Horton Lecture Fellowship in Sociology at the state university; the Americanization Center in the alley off Grant Avenue (where the elder Horton once owned some highly profitable houses of prostitution); the Clifford Horton Endowment for the Advancement of Industrial Peace; and many others. This was in addition to his membership on the board of practically every charitable and cultural and civic organization in the city. Clifford's life had been one board meeting after another.

A citizen with a finger in so many pies was naturally not permitted to have a perfunctory funeral. His body lay in state all one day in the City Hall — an honor usually reserved for defunct politicians — while thousands filed past his bier. In San Francisco there has always been a numerous group who can be depended on to show up at any public function, provided only that it has been prominently mentioned in the newspapers and that admission is free. Both these conditions of course prevailed at Cliff's funeral, and the turn-out was remarkable. He would have been gratified had he been permitted to know that so many had personally paid their respects to his memory, but he would also have been ill at ease. He was by nature an austere man with a distaste for display. He detested crowds and he appeared at public gatherings only when his admirable social sense informed him that he could not properly remain away. He was never at his ease among strangers, particularly among those of the lower orders. His manner then was likely to be so reserved that in some quarters he gained a reputation as a purse-proud snob. This caused him a great deal of regret; he would have liked to be popular in the hearty, back-slapping manner of his friend Casebolt. Besides, he had a real interest in the problems of those less fortunate than himself and a genuine desire to improve their lot. But he preferred to deal with them at second hand. Like many another philanthropist he loved the common man as a type and heartily disliked him as an individual. When some recipient of his generosity waylaid him on the street or in the corridor outside his office, Clifford could never quite conceal his distaste for the fellow. He always broke away at the earliest possible moment. Gratitude is one of the most admirable of human virtues and by no means the commonest, and the sentiment is not less beautiful when it is expressed in a breath that smells of garlic and stale wine, by a man whose shirt has been too long away from the tub and whose affably extended hand needs scrubbing. Clifford realized all that. But he was naturally fastidious, and personal untidiness revolted him. He often wished that the deserving were more sanitary.

His will contained a diplomatically worded paragraph concerning Aunt Julie. It stated that through the liberality of their father she already had an income ample for her needs during the remainder of her life. His executors were instructed to permit her to select from his personal belongings any article of furniture, piece of jewelry or *objet d'art* she might wish as a token of brotherly affection. Aunt Julie, who had hoped for half a million, swallowed her disappointment and, with no hesitation, chose as her memento Clifford's beautiful little Titian Madonna, the only really valuable painting in his mediocre collection.

The long document contained this clause:

" Because I have long felt that the present pre-eminent position of my beloved city is mainly due to the courage and enterprise of her pioneer citizens, and in order that San Franciscans of this and succeeding generations may have placed before them the inspiration to be found in the career of one of the first of the pioneers, I bequeath the sum of Ten Thousand Dollars for the purpose of having prepared and written and published a suitable life of my father, James Horton, and I direct that the disbursal of this sum be under the exclusive supervision of my friend Dr. Henry Custer Casebolt."

V

When the will was published Casebolt granted an interview, in which he spoke of Clifford's bequest with a good deal of enthusiasm. No city, he stated, has a more inspiring past than San Francisco, and among those who had forged the metropolis none was more worthy of remembrance than James Horton. His story was one that well deserved to be told. By directing that his father's life be written, and by providing so liberally for the work, Clifford had performed not the least notable of his services to the city. Casebolt made it clear that he would undertake with pleasure the responsibility of seeing that the fund was wisely expended. When he was asked to whom he intended to entrust the writing of the life, he replied that he was keeping an open mind on the point. There were many men and women in California well qualified for the work. It was his aim, however, to find exactly the right person, and that might take time. There would be no hasty decision.

As a matter of fact, it took Casebolt almost three years to make up his mind. Meantime he was subjected to a great deal of annoyance. California contains an uncommonly large number of men and women who aspire to literature, and it was not long before the ambition to write a biography of James Horton was burning in the breasts of practically all of them. Their demands proved a strain even on Casebolt's good nature, but it must be said that he behaved admirably.

When we chanced to meet one day at the house of a friend (who always invites a few authors to her cocktail parties in the erroneous belief that they tend to brighten the conversation), Casebolt told me that he was still interviewing applicants.

" I see them all, and I answer all their letters," he said. " It's a lot of work, but I want to be fair. Most of these people have no qualification for the job and I have to tell them so, but I hope I do it kindly. Few of them have any real interest in Horton. They're thinking mainly of the money."

I looked sympathetic.

"I try not to be cynical. I tell myself there's always a chance that someone with exactly the right equipment and viewpoint will show up."

Casebolt fixed me with a solemn gaze. "You know, Walter, I'm awfully keen on this matter. I simply can't permit myself to make a mistake."

My friend's expression of noble determination was a little more than I could stomach. "Nonsense," I protested. "Horton wasn't Napoleon. There must be dozens of fellows who can do a decent life of him."

"I'm sure you're right. Some first-rate biographical writing is being done on the Coast these days. But my problem's to find the right man."

"You might have a raffle."

"I've been trying to follow a somewhat more — ah — scientific method. There are many factors to be considered. It wouldn't be wise to choose a man solely on the basis of his technical competence, although that's important, naturally. But his viewpoint's important, too; his attitude toward Horton and his period. As I see it, no man can write convincingly about the old man unless he has a sympathetic understanding of his environment. Jim Horton was a very complex individual. Most of his contemporaries completely misjudged him."

"So far as my observation goes," I said, "most of his contemporaries thought he was a son of a bitch."

"He wasn't popular in many quarters," Casebolt admitted, "and it was his own fault. He cared little for public opinion. His methods were direct. He was no diplomat. But he got things done. You'll have to grant that he helped immensely to build up the city. I want a man who not only recognizes that but who will give it the importance it deserves."

" I take it you're not looking for a muckraker."

" Certainly not. On the other hand we shouldn't try to whitewash the old man. We must strike a balance. I want someone who'll put the emphasis where it belongs: on Horton's really great services to the city and state. To do that properly, some of the less attractive phases of his character will have to be minimized, certain imperfections overlooked."

" For ten thousand dollars," I observed, " a writer will overlook a great many imperfections."

" That will occur to many people. I've foreseen that danger. In a way it's too bad Cliff was so liberal. The fact that so much money is involved only confuses the issue."

" Why don't you have a whirl at it yourself? "

Casebolt looked startled. " What's that you say? "

" Why don't you write the old man's life yourself? "

Casebolt shook his head decisively. " No, Walter, that's out, definitely. I'll admit I've thought about it, but I've put the idea aside. I'm not competent."

" Nonsense. You're just being modest. No one can hold a candle to you in that field. You're the logical man."

Casebolt gave me a pained smile. " That's nice of you, Walter. Of course it's true that I've some familiarity with the period. And I know the way the thing should be slanted, if you understand what I mean. But, damn it all, a man can't appoint himself to a ten-thousand-dollar job. There'd be a terrific row."

" Why worry about that? You're expected to find the most competent man, aren't you? "

" Decidedly."

" Well, who's better qualified than you are? "

There are times when Casebolt overcomes his natural modesty, and this was one of them. " I can't think of anyone," he admitted.

" Then appoint yourself. You can't honestly do anything else."

He looked at me hard. " I can't do it, Walter," he said. " I haven't got the moral courage."

But it presently grew clear that Casebolt's moral courage was stronger than he thought. Not many weeks later the papers announced that the uncertainty as to who would be James Horton's biographer was at an end: Dr. Casebolt himself would do the job. In his statement Casebolt made it clear that he was shouldering the task reluctantly. He was all too conscious of his limitations; to do full justice to the subject required an abler pen than his. But he would do his best and he hoped the public would look charitably on the book's shortcomings.

His statement made an excellent impression. It was straight-from-the-shoulder talk by a man who had faced a difficult problem and had solved it according to the dictates of his conscience. To be sure, a few of the town's writers professed to be disappointed. There was bitterness and some profanity in the sordid dens where the literati forgathered. But their abuse was perfunctory and not ill-natured. Not one of them had seriously believed that Casebolt would let that ten thousand slip through his fingers.

Chapter 2

I STOPPED half-way up the hill and looked at the house where Juliet Horton has lived since she was a girl of ten.

San Franciscans do not need to have that house described to them. Of the wooden mansions of the seventies it is among the few, and surely it is the most pretentious, now standing. It was one of the caprices of the great fire of 1906 that it devoured the surrounding area for blocks around and left unscathed a small group of houses on the crest of Russian Hill. Of recent years tall apartment buildings have changed the contours of the hill and in a measure screened Aunt Julie's house from view, but any citizen past fifty can recall how completely it once dominated that part of the city.

I was interested to see recently, in a magazine devoted to describing the homes of the wealthy, several pages of photographs of Aunt Julie's house. There was also a text, in the first paragraph of which the author stated that the Horton Mansion, as he called it, was one of the finest examples of mid-Victorian architecture in the country. The respect with which he referred to the structure's historical significance and his use of such phrases as "American rococo" and "validity of conception" must have impressed others besides me. The article appeared as recently as 1939, yet at that time most of us still believed that anything mid-Victorian was worth noticing only as further proof of the lamentably bad taste of our grandparents. We had been regarding Aunt Julie's house as an eyesore for so many years that it was a shock to find a reputable magazine devoting several pages to a non-satirical description of its attractions.

It must be said that we were not inclined to argue the point. If the Horton house was something of which we should be proud we were prepared to be proud of it. Within a few days after the magazine appeared there was a marked increase of traffic on Aunt Julie's street. Almost any afternoon it was possible to see a number of cars parked on the level spot at the top of the hill while their occupants regarded the structure across the street. Those who looked long enough at its bulges and depressions, its bay windows and porches and pillars, its high central tower rising above the mass of lesser towers and peaks and dormers of its extraordinary roof, grew convinced that this might well be a work of importance. Its designer had clearly been a man of no ordinary imagination; it seemed reasonable to conclude, therefore, that he may have been a genius. This theory gained weight each time one looked at the place. It was not long before Aunt Julie's ugly duckling had become one of our local swans. When the Chamber of Commerce presently issued a new booklet descriptive of our scenic charms, we were glad to see that a photograph of the building (caption: "Historic Horton Mansion, Russian Hill") had been included, along with views of the Ferry Building, Seal Rocks, Coit Tower, and the bay bridges.

Aunt Julie regarded these developments with sardonic pleasure. For nearly thirty years her friends have been pointing out to her the absurdity of an elderly maiden lady of unsocial tastes continuing to live in a house that contains thirty-four large rooms. When, soon after their father died, Clifford fitted up his charming flat on Powell Street, just off California, he tried to persuade her to take the floor below, which was identical to his in floor-plan and had a view equally fine. She refused to budge. These modern flats, she said, were well enough for those who liked them, but personally she needed space enough to swing a cat; she saw no reason why she shouldn't stay where she was. As a matter of fact, she gets along very well. She has an odd assortment of servants: a Japanese butler, a Chinese cook, a Swedish maid, an Italian gardener, and an Irish chauffeur. She rules them with an iron hand, yet they are all devoted to her; they pamper her outrageously and run the place perfectly; her infrequent dinners are something to remember. She does exactly as she pleases. When she feels like dining out she calls up her friends and tells them when to expect her. When she wants to stay home she demands that they come to see her. (I was even then responding to one of her peremptory summonses.) When she wants to be alone her Russian Hill refuge is as impenetrable as a fortress.

Although she seldom spends a dollar on her income-producing property, Aunt Julie keeps her fantastic residence in excellent repair. The steep garden is beautifully tended. The lawn is like velvet, the gnarled magnolia trees have the best of professional attention, rose bushes are staked against damage by the afternoon winds that whip about the hill, and the old-fashioned paths of black and white marble are scrubbed daily. Even the conservatory (see the *Home Magnificent*, October 1939, page 26), which juts out from the sunny southeast corner — it is shaped like a mosque, with red and blue panes, etched with fleurs-de-lis, set into its roof — is kept in a state of dank perfection. Regularly on the first of each June a dozen painters appear on the hill, ladders and scaffolds are put up, and the entire exterior receives two coats of brilliant red paint. There was a time when we regarded Aunt Julie's annual painting of her house in so conspicuous a color as another of her nose-thumbing gestures at public opinion. We felt that she might in all decency have allowed the place to weather to a neutral shade that would blend with its surroundings and so soften its horrid outlines. Instead she kept it a glistening red so that it stands out on the hill like an inflamed thumb and affronts the eye for miles around. But when mid-Victorian architecture presently ceased being monstrous and became quaint and picturesque, many of us had to eat our words. Aunt Julie had not been being nasty all these years; she had been preserving a work of art.

It may have been because they wanted to make amends for having misjudged her motives that the ladies of an important civic club recently passed a resolution of thanks to Aunt Julie for having " preserved for posterity an integral part of our city's heritage." A copy of the resolution was sent her and she responded by inviting the members to hold their next meeting in the house itself. Forty ladies sat down to luncheon in the big dining-room. They admired the famous paneling of redwood burl, the paintings of fishes and fruit and wildfowl on the walls, and furtively examined the Horton silver and crystal and linen. Later they applauded warmly when their president, Mrs. Stanley Spofford, wife of the Supervisor, rose and expressed her conviction that a house of such historical and artistic importance should eventually be owned by the city and preserved for the benefit of future generations. Aunt Julie took but a perfunctory part in the handclapping that followed. From her standpoint, Mrs. Spofford had made two mistakes of judgment: she had implied that their hostess might not live forever (a proposition Aunt Julie was unwilling to grant), and she had hinted that it would be a good idea if she would give the property to the city after her death.

From long experience Aunt Julie has learned to recognize the roundabout methods of those who hope to plant the seeds of philanthropy in her head. She makes it her business to nip such nonsense in the bud. When it came time to say a few words, she thanked her guests and stated that she was glad to give them this last opportunity to see her preposterous old house. It was a last opportunity because the place was soon to be torn down. The house, she added, was too big for her simple needs and its upkeep was more than she felt she could afford. The hill had become an apartment-house district; it was bad business to continue to use so valuable a site for a private residence. She had instructed her architect to prepare designs for an apartment building; his plans were complete and the work of clearing the site would begin soon. Aunt Julie added that she had lived so long on the hill and that it held so many pleasant memories for her that she dreaded the day when the wrecking crew would arrive. But the world moved onward and one must keep up with the parade. She added sagely: " I've never been one to stand in the way of progress."

The meeting broke up on a note of pleasant melancholy. Aunt Julie took her guests on a tour of the grounds and watched them depart, a courageous smile on her face. At the moment she must have believed that every word she had uttered was true. Not until weeks later did it grow clear to the ladies that her announced intention of tearing down her house was sheer invention. Aunt Julie had made it up as she went along. She told me about it later, a reminiscent chuckle in her ancient throat. " Serves 'em right," she snapped. " Pack of meddling busybodies. Give my house to the city? I'll put a match to it first."

ii

We had not met for several weeks and, as she usually did under such circumstances, Aunt Julie began by remarking that my color was bad and that I had reached an age when a total physical breakdown need surprise no one. Although she esteems herself proof against the ravages of time, she is far from believing that her friends enjoy a like immunity. When she greets acquaintances — most of whom are getting on in years — she looks them over with an eye alert for evidence of approaching collapse, and she is usually able to point out signs that the inevitable is close at hand. This puts the more susceptible of her friends in a morbid frame of mind and permits Aunt Julie to take command of the situation and to advise them cheerfully on how best to spend what few remaining days may be granted them.

But that was an old story to me and I was not disturbed. I told her I had never felt better in my life.

She gave me a sympathetic glance. " I admire your spirit, Walter," she said. " A stiff upper lip is half the battle. Are you sure you're getting enough exercise? But of course you must also be careful not to overdo. I do hope you didn't walk up the hill. I'm always having to warn my friends against that. Bad for the heart."

" I'm sixty-three and I feel thirty. My doctor's amazed every time he sees me. You should hear him brag about my heart."

" Maybe your appearance deceived me," Aunt Julie granted. " I've heard that perfectly well people sometimes have that ghastly, drawn look. Just the same, I hope you'll be careful. If there's one age that's more dangerous than any other, it's the late sixties."

I pointed out that sixty-three was not the late sixties.

" I'm not trying to alarm you, Walter. If you get safely through the sixties there's no reason why you can't feel safe for another few years."

" Thank you, Aunt Julie," I said. " You've taken a load off my mind. Aren't you going to offer me a drink? "

" Hedrig is bringing one now. I'm having a glass of

sherry to keep you company. Sit down and tell me all the scandals."

It must be said for Aunt Julie that she is never inclined to labor a point. Once she has convinced a caller that he has one foot in the grave, she washes her hands of the subject and passes on to more interesting matters.

She had received me, as usual, in her upstairs sitting-room, a spacious but cluttered chamber that overlooks Alcatraz Island and the Contra Costa hills. Its walls are loaded with ornate gold frames containing paintings by late nineteenth-century artists of no importance whatever. The carpet has an all-over design of red and yellow roses on a green background, and a number of small Oriental rugs are placed at strategic points where the wear is likely to be heavy: opposite the door to the hall, before the fireplace, in front of the horsehair sofa that faces the semicircular bay window in the northeast corner. In an alcove to the right, which one enters through an arch screened by a portiere of glass beads, stands the walnut desk before which Aunt Julie spends several hours each morning at the congenial task of administering and increasing her fortune. The desk is a model of tidiness. Neat stacks of papers are on her right and left, her pen rests on the antlers of her deer's-head inkwell, and the telephone and her little black book of interest tables are close at hand. She keeps her checkbook in a drawer of a small table on the opposite side of the alcove, which she cannot reach without getting up from her desk. Aunt Julie is a practical psychologist of sorts.

There was an oak log in the grate. She had been sitting before it, toasting her venerable shins and reading the afternoon paper. Her still abundant hair was gathered loosely about her head, and her small blue eyes looked out with shrewdness from beneath heavy brows. The newspaper, carelessly folded, lay on the table beside her rocking-chair. On the table, too, were a reading-lamp, containing a very bright light, a pack of the cheap Russian-type cigarettes she has smoked for many years, and an ashtray loaded with butts. Although there were two vertical red marks on the bridge of her nose, her spectacles were nowhere in sight. Before the world Aunt Julie maintains the fiction that her eyes are as good as when she was twenty. She wore a black silk kimono.

Hedrig appeared and made room for her tray on the table. The tray contained Aunt Julie's glass of sherry, a bucket of ice-cubes, a syphon, and a bottle of Scotch. The maid handed Aunt Julie her wine, emptied the ashtray, and went out. I helped myself to a drink and sat back, tinkling the ice in the glass while it cooled, and said nothing.

Aunt Julie sipped her sherry and looked into the fire. " Maybe it's a sign that I'm in my dotage," she presently remarked, " but lately I've been thinking a good deal about the past. I find myself remembering all sorts of nonsense that happened when I was a child. Do you do that? "

" Now and then," I admitted. " But I don't encourage it. I've never found reminiscing a very rewarding occupation."

" I suppose not," said Aunt Julie. " But then, you've got less to remember. Can you recall anything at all about the old town? I mean a long time back."

I considered. " That depends on what you mean by a long time. I was born in 1877. My memory's fair. I can recall plenty."

" What, for instance? "

" Well, I remember the day Judge Terry was shot. That was about '89. And the Durrant case — which was later, of course — and the trial of Dr. Bowers, and — " I paused.

" Your memories seem to run to murders," she commented. " I didn't realize you had a bloodthirsty streak in you. What else? "

" Quite a few things. Woodward's Gardens. The Midwinter Fair, especially the Ferris wheel. The steam dummy that used to run to the Cliff House, and the Bird Man out in front of the baths. Billy Emerson. Some of the Mechanics' Institute Fairs. The Washington Street Grammar School. Chinese New Year. White Hat Mc-Carthy. The murder stories in the old *Morning Call*. They always had sketches of the corpse lying in a pool of blood on the parlor floor, and dotted lines showing how the murderer had gained entrance. Ned Greenway. Emperor Norton, of course. I heard Patti sing at the Grand Opera House."

" That would have been the time Mapleson brought her out in '86," Aunt Julie said. " Her voice was gone then. Most of the singers were past their prime when they got out here, and the actors too."

" That's not what the books say," I pointed out. " According to them, San Francisco got the cream of the lot. Everybody knows that no artist felt that he had arrived until we had put our stamp of approval on him."

"Rubbish!" snorted Aunt Julie. "We were always flocking to hear nobodies, and paying far too much for the privilege. Three quarters of the people we went crazy over should have been run out of town, and their managers too. They played us for suckers."

"You won't find many old-timers will agree with you."

"What's that got to do with it?" she snapped. "I'm not in the habit of agreeing with numbskulls."

Aunt Julie lit another Obak. One of the pleasures of her later years has been to poke fun at the belief, now universally held, that the pre-fire town was a charming and romantic place. She holds an exactly opposite view. By her theory, San Francisco from the fifties until the early 1900's was a moral and cultural stink-hole, filled with sights and sounds and smells that affronted the senses, and overrun by a gang of scoundrels whose ignorance was exceeded only by their arrogance.

I have never supported her in that heresy. San Francisco was no better or worse than other American cities of the period. In the several novels I have written about the early town I have tried to keep in mind that people then were very much as they are today. A man who wore a dickey and rode on the horse-cars was surely a no more romantic — or sordid — figure than his grandson who fancies purple sports-shirts and drives a Chevrolet. The result of this sensible point of view is that the books pleased nobody. Citizens used to write me stating that I had libeled the best town in Christendom and the most romantic era in history and that I deserved to have my head punched. On the other hand, Aunt Julie (an industrious novel-reader) told me I was no better than the other old-maid worshippers of the heroic pioneer, and when was I going to get onto myself and stop writing such nonsense?

But on the whole I feel that Aunt Julie's stand deserves to be encouraged. If a lively minority is valuable in politics, it is worth something too in the comparatively unimportant matter of evaluating the past with impartiality and candor. There too we need an alert and vocal opposition. In her small way Aunt Julie does what she can to fill that need.

iii

I finished my drink and refused another. I well knew why I had been asked over that afternoon, but Aunt Julie seemed in no hurry to come to the point. I took the bull by the horns.

" I got a letter from Dr. Casebolt this morning," I said. " He sent you his warm regards."

" If he wants to send me his regards he knows my address," she snapped. " What does he want? "

" He's anxious to know what you think about his new book."

" If he doesn't know what I think of it he's a greater donkey than I thought. I suppose he sent you a copy, too. Did you read it? "

" A bit here and there. It came only yesterday. I've looked at the pictures."

" Well? " said Aunt Julie.

" I think it's a very competent job. It seems temperate and thorough, and the illustrations are excellent. I've no doubt every word's in the best of taste. It certainly won't hurt his reputation."

Aunt Julie's reply was a contemptuous snort. " You know as well as I do that it's a disgraceful performance. It makes me sick every time I look into it, and I've got a strong stomach. And it's supposed to be the life of James Horton! Father was no saint and he never had any idea of being a good citizen, but he wasn't a hypocrite. I never trusted that man Casebolt. Clifford used to bring him around, but I put a stop to it. He's a ghoul. He robs the dead of their honest vices."

" He belongs to the school of biographers who believe a man should be remembered for what he got, not how he got it," I said. " They're careful to preserve a decent reticence about matters that don't look well in print. Many of them make a very good thing out of it."

" If they don't intend to tell the truth, why do they bother writing books in the first place? Reading that nonsense of Casebolt's has got me thinking about the things I can remember. I've lived in this town a long time. If I say it myself, I've had an interesting life and I've known what was going on. It wasn't much like what gets into the books."

" You should write your reminiscences, Aunt Julie."

It has been my observation that few persons are displeased when it is suggested to them that they waste their time in so frivolous a pursuit as writing a book, and fewer still are able to conceal their belief that if they permitted themselves to engage in such folly the result would open people's eyes. It was clear that Aunt Julie was no exception.

" What ever put that idea into your head? " she demanded.

" I'm perfectly serious."

" I can think of more useful ways of occupying my time. But that doesn't mean that I wouldn't be helpful to someone who wanted to write about Father as he really was. I could tell him things."

" I'm sure you could."

" But I wouldn't work with a sentimental fool. He'd have to be a man of sense."

" That narrows the field."

" I might be inclined to take a chance on you, Walter," said she.

I shook my head. " I'm a fiction-writer. Biography's not in my line. Besides, Casebolt has already done the job."

" You've lived here all your life. You should know the town. You must remember Father well; you were at the house often enough when he was alive. You knew Chris Winton. You practically grew up with Clifford, and you've known me fifty years. What else do you want? "

" I don't know the sixties and seventies."

" I do."

" I'd be afraid of you as a collaborator. You've got no reticences. You'd break all the rules."

" Nonsense. I'll send you over some things I've got stored in the garret, letters and such. Things that Casebolt never saw and wouldn't have used if he had. You look them over, then come back and tell me what you think."

" I'll tell you now," I said. " I like living here. I don't want to move."

This whole scheme, I reflected, was typical of Aunt Julie. When it serves her ends she never hesitates to commandeer the time and talents of her friends. I could understand why she wanted such a book written; my knowledge of her history gave me the key to that. She did not want Casebolt's story, with its evasions and suppressions and prettifying to stand as the last word on the Hortons. That was the story as Clifford had wanted it told; it explained Clifford and justified all he had stood for. It didn't explain Aunt Julie. By Casebolt's version she was, in fact, unaccountable, a sort of renegade member of one of San Francisco's most admirable families. But there was more to it than that. Besides a natural desire for self-justification, she has a tough sort of honesty, a genuine respect for the truth. I could see why she wanted the real story told. But I was not going to be badgered into doing the job for her. I wasn't roped in that easily. That was final.

As I walked down the hill the street-lights were coming on. From the high Vallejo Street corner the entire heart of the city was visible: the massed office buildings downtown, their windows glowing; the miles of docks pointing angular fingers into the bay; the squat, steep-sided cone of Telegraph Hill, in the lee of which the squalid village of Yerba Buena had come into being hardly a century before. No, I was not going to fall into Aunt Julie's web. Yet — why deny it? — there was a certain temptation in the picture she had drawn. To try to present a family, and a city (one couldn't write of the

Hortons without telling a great deal about San Francisco), clearly and with honesty; to ignore the tags and labels that had been applied to both by others; to avoid being taken in by the sentimentality and downright violence to the truth that over the years had solidified into tradition — to reconstruct an era as it was, not as it was conventionally believed to have been — there was a job to do, or to try to do.

I shrugged and walked on. Writers are given to such grandiose daydreams; the sensible ones stick to the jobs they know are within their capabilities. No, Aunt Julie's challenge was not for me. I dismissed the matter from my mind.

That evening I took up the *Life of James Horton* and read the first two chapters with close attention. Every now and then I found myself reflecting: " Now, if I had been doing that, I should have treated it thus and so." Presently I took out a pencil and began scribbling notes on the margin.

It was a dangerous procedure and I knew it.

The next morning I called Aunt Julie by telephone and told her I had decided to put down on paper some of my memories of James Horton and his friends.

Chapter 3

BUT I soon discovered that for me to put Horton in a book presented many difficulties.

It is true I had once seen a good deal of him, but that had been during the latter part of his life; of his early and middle years, when he was making his way in the world, I knew nothing at first hand. Yet I realized that if the man himself were to be explained these formative years could not be ignored. I have never had much taste for the dull routine of research, but in this case I did not see how I could avoid it, and I spent the next two weeks assembling such information as I could put my hands on. The result of my labors, such as it is, will be found in this chapter and in the chapter that follows it.

The outlines of Horton's career are set forth in a number of the standard California reference books. He was born near Galesburg, Illinois, on March 20, 1840. He arrived in California in 1854. He married Anita Wilkes five years later. The union was blessed by two children, Juliet, born in 1863, and Clifford Wilkes, eight years later. His wife separated from him in the mid eighties. They were never divorced. She survived him by a number of years, dying as recently as 1923, aged eighty-seven. Horton himself died in 1912.

One of the many illustrations in the *Life of James Horton* is a reproduction of a daguerreotype of Horton and his bride. It shows that at that time (1859) he wore a thick mustache and prominent sideburns that reached well below his ears. These, and his abundant hair, which he parted on the side, gave him a look of dignified ferocity far in advance of his years, which were nineteen. He is standing, not very gracefully, beside his seated bride. One hand rests on the back of her chair and the other clutches a pair of gloves and a high-crowned felt hat, holding them at about the level of his navel. He wears pointed shoes, half buried in a bearskin rug; his long legs are enclosed in baggy broadcloth trousers, and on the lapel of his coat is a white rose. He looks like what he was: a young man of the late fifties standing for his wedding picture.

The naïve, round face of his bride wears an expression of amiability that is hard to reconcile with what is known of her disposition in later years. Making allowance for the state of the photographic art at the time, it is apparent that she was an attractive girl, but not a beauty. Her snub nose and black hair, parted precisely in the middle and gathered in buns over her ears, gave piquancy to a face that was otherwise a bit on the stolid side. She was a big girl. The arm holding the cabbage-like bouquet is strong and muscular, and her hips and breasts have the fullness demanded, and somehow achieved, by all the young women of her time. She weighed about a hundred and

sixty pounds, and she promised to fill out as she grew
older.

In his later years Horton was not given much to reminiscences of his childhood and one is left in doubt as to
his adventures while crossing the plains. Casebolt devotes a chapter to the journey and he manages to make
it seem a heroic enterprise, but it is clear he had little
information that bore directly on the Horton party. It
is true that '54 was late for Indian attacks and that by
then the passage from Salt Lake to the Sierra had been
robbed of most of its dangers, but not of its discomforts.
It was a slow, tedious journey. It was hot and dusty and
uncomfortable. The food lacked variety, the hours on the
road were long, and the scenery monotonous. Theirs was
probably a typical crossing, and that means, if one can
believe the diaries of the men who made it, that it was
something one got over with as quickly as possible. The
impression one gets from reading such narratives is one
of universal boredom. The monotony and discomforts
of the trip got on the nerves of the Argonauts and they
behaved as people who are bored and uncomfortable usually do. Their odysseys contain far more frequent references to petty bickerings than to high adventure. Where
one party fought Indians or thirst, a score fought among
themselves. I have yet to read an overland diary, written
while the pioneer was actually on his way to California,
that gave any indication he considered himself engaged
in a romantic enterprise. Where you find one writing:
" We are the vanguard of civilization," a hundred com-
plain of sand in the cornmeal or confess to an eagerness
to punch some fellow forty-niner in the nose.

But Casebolt belongs to the romantic school of historians, and his pioneers are never less than seven feet high. He imagines young Horton playing a manly part in the adventure, carrying water from the streams at camping time, standing guard at night, and searching the horizon during the long days for signs of savages in ambush. It may be so. It may be that, as Casebolt states, James arrived in California a seasoned young pioneer, aware of his responsibilities and eager to do his part in the building of a new commonwealth. Casebolt puts into his mouth a suppositious monologue, delivered while he stood in a notch in the mountains above Placerville and first beheld the broad acres of the promised land. That speech reveals a command of the language far beyond any Jim Horton exhibited in later life. But Casebolt's pioneers always make speeches when they first catch sight of California, and what they say usually sounds like an excerpt from a political oration.

ii

In the late eighties the California historian Hubert H. Bancroft induced Horton to dictate some recollections of his early days in the state. The document (it is called the *Horton Memoir*) is now in the Bancroft Library in Berkeley. It is really the transcript of an interview. Bancroft sent one of his young men to Horton's office and the young man asked questions and took down the answers in shorthand and later transcribed them, omitting nothing except the profanity. The result has a salty quality that I have always found entertaining. When I have occasion to visit the library I sometimes ask to have the document brought out and I spend a pleasant hour browsing through it.

In the early pages of his *Memoir* Horton has several things to say about his first years on the Coast. I quote them here, not because they throw light on his movements during the period (he is usually hazy on places and dates), but because they reflect a certain directness and candor that was one of his characteristics.

He is here reviving a boyhood memory:

The first real money I ever made, except for odd jobs, was when I went to work in a bakery in one of the mining towns. The bakery was run by a Mrs. Shelbee, a big, rawboned woman from Missouri, with a voice like a man. My job was to cut firewood and carry water and make myself generally useful. Sometimes I spent a whole day peeling apples. My wages were three dollars a week, but I used to help myself to all the cookies I could eat, and sometimes she gave me a pie or a loaf of bread to take home.

She had a friend that was working a claim about three miles up the creek. She had set her cap for him and every day or two she sent me up with a basket of cakes and pies, &c. On the way I had to pass a dozen other claims. The miners would ask what I had in the basket. They knew all about Mrs. Shelbee and her friend. Sometimes I would lift up the flour sack and let them look inside. There was always more than one man could eat, and it got so I would sell off a few cookies or maybe a cake. This kept on until pretty soon there wasn't very much left in the basket by the time I got through. One day Mrs. Shelbee's friend said to me: " Your boss is getting stingy as h—." That set me to thinking and when I got back

I made her a proposition. I said if she would get a bigger basket and fill it with bread, cakes, &c. I would go out among the miners and sell them. She fitted me out with as much as I could carry comfortably and I went up along the north fork and peddled it from claim to claim. It sold like hotcakes. By noon I was back in town with my empty basket. Mrs. Shelbee said, fine, this afternoon you can go out on the Middle Fork. I said all right, but that it was hard work and I wasn't going to continue for three dollars a week. We talked it over and she offered me a 10% commission and no wages. That was agreeable to me. From then on I made two trips a day. I had a bell that I used to ring when I got near the claims and the miners would crowd around. I had the first bakery route in the mines. My commissions ran from $2.50 to $3.00 a day, but that wasn't all. Sometimes I raised my prices a little, which I considered legitimate. It was hard work toting that basket around, and I was frequently doing something extra for the miners, like bringing out their mail or some tobacco. It wasn't long before I was averaging $25.00 a week. I paid $60.00 for a mule and packsaddle and after that I was able to go four miles from town, each way. That went on until the rains flooded the diggings and my customers had to quit for the winter. I ended up with $150.00 cash, besides the mule, and I don't think I was a day more than twelve.

Horton was older than twelve, but the point is unimportant.

A few pages farther along in his *Memoir* Horton makes it clear that he was sometimes less prosperous than he had been during the months he had operated his bakery route. He recalls that soon after they reached California, his father, Samuel Horton, met a man named Francis Diggies. Diggies, who had been in the gold fields since

'49, suggested a partnership and the elder Horton agreed. Samuel put up a half interest in his team and wagon, and Diggies placed his experience as a miner at their joint disposal. The venture was unsuccessful. Horton's comment on his father's partner is a shade ironical. " Diggies knew all about where gold was to be found and how to find it, but he had the worst luck of any man that ever lived. He had come within an ace of making a dozen fortunes, yet he never had a dollar in his pocket. Somebody always euchred him out of his claim, or the water failed at the wrong time, or a flood washed out his dam, or he just got discouraged and quit, whereas if he had sunk the shaft another six inches he would have taken out $22,000.00, which is what the fellow who came along after him did."

The association lasted five months. During that time the Hortons saw most of the camps from Placerville as far south as Mariposa. Diggies was never one to stay long in one place. While Samuel and young Jim worked the claims he had picked out, Diggies went about examining rock formations and studying the slope of the hills and questioning travelers who happened by. Then he would come rushing back and insist that they pull up stakes and hurry somewhere else. Usually it was a long way off.

Horton continues:

One night Diggies had a dream about a tree that had been blown down by a storm. It lay across a canyon and the ground about its roots was sprinkled with nuggets, big ones. The tree was somewhere up Downieville way — he never explained how he knew that. He woke us up and said we should start right away. There wasn't a minute to lose because the nug-

gets were out in the open and anyone who happened along could see them. We would have gone, too, if my mother hadn't put her foot down. By that time she had had enough of Diggies. She gave him to understand that we weren't going on any more wild goose chases. That didn't feeze Diggies. He sold back his half interest in the outfit for $15.00, which was all my father had left, and started off that same night, on foot. That was the last we saw of him. We used to wonder if he ever found his tree. He was crazy as a loon, of course, but no crazier than lots of others. Hundreds of people were running around in those days that would have been locked up if they had been in any business except gold mining. I got my belly full of prospecting that summer. It was years before anybody could interest me in a mining property.

Casebolt states that young Horton was often hungry during that period. I quote a characteristic passage from the Life:

The growing boy lost weight and the healthy color faded from his cheeks. His clothes would have been reduced to rags had it not been for the care of his pioneer mother, whose patient fingers added patch upon patch and so contrived to make both serviceable and neat a costume that in the eyes of a less resourceful woman would have been deemed fit only for the ragbag.

These details are certainly imaginary. But there is no reason to believe they are very wide of the truth.

iii

When his association with his rainbow-chasing partner ended, Samuel gave up his hopes of sudden wealth and began hunting for work. But times were bad and jobs not easily come upon. The first gold excitement was over. The placers were being worked out and quartz mining, which later became important, was just beginning. Samuel was able to pick up only an occasional day or two of work, at low wages. Between times he worked abandoned claims along the creekbeds. Sarah, his wife, and young Jim helped; between them they managed to pan enough gold to keep them from starvation.

After a few months of this, Sarah Horton grew convinced that she had seen enough of the Mother Lode. She decided to go to Stockton; somehow she raised a few dollars to support her and young Jim after they arrived. A friendly teamster permitted them to make the trip in the bed of his empty freight-wagon. Sarah was a Clifford and the Cliffords did not share the Hortons' taciturnity. In her later years she delighted to tell how, with a discouraged husband and a young child, she had waged her revolt against poverty. As a child, Juliet was the loyalest of her grandmother's listeners, a diminutive audience of one who never tired of hearing more. Aunt Julie likes to think that she closely resembles her paternal grandmother, which is an erroneous belief, but harmless. It was from her that I learned the outline of what follows.

Sarah reached Stockton in July of 1855. She carried their joint belongings tied in a bundle, and a borrowed capital of less than five dollars. Her husband remained in the foothills. They were separated by only fifty miles, yet they did not meet again for nearly a year. Stockton was then a haphazard town of about four thousand, the main supply depot for the Southern Mines, and the center too of a farming region that was already spreading over the rich San Joaquin delta.

The freight-wagon deposited them in a corral at the edge of town. Sarah swung the bundle over her shoulder and started down the dusty road toward the business center. The July sun was already hot and the bundle grew heavy. After a time they rested on the steps of a house. The house was one of a row of identical wooden structures that stood, barren and weathered, on the cracked earth, surrounded by dry weeds.

They presently heard the sound of someone wielding a broom inside, then the door opened and a young woman confronted them. She was dressed in a pink wrapper, with pink satin slippers on her stockingless feet. She seemed a figure of extraordinary luxury. She addressed them in a tone of surprised curiosity:

" What the hell are you doing on my porch? "

(I repeat the dialogue as Aunt Julie heard it from her grandmother.)

Sarah got to her feet and shouldered her bundle.

" We was just resting," she stated with dignity. " I didn't think you'd have any objections. Come, Jim."

" Hold on," interposed the stranger. " I wasn't chasing you away. It surprised me to open the door and find you two sitting there like a couple of goddamned hoot-owls on a fence."

She leaned against the door-jamb and swung the broom-handle in a lazy arc.

Sarah didn't mind the casual profanity, but she was beginning to suspect that this young woman might not be virtuous. Her wrapper was silk and elaborately embroidered and it had obviously cost a good deal of money. Sarah could see a handsome figured carpet in the hall and a picture in a gilt frame on the wall.

"Thank you," she said stiffly. "We're rested now. We just arrived in town and I've got to find a place to stay."

The young woman in the doorway regarded her shrewdly. Sarah, who would have preferred to have this stranger think she had arrived grandly by stage, had a suspicion that she knew they had come in on a freight-wagon.

"We just got in this minute," she went on. "I'm a stranger here and I'd be obliged if you'd direct us to a respectable boarding-house, not too expensive." She put a slight but sufficient emphasis on the word "respectable."

The girl leaned her broom against the door and folded her arms within the sleeves of her wrapper. She regarded them with lazy interest.

"You shouldn't be chasing around in this heat, loaded down like a blasted pack-mule."

Sarah eased the bundle from her shoulder and dropped it in the dust.

"My husband's employed in the mines," she lied. "He can't join us for a while." With one hand she smoothed her skirt, rumpled by a night in the wagon.

James, his bare feet covered to the ankles in the hot dust, began to whimper. It was long past time for breakfast. Confronted by this crisis, Sarah dropped her airs and smiled on the stranger.

" I haven't got much money and I've got to get a job right away." The ice broken, she hurried on. " I've thought some of starting a restaurant. I had some boarders up near Murphy's last fall. I was doing well until the floods drove them out of the creek. They was working a placer claim. Ever since then I've had this restaurant idea in the back of my mind. Mr. Handy says I can count on him for a customer. He says he can't get a good meal in Stockton."

" Oh. So you rode down with Ed Handy? "

Sarah nodded, abandoning pretense. " I didn't want to spend the money for the stage. We was very comfortable. Mr. Handy spread some straw in the wagon and we slept all right."

The young woman nodded approvingly. " Now, wasn't that fine of him! I'm going to congratulate him for being such a gentleman. I never saw a teamster yet that didn't have a heart as big as an ox. If he hadn't forgot he might have offered to see that you and the kid got some breakfast. The low-down hyena."

James began crying in earnest. Sarah picked up her bundle again. " We'd better be getting on. Take my hand, Jimmy."

The stranger ignored Sarah and addressed James. " How would you like some rolled oats with cream, and some pancakes and bacon on the side? "

Jim stared at her; his jaw dropped. She stood aside and waved down the hall. " Run on back to the kitchen. Tell the Chinaman I said he was to fix you up."

James was through the door like a whirlwind. " Say thanks to the lady," Sarah shouted after him.

She regarded the other doubtfully, then she shrugged and followed James inside, carrying her bundle.

" I'm Mrs. Horton," she said.

" Mrs. Briggs," replied the other.

They shook hands solemnly.

It was the beginning of a friendship that lasted forty years. Cora Briggs was then embarking on what can only be called a distinguished career. Her rise, in less than two decades, from the little Stockton brothel where she entertained Sarah Horton and Jim at breakfast in 1855 to her luxurious establishment in San Francisco, constituted one of California's most widely known success stories. Moreover, everyone agreed that Cora deserved all the good things that had come to her; even her competitors admitted that she was a credit, as well as an ornament, to the profession. To use the term " disorderly house " when referring to one of her sedate establishments was a ridiculous perversion of the language. From inmates and customers alike she exacted an almost painful degree of decorum; it was far easier to imagine a brawl marring a convention of bishops than one of the circumspect gatherings in her Dupont Street parlor. To be sure, Cora herself retained to the end her deplorable tendency toward profanity, but no such freedom was permitted anyone else in her presence. San Franciscans still recall the visiting colonel during the Spanish War who, in the heat of an argument over the conduct of the Cuban campaign, referred to the general staff as a set of " pusillanimous bastards," and was brought to his senses by the downcast eyes and rosy blushes of every girl in the room. Whole generations of college students repeated a remark she once made in the nineties: " If you young gentlemen can't treat my girls with as much respect as you treat your other teachers, you can get the hell out of here and stay out."

But that was far in the future. Cora was responsible for the fact that Jim's mother was able to establish herself in Stockton. She assumed charge of her affairs, mapping their campaign over the breakfast table. She sent them off to a boarding-house keeper with a note in which she guaranteed their bill. She made inquiries among her customers and succeeded in finding Sarah a place as a cook in the family of an agent for one of the steamship lines that plied between Stockton and San Francisco. Sarah lived in a shack in the rear of her employer's house and Jim was sent to the public school. He had never been inside a classroom before; he had to begin at the beginning. But there were others of his age and size in the primary class and he did not mind. He was a conscientious student. At the end of a year he could read and write as well as the average boy of his age, and could do arithmetic rather better. He had a talent for figures. Before and after school he helped his mother, who presently embarked on her restaurant venture.

She bought, for five hundred dollars, the equipment and goodwill of an establishment called the Valley Grill. She handed over one hundred dollars, her entire capital, as a down payment; Cora Briggs again came to her aid by guaranteeing the balance. The venture was unsuccessful. Sarah could not understand why, for the location was good and her meals were better cooked and not more costly than those of her competitors. Yet, although the sidewalks outside were normally crowded with passers-by, few came inside. It was then that young James again manifested the business sense that distinguished him in later life.

Horton relates the incident in his *Memoir*, and Casebolt has repeated and elaborated the story in his book. I quote Casebolt's version:

For some days his mother had observed that the boy went about his tasks with a thoughtful countenance. This was so unlike his usual boyish frankness that his parent would surely have noticed the change had not the knowledge of her impending failure absorbed her thoughts. She may have observed, too, that for a week or more James had, whenever no pressing task awaited his willing hands, absented himself on mysterious errands that sometimes consumed several hours. If the harassed woman noticed these unexplained absences from duty at a time when her affairs were rapidly approaching a climax, she wisely forbore to chide him for his apparent neglect of their common interests.

One evening as Sarah Horton, after the last customer had departed, sat regarding the disappointingly meager total of the day's receipts, young James spoke:

" Mother," the lad stated, " I believe I have discovered the reason why our enterprise has failed to prosper as well as we had hoped."

[*Casebolt's conversations usually sound a bit stiff, but one always knows what he is driving at.*]

The woman roused herself from her reverie and smiled at her son. " Have you, James? " she asked encouragingly. " Tell Mother."

" For the past week," the boy continued, " I have been standing outside the other restaurants and trying to determine why the public patronizes them. I believe I have discovered the reason. I have noticed that it is chiefly those from out of town who visit restaurants, and that these do so as soon as they arrive. The restaurants on the edge of the business district are, therefore, the ones that get the bulk of the business, especially those on the streets leading to the main out-of-town roads. I think our business would prosper if we could find such a spot. In fact, I have found a location that I believe will be desirable. Won't you come and look at it? "

" Willingly, my son," replied his mother.

As Casebolt tells it, the incident bears a marked resemblance to one of the exploits of Little Rollo. Yet that was probably about the way it happened. Jim Horton had discovered why customers patronized some restaurants in numbers and others hardly at all. I believe the making of such surveys is now a recognized procedure in the retail trades, but it could hardly have been common in Stockton in the middle fifties. It is possible to attach too much importance to the incident, yet it indicates a degree of shrewdness unusual in one of his years. Horton's talent for business manifested itself early.

Sarah did not, however, avail herself of the opportunity to put Jim's deductions to a practical test. Samuel Horton presently came down from the Mother Lode, and the united family moved on to San Francisco.

iv

They reached the metropolis in the fall of 1856.

San Franciscans will not fail to grasp the significance of that date. If Samuel had arrived a few months earlier, and if he had had the good sense to ally himself with William T. Coleman's band of courageous men who were engaged in driving the rascals out of town, Samuel's prestige, and that of his son and grandchildren, would in later years have been far more secure.

The fact that no certificate of membership in the Second Vigilance Committee appears among the illustrations of the *Life of James Horton* must have caused its author real distress. Casebolt has a particular liking for that energetic organization. It would have done his heart good had he been permitted to devote a page or two to a summing up of the Committee's stand for civic decency, and to heap a few more coals of fire upon the heads of the misguided men who held out for law and order. His book, indeed, betrays a slight impatience with Samuel because he failed to reach the city sooner than he did, and no one will blame Casebolt for that. Few things annoy a biographer so much as to find himself saddled with a subject who habitually misses the bus.

As for Samuel, I doubt if his tardiness ever gave him any concern. Not much about him has been preserved, but what is known encourages the belief that he was not one to cry over spilled milk. During her last years his wife Sarah lived with the Hortons. After I had started this random narrative, I asked Aunt Julie to jot down some recollections of her grandmother. From them I quote a passage that bears on Samuel:

Grandma Sarah [writes Aunt Julie in her dashing hand] *used to say that Sam'l was an outdoor man and that he never took to towns. There was an iron foundry near where they lived and Sam'l worked there off and on. But it wasn't steady and he spent most of his time fishing off the end of the docks. He still had the gun he had carried across the plains, and when there was money for powder and shot he went hunting for cottontails. The fish he caught were full of bones and tasted of coal-oil, but these and the rabbits kept them from going hungry. Grandma Sarah said that Sam'l never got the gold fever out of his bones. When the Fraser River excitement began, nothing would do but that he had to go. He made a deal with a foreman at the foundry. The man paid his passage to Victoria and Sam'l agreed to send him half of what he earned. Grandma Sarah saw him off on the boat. She used to say that she knew then she would never set eyes on him again, and she was right. One day a long time afterwards she had me drive her down to Seventh Street so she could see the house where they used to live. It had been torn down and there was a blacksmith shop on the spot. We never did learn for certain what happened to Sam'l. Once we heard a rumor that a man who looked a great deal like Sam'l was living in a little town in Idaho, but he had a wife and children up there, and Father thought it just as well not to go into the matter any further. Grandma Sarah would never admit it, but she suspected that Sam'l had deserted her for somebody else. He always had an eye for the ladies, she used to say.*

When Samuel disappeared into the northern darkness the support of the household fell to young Jim. He proved equal to the responsibility. His operation of the bakery route is proof enough that he had the money-making faculty. The sound of silver clinking in his pocket was the kind of music that, once heard, he was unwilling to forgo. And of course he was not at a loss as to how to proceed when he reached a city where opportunities grew on every lamp-post. Even before his father left, Jim had learned that old iron and lead and copper had a market value; that had long been the basic fact in the economy of small boys all over the nation. He had a cart that he pulled about on foraging expeditions after school and on Saturdays. When it fell to him to pay the bills at the Seventh Street cottage, he merely developed what had been the means of raising an occasional half dollar into a steady source of income. Each morning he set off on tours that took him all over the city: along the waterfront, through the warehouse and wholesale district, in and out of downtown alleys. At nightfall he pulled his loaded cart from one to another of the junk-dealers' yards that then centered about Fourth and Howard streets, and bargained for the sale of his loot.

In his *Memoir* Horton devotes a paragraph to that period. This is what he recalled about his start in the junk business:

I was big for my age and strong as an ox, but it was hard work pulling that cart about. The wheels would sink in the sand or get caught in the cracks in the streets, which were made of planks in those days. Besides, fifty or sixty pounds was about the limit of what it would carry. If I found something that weighed more than that I had to leave it, unless it was something I could break up and tote off in pieces. Whatever

I couldn't handle I hid in the bushes or covered with trash. It got so I had old metal cached all over town. I was waiting until I could buy a horse and wagon. That took me five months and it was a pretty poor turnout even for a junkman. I wasn't satisfied until I could sell it and get a decent outfit.

I am no expert in such matters, but it seems to me that a young man who cruises about a city with his eyes peeled for whatever will make a few cents' profit is on his way to success. Horton's progress was rapid. Within a year he had rented a lot on lower Folsom Street and had filled it with abandoned ships' gear, discarded boilers and machinery, scrap metal of every salable description. San Francisco must then have been a junk-dealers' paradise. Its inhabitants were traditionally improvident; they cheerfully tossed out whatever they could not immediately use. Young Horton prospected the town's alleys and vacant lots as industriously as any miner ever searched a Sierra canyon, and with a better average of success. He sometimes struck a rich pocket. One such (as he states in his *Memoir*) was when he explored the hulk of a Chilean schooner rotting in the mud off Hunters Point and discovered that her bottom was covered with sheet copper. Again, he undertook to clear the site for an industrial plant and learned that the chimneys and foundations of the wrecked cottages were highly salable, there being a shortage of bricks in town at the time. By then he had given up his prospecting trips and was himself bargaining with the itinerant peddlers.

An important turning-point came soon after. I quote again from the *Memoir:*

◆◇◆◇◆◇◆◇◆◇◆◇◆◇◆◇◆◇◆◇◆

I did a lot of business on the waterfront and I made it a point to keep an eye on what was going on there. One day I noticed an English ship that had just come in. She was anchored out in the bay and I could see that the crew was tossing her rock ballast overboard. She was in the grain trade. Not much freight was consigned to the coast from Europe and many of the ships had to come out in ballast. Her name was the Robert A. Wagoner. I got in a boat and rowed out to her and hunted up the captain. I had just sold 6,000 bricks for $32.00 a thousand. I was interested in that kind of a deal.

I said to the captain that I understood they manufactured bricks in England and that I was anxious to know what they were selling for. He said that he couldn't tell me but that he would find out and let me know on his next trip. I said no, that wouldn't do at all, that the next time he came out I wanted the bricks and not the price. I said: Suppose on your next trip you take a cargo of bricks for ballast instead of rock that you have to throw overboard when you get here, what will your rate be? He named a rate; it was low. I said: I tell you what I want you to do. I want you to buy $2000.00 worth of bricks — I had a sample along to show him what I wanted — at the best price you can get, and bring them out as ballast. He looked at me. I was eighteen and looked young for my age. I had on the kind of rough clothes you have to wear in that business. I didn't look as if I had $2.00, let alone $2000.00. I could see what he was thinking. I said: Look here, when do you plan to go up to town? He said he was going that afternoon. I said: All right, you meet me at 2 o'clock at Sather's Bank and I'll give you a draft on London for $2000.00 and we can sign the papers. When he showed up I had the draft waiting for him. We had the papers made out at the bank and after we both signed them he began to thaw out. He was only about twenty-five himself; his name was Captain Gerald

Hargraves. We stepped across the street and had a drink. We became good friends. For years he made it a point to look me up whenever his ship docked at San Francisco. We often laughed over that shipment of bricks. It was a pretty big thing for a boy of eighteen.

v

Horton sold his bricks. He made a profit and imported more. It occurred to him that an importer of bricks might profitably import other things that buyers of bricks would logically want. He extended his acquaintance among the agents and masters of the European grain ships. Because they were offering low rates for the long western haul, he placed orders for other building materials from European countries: lime, nails, bolts, strap iron, corrugated tin roofing. These materials were soon being deposited in volume on the adjacent wharves and trucked to the Folsom Street yard. The character of his business changed. He built a shed to store his lime and cement. His stacks of bricks and iron encroached on the area occupied by heaps of old metal. The success of his initial venture as a wrecker caused him to branch out into that field — then an active one, for whole sections of the city were being torn down and rebuilt. Lumber salvaged from these operations so filled his rented lot that he had to look for more space.

In the early sixties Horton made his first investment in San Francisco real estate. He signed a five-year lease on the lot he occupied and on the property adjoining it to the east. The lease contained an option to buy at the end of the second year; the price was thirteen thousand five hundred dollars. The enlarged space had a frontage of a hundred and fifty feet on Folsom Street and a depth of two hundred feet — more than half the block. The option was taken up early in 1864, partly with money borrowed from the Bank of California.

The *Memoir* contains Horton's circumstantial account of that transaction:

I walked into the bank one morning and told the clerk I wanted to speak to Mr. Ralston. The clerk knew me; he knew I always kept a satisfactory balance with the bank. He didn't hesitate. He said: Just a moment, Mr. Horton. I'll tell Mr. Ralston you're here. I watched him go into the private office. The door was open and I could see him standing in front of the desk while he talked. He came out and held the little gate open. I walked in. I knew Ralston by sight but I had never exchanged a word with him. He was writing a letter; he didn't look up until he had finished it and addressed the envelope. When he saw me he looked surprised. He said: Who let you in here? I said: Your clerk let me in. Well, he said, who are you and what do you want? I told him that my name was Horton and that I wanted to borrow $8000.00. He asked if I personally wanted to borrow it. I said yes, I wanted it myself and that I had security. He wanted to know how old I was and I said I would be twenty-one in two weeks.

He told me to sit down and we went into the proposition. He sent out and got the record of my account. He wanted to know how much business I did and what shipments I had on the water and why I wanted to buy the property instead of renting it. I saw that if I wanted that loan I would have to put my cards on the table. There was a sheet of paper on his

desk and I took a pencil and drew a rough sort of map. In one
corner I drew the Pacific Mail docks and in the other corner
I put Montgomery Street and the business district. Then I
drew circles connecting the two. I showed him the circles
and said: That's where the traffic has to go to get to and from
the docks. It was a very roundabout way; there were no
through streets beyond Market. Then I drew a straight line
between the two corners. I said: Some day they will put
through a direct street and it will open up this whole district.
I had put a cross on the spot where my yard was; the straight
line passed just to the southeast of it. He took the map and
studied it. He said: You come back again in two or three days
and we'll let you know. I didn't wait two or three days. I
went back the next afternoon and he said: Well, Mr. Horton,
we will lend you $8000.00, but see that you don't close the
deal until after your birthday. The bank never lends money
to minors.

In five years Jim Horton was one of the substantial
young men of the city. I shall not trace all the steps of
his rise. In the field of American biography there are
hundreds of fat volumes that follow in detail men's progress from office boy to chairman of the board; I have no
wish to add to their number. There are, however, a few
points in which Horton's scramble upward differed from
that of the majority. Besides, not every rich man has left
behind so frank a narrative as Horton's dictation. I therefore quote another passage from the *Memoir*, one that
relates the circumstances of his entry into the wholesale
machinery business.

A few words of preliminary explanation are necessary.
On October 21, 1868 San Francisco had a major earth-

quake. Chimneys and building fronts were shaken down, several scores were killed or injured, and the shock to the morale of the inhabitants was severe. There had been several lesser shakes during the preceding weeks. When this climactic quake occurred certain citizens decided they had had enough. They wound up their affairs, sold their property, and left town without any delay. This group was small in number, but it chanced that some of them had large holdings in real estate. Their action in tossing it on the market caused a sharp, though temporary, drop in property values.

One of the group was a young man named Albert Luning, the representative of a Pennsylvania manufacturing concern. Luning had chanced to be walking down Kearny Street when the earthquake struck. The façade of the building he was passing tilted outward and crashed to the sidewalk. Luning jumped to safety and escaped without a scratch. None the less the incident made a distinctly unfavorable impression on him. A few hours later Horton, who sometimes did business with him, walked into Luning's office on Commercial Street. The *Memoir* continues:

He was sitting just inside, with both doors open so he could get out in a hurry. He had a box set up on end in front of him, with pen and paper, and he was writing. I asked him why he didn't work in his office. The office was in the back. He said: Go look at it. I walked back and looked inside. Everything had been shaken down; he hadn't made any attempt to straighten it up again. I went back to where he was sitting. What are you doing? I asked. Seeing him sitting there writing made me curious. He said: I'm writing my will. I looked at him and I couldn't help laughing. He picked up the sheet of paper and showed it to me. It was his will, all right. I said: I want to place an order for that medium hoist I was talking to you about. He put down his pen and looked at me. He said: If you take my advice you'll get out of this town as fast as ever you can. How do you know the next earthquake won't be twice as bad? I said: I'll cross that stream when I come to it. I told him I had a going business and that I was making money and intended to make more. I asked him if he expected me to walk off and leave it. He said: All that won't do you any good if a brick wall falls on you. All right, I said, I'll take my chances. How about ordering that hoist for me? He said: To h— with the hoist. I'm getting away from here as soon as I can. That's all very well, I said, but who's going to take my order for the hoist? He kept on writing. That's for the firm to say, he said. I've tendered my resignation.

I thought things over. It was a good company and Luning did a large business. They manufactured mining machinery and logging equipment and the like. A lot of that sort of thing was being sold out here then. I said: If you are leaving I would like to have the opportunity to take over the agency. He said: I don't know as to that. I've got no authority to appoint anyone.

I saw I wasn't getting anywhere. I said: What about your house? I happened to know that he lived on the Clay Street hill. He looked at me. He had forgotten all about his house. I said: I might be interested in buying it if the price is right. He said: You make an offer. You won't find me unreasonable. I had never been inside the house but I knew what it looked like on the outside. It was a new cottage with a bay window and a picket fence in front. I named a figure that I knew would interest him: $2250.00. I added: But I don't want it unless I get the agency. He thought it over for a few minutes, then he said: All right, I'll appoint you my successor pro tem, and I'll give you a good recommendation. He found the letter to his firm and tore it open and wrote another half page, saying what he had done and recommending me highly. We shook hands on it. I spent the rest of the day there and made him show me the ropes. We signed the papers the next day and I paid him his $2250.00. He went down and bought tickets for his wife and children and himself on the next steamer for the East.

I found myself in the wholesale machinery business. I've never had any reason to regret it.

When Horton took over the agency of the Keystone Iron Works in 1868, large-scale development on the Comstock was just getting under way. Mining equipment of all kinds was in brisk demand. The fever of speculation was rising in San Francisco, silver stocks were booming, and there was ample money to spend for development, including machinery. Horton found that he had got into a business that held opportunities for profits beyond any he had imagined.

The Folsom Street yard saw little of him during the next few years. He applied himself to learning the machinery business and to cultivating a new group of customers. He made himself agreeable to the dozens of mineowners and operators and speculators whose offices were springing up along Montgomery and California streets. He made frequent trips to Virginia City to oversee the installation of Keystone hoists and pumps and transmission machinery. He was usually willing to make a confidential deal with a mine superintendent or other official who thought he deserved a commission on the business he gave out, but who felt that the transaction would not look well on the books of the company. The number and size of the orders he sent back to the Keystone Iron Company must have caused the Scotch owners to thank their stars for the earthquake that had scared their former agent out of town.

Horton repeated on a larger scale the methods he had followed in his brickyard. He began handling other types of mining equipment. He imported a shipload of wire rope from England and presently added a line of leather belting. In the spring of 1870 he made a flying trip east (over the new railroad) and returned with the agency for a new portable steam engine. When this proved useful in the expanding lumber industry he added other logging and sawmill equipment. He varied his sales trips over the Sierra by visits to the redwood forests of Humboldt and Mendocino counties and the Santa Cruz Mountains.

The machinery showroom on Commercial Street was presently outgrown. Meantime the former junkyard across the town flourished, for the building boom continued. By 1872 Horton had seventy men working for him. That year he bought another lot adjoining the Folsom Street property (he then owned the entire block) and began construction of the big brick warehouse that long remained a landmark in that end of town. Its sign: " James Horton: Mining and Lumbering Equipment," was familiar to thousands of San Franciscans before the fire. The tall letters were clearly visible from Market Street.

vi

Horton's name began to appear rather frequently in the local newspapers, proof that he was becoming a power in business circles. Years later he recalled with pride that he could walk into any office in town and address the boss by his first name.

I often [he states] had occasion to see John Mackay. Whenever I stepped into his office it was always Hello John and Hello Jim, and no standing on ceremony. I don't remember that anyone put on airs. Jim Ralston would stop you on the street and talk for half an hour, and if you happened to step into the Bank Exchange any afternoon Jim Flood would clap you on the back and buy you a drink, and it was like that wherever you went. If you met Senator Hearst or Lucky Baldwin or Charley Crocker, or Friedlander, the wheat king, you wouldn't know they had a dime. Of course some of the big men, like Fair and D. O. Mills and Senator Sharon, didn't go in for back-slapping, but that was because they were reserved by nature. I was that way myself, to some extent. . . .

In his business dealings Horton belonged among the conservatives. During a period noted for its plungers, when men risked sizable fortunes on gambles that might make them millionaires in three months — or paupers in half the time — he played for smaller but surer stakes. He once stated that during the first ten years of the Comstock era he never invested a dollar in a mining stock. " I could have afforded it as well as the next man," he added. " I was well fixed before I could cast my first vote.

But I worked hard for my money. I could never see any sense in throwing it away."

The Memoir continues:

Friends used to come up to me and say: Jim, you ought to be in this. They would refer to some mine they were pushing. I frequently got confidential tips from some of the biggest men in the city. I wasn't interested. I had seen too many men with promising businesses get wiped out and have to start over again. One man said to me: Jim, you've got to take risks if you're going to get anywhere. When you play for big stakes you can't be afraid to put your chips on the table. I'm worth half a million today and eighteen months ago I couldn't pay my room rent. He was widely known; you'd recognize his name if I mentioned it. But he was a gambler, pure and simple. I said: That's all very well. But some day you'll put your chips on the wrong card. He laughed at me. He said: I'm going to make a million and a half and then I'm going to sell out and put my winnings in income property and build myself a house on Nob Hill and live like a king. I won't do another lick as long as I live.

Well, it wasn't three months later that this mine he was interested in went under and he lost every dollar. He came to see me. He had $65,000.00 worth of machinery on order and no money to pay for it. I cancelled the order. Then I said: Well, what do you think now about putting your chips on the table? He sat there in my office and looked at me and pretty soon he began to cry. I can see him now, sitting there with the tears running down his cheeks and into his beard. Whenever people come to me with ideas for making a fortune easy, I tell them about M— and how he sat across my desk that day, and how later that afternoon he drove out to the beach and blew off the top of his head with a 44 rifle, which is what M— did.

In his treatment of that period, Casebolt is at pains to point out that Horton steered clear of the pitfalls that brought disaster to scores of less prudent men.

The temptation to join in the prevailing orgy of speculation [he states in the Life] must at times have been strong indeed. All through these exciting years . . . information that would have been deemed invaluable to thousands who were playing the market came to him through his business and social contacts. It was a situation that might well have turned the head of men of greater age and wider experience. In the space of a few years he had seen men, many of them of very limited capabilities, rise from humble beginnings to positions of extraordinary wealth and power. . . .

Few can doubt that if James Horton had chosen to emulate these men; that if, like them, he had devoted his initial fortune to acquiring control of any one of a dozen Virginia City properties, and then had brought to bear his marked talent for organization and finance, his name would today be listed with those of the Bonanza kings themselves. But James was opposed to speculating and he stood by his principles. It required a high degree of moral courage. . . .

Here again the discerning reader will observe that James disappointed his biographer by his failure to become a Bonanza king. But Casebolt makes it clear that although Horton's part in the Comstock won him little fame, his services were important, and the financial rewards were far from insignificant. I quote again from the Life:

◇◇◇◇◇◇◇◇◇◇◇◇◇◇◇◇◇◇◇◇

By 1875 Horton was, by the standards of his day, a wealthy man. We may judge as much from the fact that his new residence — which in cost and in its princely proportions and appointments did not suffer in comparison with any in the city — that year began to rise on the topmost peak of Russian Hill. Further evidence, if such be needed, may be found in the magnificent Horton Block, already completed and occupied on lower Market Street, and universally acknowledged to be the finest (though not quite the largest) office building west of Chicago. From our knowledge of Horton and his methods, we may infer that these two structures were built entirely out of surplus funds. Horton was too prudent a businessman, and too familiar with the unstable conditions of the period, to permit himself to go deeply in debt, or to allow his working capital to fall below the level of safety. . . .

A reading of these excerpts from the *Life* may explain the feeling I had when I first read the work. As Casebolt tells it, Horton's career closely parallels that of an Oliver Optic hero. It is a tale of virtue rewarded, of a poor but honest boy's triumphant progress from rags to riches.

I had some acquaintance with Horton during his last years. That was after success and creeping infirmities and a growing boredom had done their best to tone him down. Even in his old age he could not by any standard have been called a benign old gentleman. He had excellent qualities. He minded his own business and encouraged others to do likewise. Most rich men of his day knew exactly how to remake the world; if Horton had such a formula he kept it to himself. I have never known him to pretend to wisdom on any of the many subjects of which he was ignorant. He was not a particularly intelligent man, but he had a native shrewdness and hard common sense, and forty years of experience had taught him how to safeguard his own interests.

When I was a newspaper reporter I was once sent to his office to interview him. I was instructed to get a statement endorsing a bond issue to purchase land for a new school, a project which my paper was supporting. I explained my errand and without hesitation Horton dictated a few sentences warmly endorsing the plan. I was surprised and delighted. The bond issue would raise the city tax rate and cost the old man a considerable sum of money. I complimented him on his support of a needed civic improvement. He leaned back and looked at me. "Don't let this get any further," he said, "but my support will do your bonds more harm than good. When people find I'm for them they'll think I must be making money out of the deal. They won't be able to get to the polls fast enough to defeat them." He was then past seventy and as close to mellowness as he ever got.

A year or two ago, in the newspaper room of our public library, I chanced to come across the following:

CARSON CITY, APRIL 11: — R. G. Burgess, representing the stockholders of the Canfield Mine and Milling Company, Gold Hill, today filed suit in the District Court against Covington Burt, until recently superintendent of the company, and several others, on charges of conspiracy and embezzlement in connection with the construction and equipment of the company's mill at Gold Hill.

The complaint states that Burt conspired with certain firms and individuals to defraud his employers by presenting bills for milling machinery made out in amounts in excess of its value and in some instances for material that was never delivered at all. In addition to Burt, the following were named defendants: A. L. Hartwick and J. Costello, Virginia City; Williams and MacBane, Sacramento; the Gorham Iron Works, James Horton, and Livermore, Harrison & Co., San Francisco, and several John Does.

The item appeared in the *Alta California* for April 12, 1871. I copied it and mailed it to Casebolt, who was then engaged on his *Life*. He acknowledged its receipt promptly and with his usual courtesy. His reply ended with these words: " Obviously this lawsuit was the result of a private quarrel between Burt and the stockholders. The standing of the San Francisco companies named is in itself a guaranty that they would not knowingly have been parties to such a transaction."

With that I found it difficult to disagree. The companies were among the most respectable in town.

I shall end this chapter with yet another excerpt from Horton's *Memoir*. The passage is one of my favorites. Horton's interviewer had asked him an inevitable question: to what did he attribute his success? This is the old man's reply:

Up at my place at Calistoga I've got a fishpond. When it was first built my gardener came down to buy some fish to put in it. The man in the store sold him two dozen carp. He said that the fishponds in Europe all had carp in them and that that's what should go in mine. My man bought the carp and they were sent up on the train in a barrel, with a sack tied over the top. The next time I went up I went out to see how they were getting along. I stood at the edge of the pond and looked at them. They had made themselves at home. I don't know if you ever saw a carp, but it's a big, lazy fish; it doesn't move about any more than it has to. It just floats around, opening and closing its mouth, and once in a while giving its tail a flip. When I got back to town I went into that fish store myself. I asked the man if he had any fish that didn't like carp. At first he didn't know what I meant. I repeated that I was looking for some kind of a fish that didn't get along with carp. He thought a long time. Then he said he thought that Alaskan snappers didn't like carp. All right, I said, I want you to send one of your snappers up to my country place. He said: Did you say one snapper, Mr. Horton? Yes, I said, one. I wrote my gardener and told him to keep the snapper by himself until I came up. I wanted to put him in the pond myself. I had some visitors that week-end, and Sunday afternoon we went down to the pond and I took the can that the snapper had come in and dumped him into the water. He was a very active fish. In a few minutes he had been all around the pond a dozen times. I thought to myself: He already knows more about that pond than those carp have learned in three weeks. He ignored the carp and, so far as I could see, they ignored him. I was disappointed. I told my gardener to drop some fish food into the pond. He did, and then things began happening. The carp came hurrying over with their mouths open, but the snapper got there first. When the first carp came up, the snapper was at him like a terrier. He hit him so hard that the carp jumped clear out of the water. Then he went after the others. For a few seconds the water was white where those carp churned it up trying to keep out of the way. In less time than it takes me to tell you, the carp were down at the far end of the pool and the snapper was helping himself to the food. I turned to my friends and said: We can learn a lesson from that. Ever since then, whenever anybody asks me *how to get on in a business way, I tell him that story. The world, I say, is full of carp. If you want to amount to something you've got to be a snapper.*

On Horton's Memoir there is a penciled note in the margin opposite this tale; the handwriting is Casebolt's:

WARNING: Horton is here having a little joke with his interviewer. Casey's Dictionary of Fishes (London, 1907) lists no such fish as the Alaskan snapper. A. L. Hargraves, Professor Emeritus of Zoology, Willamette University, and a noted authority on the fishes of the Pacific Northwest, wires on September 17, 1938: " With reference yours of seventeenth. Stop. American ichthyologic literature contains no reference to species having characteristics so-called snapper. Specimen described almost certainly hypothetical. Stop. Best regards. Stop. Hargraves."

Cum grano salis!

Chapter 4

ALTHOUGH there was a time, during the middle and late nineties, when I saw Horton frequently, I was of course never in his confidence. The difference in our ages would have prevented that, even had he been in the habit of discussing his affairs with others. For several years I regularly spent one evening a week on Russian Hill. I went, not on Horton's urging, but on Juliet's, and the reason she invited me was because the conversation of her father's friends often bored her, and she liked then to have someone about her who knew nothing about business and cared less.

I met that qualification to perfection, yet I doubt whether I was a very entertaining companion. I was a full ten years younger than Julie — I had just turned twenty — and my lack of knowledge of the world was little short of staggering. In those days I had a great deal of respect for what was called the finer things of life. I had a soul above the sordid concerns of trade. I could talk with authority of the more pretentious plays (which I saw from the gallery); when the opera came to town I went as often as I could get free tickets, and if I stayed away from a concert or a lecture it was because no passes were to be had and I did not have the cash to pay my way. I knew enough about what had recently been happening in the world of art and architecture to discuss superciliously the houses to which I was invited, and I regularly visited Doxey's Book Store to leaf through the *Yellow Book* and other advanced periodicals on his magazine rack. Besides these accomplishments, I played a fair hand of euchre (a game for which Aunt Julie then had a passing enthusiasm) and I was always willing to complete a foursome.

Thus I was brought into frequent contact with Horton. I had ample opportunity to study him at close hand and so to learn what were the qualities that distinguished him from his fellows and enabled him to reach his pre-eminence. I did nothing of the sort. As a matter of fact, I was not at all interested in him. Nothing he said struck me as particularly worth listening to, and he certainly didn't look distinguished. His was a physical type once common in San Francisco but now strangely rare: gaunt and fragile-looking, but strong as an ox and virtually indestructible. He looked like what he was, an Illinois farmer who had prospered. When I thought of him at all it was to wonder that a man of his wealth should look so much less impressive than a millionaire ought to look (I had noticed that in others besides Horton), and that he seemed to take so matter-of-fact a view of his accomplishments. I was sure that if I had been in his boots I would have cut a far more dashing figure.

It was not until some years after his death that I began to pay him close attention. My thoughts turned to him then because a curious thing happened: he began to be regarded as an important and significant figure. One saw his name quite frequently in books or magazine articles that dealt reminiscently of the upbuilding of the city. There it was mentioned on equal terms with the Parrotts and Haggins, the Fairs and Sutros and Floods and the other early citizens to whose careers our youth of to-day are often urged (with what result I know not) to look for inspiration. Naturally, my own interest increased. It is always a surprise to discover that an acquaintance whom you used to consider not worth a second thought has become a historic figure.

Several years ago a young woman called me by telephone from Berkeley and announced that she was preparing a doctoral thesis on James Horton, and could she have an appointment? She arrived the following afternoon, leaned a briefcase against her chair, balanced a notebook on her knee and asked me to tell her what interesting things I could recall about the great man.

I tried to think of something significant.

" He liked apples," I said. " He used to keep a bag of them in his desk. While visitors were talking he would take an apple out of the bag and pare it with a jackknife and cut it in quarters and lay the quarters in a row on his desk and eat them. He never offered his visitors any."

She didn't seem very much interested in that.

I tried again. " He once said that the belief that the Chinese are scrupulously honest in their business dealings is false. He said that so far as he could remember he had never done business with a Chinaman but that the latter had tried to cheat his eyes out."

The young woman said nothing. She made no notes. I began to see that I was on the wrong track and I asked her what sort of information she was looking for. She replied that she had recently been at the State Library in Sacramento and had copied out the references to Horton in the newspaper index there, and that she had been reading the references and making notes. She nodded toward the briefcase. The notes were in there.

I told her I doubted if I could add anything to what she already had.

She then said that when she was leaving the library one day, she had noticed an inscription on the pediment of the building across the courtyard. The inscription read: " Give Me Men to Match My Mountains." It was a quotation, she stated, from John Muir. She added that it had occurred to her that the phrase might serve as a theme for her study of James Horton. She had copied it down and she planned to put it in her manuscript, on a page by itself, just after the title-page and in front of the introduction.

I said I thought that an excellent idea.

What she was looking for, she added, were incidents of Horton's career that would confirm her theory that he was indeed a man who matched the mountains. I asked if she had any particular mountains in mind. She said no, just the mountains in general. After that neither of us said anything; we had reached an impasse. She was a solemn young woman, who hailed from a town called Dos Palos, and she was preparing for a career as a high-school teacher of history.

I disliked to see her leave empty-handed, so I made a last suggestion. "Why don't you just say that he matched the mountains and let it go at that?"

She said no, that in historical writing when one made a statement one must back it up. There must be proof, either in the text or in a footnote. I said I could understand that, and that I withdrew my suggestion. She closed her notebook and picked up her briefcase and left. She thanked me politely, but I could see she was a little disappointed at the result of our interview. I didn't much blame her.

ii

The year after the Russian Hill house was finished, Horton and his wife set off on a tour of Europe. They left San Francisco in May 1876 and later that month sailed from New York on the Cunard liner *Bothnia*. During the next three months they followed the conventional tourist routes. They visited the English cathedrals and the Paris galleries. They admired the scenery of the Alps and the Black Forest. They attended the opera in Naples and listened to band concerts at German spas, and the trains on which they traveled and the hotels where they stopped were full of other tourists bent on exactly the same errands.

Wherever they went they bought furniture and bric-a-brac for their new house: tables and sideboards in London, china and porcelain figures in Paris, marble benches and busts and bird-baths in Pisa, paintings in Paris and Florence and Rome. They returned late in September on a French boat (which they thought inferior to the *Bothnia*) and reached home on October 18th.

It was Horton's only trip abroad. That contact with an older civilization than America's could not have made a deep impression on his mind. His *Memoir*, dictated fifteen years later, has only this brief reference to the period:

People took more stock in a trip to Europe in those days than they do now. If you walked into a man's office and said, Well, this thing has got to be settled one way or the other, because I'm leaving for Paris next week, the other man was impressed. Going abroad wasn't like it is today. Now every Tom, Dick and Harry runs off whenever he takes the notion. Nobody thinks anything about it, except that sometimes you wonder where the fellow got the money. . . .

I can't say that I was much impressed with what I saw. I am not referring to the paintings or the old buildings or scenery. They are ahead of us in such things and always will be. I have in mind particularly the way they do business, and in that I would say they're at least twenty years behind the times. . . .

In Paris the Hortons stopped at the Hôtel des Deux-Mondes on the avenue de l'Opéra. At dinner one evening Horton got into conversation with a young man at their table, a manufacturer from Lyon. His name was Henri Lafavre. He was a partner in a firm that operated a textile mill; he spoke English volubly and inaccurately. Horton was glad of an opportunity to talk business with a member of so puzzling a race. After dinner they spent a pleasant two hours in the lobby. Anita, who normally would have had no interest in such a conversation, was an absorbed listener. Like Horton, she was much impressed by the Frenchman, whose manners were charming and who listened respectfully to whatever she had to say.

During the next few days Lafavre took the Hortons under his wing. He suggested establishments where they might buy furnishings for their new home. They were impressed by the close interest he took in each purchase. It was amusing to watch him inspect a clock or a marquetry table or a pair of bronze vases, walking completely around them with his head on one side, talking and gesticulating constantly. There was no limit to his helpfulness. Anita had been buying dresses at a large and expensive store near the Madeleine. Lafavre dismissed the place with scorn and took her to a series of small shops on narrow side streets. There he argued passionately over the materials for her evening gowns, the style and workmanship of her dresses, the prices of her hats. The three went driving in an elegant rented landau. They spent a day at Versailles and one evening took a boat ride down the Seine to Auteuil. They parted as old friends.

This chance meeting had an interesting sequel. Not long after he returned to San Francisco, Horton acquired a controlling interest in the Argonaut Woolen Mills (for an analysis of that complicated transaction see pages 316–19 of the *Life*), which occupied a big wooden building on lower Harrison Street. The mills had never competed successfully with goods sent out from the textile centers of New England, and Horton and the other owners presently grew convinced that a change of management was needed. While they were casting about for a suitable man, Horton recalled his Paris acquaintance, who had come from a line of textile-manufacturers. Fortunately he had saved Lafavre's address. He wrote suggesting that the Frenchman come to California and look over the situation. Lafavre arrived a few months later. He had married in the meantime and his bride came along. He made a favorable impression and was duly installed as superintendent of the mills.

During their first weeks in town the Lafavres were guests of the Hortons on Russian Hill. Both were full of Gallic verve and they were soon leading an active social life. Helene Lafavre was plump and coquettish and, in those days, pretty and graceful. When I first knew her, years later, after she had married Hervey Richards, of the shipping family, she had put on weight, but one could guess that this dumpy, voluble little woman had once been uncommonly attractive. At fifty she was still a confirmed flirt.

During the late seventies and early eighties this couple introduced a novelty into the social life of the town. Their house on Powell Street became a sort of oasis to which many fled to escape the arid functions higher on the hill. Their parties bore the taint of bohemianism, for the Lafavres had a liking for actors and musicians and artists, but everyone had a good time. Few refused the host's invitations and fewer still, having gone once, were not eager to go again. This carefree couple had a great deal to do with breaking down the formality that characterized our social gatherings. One was sure to meet entertaining people in their crowded, hot rooms. It was pleasant to flirt with the pretty hostess and to meet on informal terms whatever touring actors and actresses happened to be in town and — the wine being good and plentiful — to observe the eagerness with which they responded to requests that they perform.

Unfortunately, Lafavre's successes as a host were not duplicated in the business field. Under his management the Argonaut Mills showed no signs of the hoped-for rejuvenation. For three years the owners met and, yielding to the superintendent's impassioned pleas, voted an assessment to pay the annual deficit. At the fourth annual meeting, having had enough, they voted instead to liquidate the business. Finding himself out of a job and, as it developed, heavily in debt, Lafavre dropped from sight. He did not go alone. Several weeks after his disappearance, one of his local acquaintances met him in a Chicago restaurant. Lafavre greeted the San Franciscan with joy and proudly introduced his companion. She was Virginia Durgan (later Vesta Hayden of light opera), who had until recently been a ballet girl at the San Francisco Tivoli.

The Hortons had been frequent guests at Lafavre's lively parties; when the blow fell, the abandoned wife took refuge on Russian Hill. The furnishings of the Powell Street house were auctioned off by the creditors and Helene presently opened (with Horton's backing) her millinery shop on Kearny Street. She had shrewdly foreseen that the combination of curiosity and sympathy would bring half the ladies in town to her store. " Helene of Paris " was a success from its opening day. It remained so long after its founder had given up active management of the business and went to preside over the Richards house on Jackson Street. She had meantime divorced the missing Henri.

i i i

It is interesting to reflect on how profoundly this care-free couple affected the future conduct of both Horton and his wife. When Lafavre came out to rehabilitate the woolen mill, Horton was in his mid-thirties. He had not led a frivolous life. Since his early teens his interests had been centered on the struggle to make a living. He had had more than average success, but it had not been a particularly easy success. It had involved scheming and persistence and hard work. In that overworked phrase (beloved of writers of problem novels), he had forgotten how to play.

Then, at thirty-five, he began spending several evenings a week in Henri Lafavre's front parlor, a chamber jammed with men and women unlike any he had encountered before. Their enthusiasms were for things that had little to do with making a fortune or holding on to one already made. Horton learned that the game he had been playing so long was not the only one that interested him. Making a profit, outwitting a competitor, wooing a new customer, or mollifying an old one, these were concerns that, followed too long and too closely, lost some of their power to fascinate.

Horton discovered that he enjoyed the evenings at the Lafavres' more than the sedate functions of the important citizens whose favor he had been cultivating. It was a quiet revolution and a thorough one. Thereafter he did very much as he pleased. This does not mean that he led an irresponsible or even a carefree life. The job of protecting and augmenting his fortune continued to engage the greater part of his interest. He found the parties at the Lafavres' an entertaining novelty, but he did not take them seriously. He was too hard-headed to be taken in by the jobless actors and musicians, the singers without roles, and the bad painters who made up the faithful regulars of the group.

His wife had no such reservations. To Anita Horton this first contact with the arts convinced her that that was where her interests permanently lay. She took to the bohemianism of the Powell Street salon like a duck to water. It brought out qualities that she herself had certainly never suspected. She had no artistic ambition of her own, and no real interest in music or painting or the stage. What she wanted was to be a patroness, not of the arts, but of artists. It was the beginning of a self-imposed task that she willingly carried as long as she could bear the burden. From the middle seventies onward, she had from half a dozen to a score of young men (she was less interested in the women) under her wing. First in San Francisco, then in New York, and later for many years in Paris, she enthusiastically handed out food, drink, shelter, advice, and coin to a succession of painters and sculptors and poets that must have numbered in the thousands. The fact that a lamentably small number of her protégés ever distinguished themselves made no difference. Whether or not they had talent was immaterial; it was enough that they permitted themselves to impose on her.

In my youth Anita Horton's odd enthusiasm was still frequently discussed. No one seemed very sympathetic. In those days art was something one absorbed as a by-product of a trip to Europe and promptly forgot after one's return. Even that fleeting tolerance was seldom extended to those who had created the paintings our travelers brought home with them; on the Coast art became respectable long before the artists did. Anita's behavior was deplored by the conservatives. The wives of prosperous citizens were not expected to have enthusiasms, least of all for the company of painters, and local painters at that. On the day she began covering the walls of the bookless library on Russian Hill with locally produced canvases she took her place among the town's lengthy list of eccentrics.

Curiously enough, this view of her was shared by the beneficiaries themselves. One of the privileges of the artist is that of treating his patrons with contempt, and Anita did not escape. She was unconcerned. If her friends accepted as their due whatever she gave them and returned neither thanks nor gratitude, she bore their treatment with good nature. Genius could not be expected to conduct itself otherwise. When they ordered her servants about and were rude to her non-artistic guests and behaved as though they owned the place, she looked on with entire content. It was a small price to pay for the privilege of having them about, of hearing them address her as Anita, and of being allowed to sit in the background while they discoursed on their problems, their hopes, and their prejudices.

iv

What Jim Horton thought of his wife's new friends is not altogether clear, but on the whole he seems to have behaved well. Anita's artistic gatherings were held during the afternoons when Horton was busy downtown, but frequently the group remained for dinner and thus came in contact with their host. A few are still living who recall those remote evenings. Billy Hendrixson, now past eighty, who has been painting clipper ships for more than sixty years, was once under Anita's wing. He remembers the Hortons well. I met him one day in front of the Marine Exchange and stopped to chat. Uncle Billy is a ruddy-cheeked viking, and one of the ornaments of the town. His white mane flows out from beneath his broad-brimmed hat, his ascot tie droops from the collar of his vivid blue shirt; he is the very picture of the venerable marine painter. In his long career he has painted thousands of ships, all plowing through the same sea, the same headlands in the background, and the same stock clouds overhead. He is our dean of painters and we are proud of him. Merely to encounter him on the streets, heading into the wind with the rolling gait he still retains after six decades on dry land, is to have visible proof that ours is an artistic city; no one minds any more that his paintings are so bad. As a spectacle he is worth a dozen of our present-day artists, who all look like stock-brokers.

I asked if he remembered Jim Horton.

"Horton? Of course I remember Horton," he replied. He fixed me with the resentful gaze characteristic of old age when it is questioned about something about which it has no direct interest. "Why d'you ask about Horton?"

"Well, he was a big man in his day," I said. "I'm very much interested in him."

"He doesn't interest me a damn bit. He was just a rich businessman. Made a pot of money and built himself a house on top of the steepest hill in town. I never went up there that I didn't cuss. D'you ever see a sailor who liked climbing hills?"

"Did Horton ever buy any of your paintings, Uncle Billy?"

"Can't recall that he did. Cliff bought one, though, a few years back. Clifford Horton, you know — the old man's son. It was a big canvas; I got five hundred dollars for it. A man could get decent prices then. He gave it to the Potrero Boys Club. I went over and made a speech the day it was hung. In the course of my talk I told how I once turned down a commission from Jim Horton. Cliff wasn't much pleased to hear that story. Not that that bothered me any."

Uncle Billy has long had a low regard for those who bought his pictures. One of the pleasures of his old age is to recall how he used to put them in their places. "All right, that's my price, and the frame will be extra. You can take it or leave it. . . ." Of recent years practically everyone has elected to leave it, but Uncle Billy is un-bowed.

I asked to hear the whole story. He propped himself against one of the stone columns of the Exchange. "There's nothing much to tell. I was a young fellow then and, between you and me, not much of a painter. Some-body brought Anita — that was Horton's wife — down to my studio; I was in the alley behind the Montgomery Block, upstairs over a barrel shop. My pictures were lean-ing against the wall. She asked to see them. I told her to help herself. I was busy and didn't want to be bothered. She carried them out and put them on a chair by the window and stepped back and looked at them. She was a big woman, not bad-looking. She was a good deal impressed. Nothing would do but she had to have an exhibit at her house so her friends could see them. There were about fifty people for the opening, but they must have come for the food. We didn't sell a blasted picture. That night she gave a dinner and everybody drank a toast and said I had a great future.

" That was the first time I ever spoke to Horton. Dur-ing the evening he took me to one side. He'd just bought himself a schooner to carry lumber from his mill up the coast. She was the first ship he ever owned and he was proud of her. He asked what I'd charge to paint her. I knew the boat. She was a dirty little pot called the *Frances Day*. I told him that before I'd paint any stinking lumber schooner I'd starve. I said if I couldn't make a living painting clipper ships I could always go back to sailing them. He offered me a hundred dollars to paint the *Frances*. 'You can't make that much in six months as a sailor,' he said. I said: ' Why don't you get somebody to paint a freight-car and hang that up? ' He said he didn't want a freight-car, he wanted the *Frances*, and would I paint her for a hundred dollars? I told him I wasn't interested. I heard later that he got someone else to do the job. He was surprised that I could be as independent as he was. I could have used that hundred dollars, too," added Uncle Billy.

It happens that this painting is still in existence. I came across it one day in one of the galleries of the De Young Museum. A plate on its old-fashioned walnut frame bears this legend: " Schooner Frances Day, San Francisco. 350 tons. Builder: Benicia Iron Works, 1871. Owned and Operated by the Horton Mill and Lumber Co." A card on the wall states that the artist is unknown and that the donor was Clifford Wilkes Horton. It is part of the museum's historical collection.

The drawing is crude but spirited. It has a quaint interest. The little craft is buffeting heavy seas, just off shore, with the surf pounding the cliffs beyond, and the wooded hills of the Humboldt coast in the background. The painting must have hung for years in Horton's Market Street office; it was probably the only work of art he ever admired. I wondered how it had been saved from the fire. I wondered, too, that Casebolt had failed to locate it and reproduce it in his book.

It gave me a certain pleasure to reflect that I had stumbled on something my industrious friend had overlooked.

ν

For many years Horton had his office on the fourth-floor corner of his Market Street office building, the Horton Block. Like everything else in the district, it was gutted by the 1906 fire, but the walls remained intact and Horton rebuilt it almost as it had been before. He made a few concessions to progress. Electric lights had come into use since it had been put up, and central heating. Horton installed both, although he failed to remove the fireplaces and marble mantels that had been a feature of the larger rooms. The old rope elevators were replaced by the grille-work cars popular at the time, which resembled gilded bird-cages. This office was the center of Jim Horton's life for forty years. By the time of the fire he had become so used to it that he had trouble transacting his business elsewhere. He rebuilt the place and moved back downtown at the earliest possible moment.

On the morning of the earthquake he was at Carrick, the now deserted lumber town on the Humboldt coast. Carrick was a company town, which meant that it was Horton's town. He was the sole owner of the Triangle Lumber Company, and the company owned the town and all that pertained to it: the mill and lumber yard and the dock where Horton's schooners were loaded. He owned, too, the store and the saloon and several scores of wooden shacks in which the employees lived. He also owned and derived a very satisfactory profit from the town's red-light district, a group of houses (rather better than the millhands' shacks) at the northern end of the business district. Finally, the company — that is, Horton — owned a huge area of the surrounding country, a green, hilly empire that contained millions of acres of redwood timber.

When Horton was shaken from his bed in the Carrick Hotel on the morning of April 18, 1906, his first concern was to put through a call to San Francisco. It was clear that this was no ordinary earthquake — it struck with particular violence on the north coast — and he knew there was need for his presence in San Francisco. He succeeded in raising the operator in Willits and had given her the home number of his office assistant, Charles Pettit, when the line went dead. Within a quarter of an hour he was in the cab of a logging locomotive on the first leg of a dash to San Francisco. It took him twenty-four hours to accomplish the one-hundred-and-fifty-mile journey. At two o'clock on the morning of the 19th he stood on the wharf at Tiburon and watched the most spectacular bonfire of the century reflected on the waters of the bay. By the time he reached town, in a rented launch, his losses in burned buildings and their contents were huge. The launch landed at the life-saving station in the Presidio. Horton hurried to Russian Hill. He was concerned not over the destroyed buildings (which were insured), but over his office records. His safe was jammed with documents, few of which could be replaced, and the safe was thirty years old and not built to withstand a major fire. He was striding through the garden to the Russian Hill house when he was stopped by a sharp challenge. Young Pettit was standing in the dawn on the front porch, a rifle at his shoulder. There had been some looting of the evacuated houses in the path of the flames; his clerk had been on guard all night.

Horton's first question was about his office records. Pettit led him inside. The glare of the fire lighted the hall and Horton saw half a dozen boxes stacked on the marble floor. The previous morning Pettit had got through the police lines with Horton's coachman and one of the carriages. They had loaded the vehicle with the contents of the safe and brought it back through the littered streets to safety.

But it was by no means certain that the Russian Hill house itself would escape. The fire had burned beyond it on two sides and seemed likely to encircle it entirely. The two men went into the kitchen, ate a cold breakfast by candlelight, and considered the situation. The horses had been taken away and no other transportation was to be had. They decided to segregate the indispensable papers, to put them in a trunk, and, if the house appeared doomed, to carry it out of the danger zone. They packed the trunk, placed it inside the front door and sat down to wait. It was then nine o'clock on the morning of the 19th. Horton, who had not slept for thirty hours, dozed in his chair. When Pettit awakened him it was well into the afternoon and the fire was burning far out toward Van Ness Avenue. Russian Hill was surrounded by ruins, but the hilltop was safe. Horton went upstairs and finished his nap.

He fitted up an office in one of the ground-floor rooms and there transacted his business until the spring of 1907. During that period hundreds of other residences in the unburned districts were being put to the same use. Banks, insurance companies, railroad agencies, the offices of corporations, all were crowded into the front and back parlors, the dining-rooms and dens and butler's pantries of wooden residences in the Western Addition and elsewhere.

The room Horton took over was known as the library, although it contained no books then and contains none today. It is on the sunless northwest side, too far back to command a view of the bay. Horton chose it because it had long been shunned by members of the household, and because one of its doors opened on a passageway that led outdoors, via what was known in the family as the side door. Callers could thus, by approaching the house from the rear and following a walk through the service yard, see Horton, transact their business, and leave, all without passing through the main part of the house.

Some objected to that arrangement. Scores of the businessmen had dealings with Horton during the period, and there were a few who found it galling to have to enter and leave by what they could only regard as the servants' entrance. In his biography Casebolt describes one such incident. One of Horton's former tenants, an importer who had occupied a building on Sansome Street, called one day to complete arrangements for leasing a new structure Horton had put up on the site. He climbed the hill and presented himself at the front door. The butler directed him to the path that led to the office entrance. The caller stated that he wished to go in by the front door, and when he insisted, the butler (who was acting on orders) closed the door in his face. When the man reached Horton's desk he was fuming. Horton asked him what was wrong.

" See here," he burst out. " My family stands as high as any other in town, and a good deal higher than some. Yet your servant had the impudence to order me around to the back door."

Horton regarded him thoughtfully. He called to his assistant.

" Mr. Pettit, show Mr. Wilson outside and bring him back again through the front door."

The two left and solemnly made the circuit of the grounds, up the front steps, down the hall, and back to the office by an inner door. By then the young man looked a bit sheepish.

" Sit down," said Horton. " Here's your lease. I made a few changes while you were on your tour."

The caller glanced through the document and his jaw dropped.

" But you've doubled my rent! " he cried. " I can't pay that."

" I didn't suppose you could," said Horton. " The fact is, I don't want you in any building of mine. In times like this any man who'll waste his time worrying about his social standing is a damned poor risk. I wish you good day, sir. Mr. Pettit, show the gentleman out the *front* door."

vi

One day Aunt Julie's elderly driver, Clarence Dawes, brought me a letter and a package. The latter was done up in a newspaper; it was so carelessly tied that I suspected it must have been done by Aunt Julie herself.

I put the package on my desk and opened her letter. I quote it in full:

DEAR WALTER: *The day after Cliff's funeral I got a call from Charley Pettit saying that he wanted to see me about something important and confidential. I thought it must be about Cliff's will, so I sent Clarence down to pick him up. When he came up he was carrying a box done up with sealing wax. He put the box on the table and made a little speech. He told me that Cliff had turned it over to him about a year before, and that it contained valuable family papers. He had told Charley to put it in safety deposit and to keep it there until after his (Cliff's) death. Then he was to hand it over to me if I was still alive. If I wasn't alive he was to destroy the box unopened. When Charley finished his piece he put on his hat and left.*

After he was gone I got to thinking how like Cliff all that was. I guessed what his important family papers were. I wasn't interested. I had Hedrig take the box up to the attic. It stayed there until today when I had it brought down again. I've spent the afternoon going through the papers. You'll find some of them amusing. They tell a great deal about Cliff. He had everything in its place — I hope I haven't mixed them up — and notes in his handwriting clipped to each item. Cliff had a tidy mind, even when he was a child. His toys were always where they were supposed to be. My stuff was all over the house. It still is.

I enclose a letter from Cliff that I found when I opened the package.

This is Clifford's letter. It is dated June 26, 1930:

DEAR SISTER JULIET: It is now ten minutes past midnight and I have just completed a task in which I have taken no pleasure but which I felt had to be done.

It is probable you will never read these lines. Before I go to bed I will seal this letter with the papers now on my desk, and when I get to the office tomorrow morning I will hand the package to Charles Pettit with instructions as to what disposition I wish made of it. Only in the event that you outlive me will you know what the box contains.

If this letter comes to your hand you will also have in your care that part of the record of our family that I heartily wish did not exist. It is, naturally, only a small part of the whole. We Hortons have little to conceal and a great deal of which to be proud. Our part in the upbuilding of San Francisco does not suffer by comparison with that of any other family in the city, and I do not except the Crockers or the Phelans or the Floods. In all sincerity I can state that I have always been proud to be a Horton. Notwithstanding the scoffing attitude you have sometimes expressed toward who we are and what we stand for, I feel that we are agreed on that point. If I felt otherwise I should not feel it my duty to pass these papers on to you.

As you know, I have for some months been devoting the greater part of my time to assembling material about Father, with the ultimate aim of having written and published a book that will assure his place in San Francisco's history. I have not talked with you as fully about this matter as would have been the case had your attitude been more sympathetic when I first broached it. I assure you that the work has been going forward. On the recommendation of Dr. Henry Casebolt, whose advice has been invaluable, I have hired two of his former students, both trained research workers, and they have been going through the files of several California newspapers during the period of Father's greatest activity. They have located and copied out a great deal of pertinent material. I have also permitted them, under the supervision of Charles Pettit, to go through Father's personal papers, which were, as you know, providentially saved from the fire. These have yielded much information necessary to a well-rounded life.

You must not suppose that by delegating these tasks to others I have failed to do my share in this undertaking. Every page of notes that my young helpers have compiled, every letter or document they have selected as having possible significance, has passed over my desk and been carefully read. On the great bulk of this I have placed my initials, followed by my Okeh, and it has been filed away, properly arranged and labeled, awaiting the future biographer.

I come now to the purpose of this letter. Not all this material will be passed on to the man who will write Father's life. I have taken on myself responsibility for withholding certain letters and newspaper excerpts, as well as a few deeds, contracts, and miscellaneous papers. You will find them all, with explanatory notes in my hand, in the box with which I shall enclose this letter. Some of it you will not find pleasant reading. Some — and I am thinking now particularly of the folder pertaining to the Fred Foschay episode — will awaken painful memories. Some of the other material I have put aside, not because the events on which they bear would, if fully understood, reflect discredit on the family, but because in the hands of one not familiar with the circumstances they might be misinterpreted. The series of excerpts from the Weekly Hornet, which appeared at the time Mother went to live in New York, is a case in point. Who today would recognize that these attacks, for which there was little basis in truth, were the result of the fact that for several weeks Father refused to buy the worthless stock of the paper? The same considerations impel me to withhold the documents bearing on certain of Father's real-estate transactions, the correspondence relating to the spur tracks on Folsom Street, and the 10th Avenue street-car franchise, and to the manifestly unfair sermons of the publicity-seeking preacher, Dr. Starkweather, because of Father's ownership of the Bartlett Alley property. These are all matters that might, without full information, be misunderstood.

I do not doubt my right to withhold this material. Virtually all of it can be explained by anyone in possession of the facts. But is there any assurance that the man who will compile Father's biography will have the necessary background or judgment? You may ask, then, why I do not destroy these documents and be done with it? I have rejected that course for two reasons. First, these are family papers and I am not their sole owner; they belong equally to you. Second, there is always the danger that at a future date some writer may undertake to publish a sensational book based on Father's life. I have already had a number of requests for information from individuals who were planning to write about him. In each case I have succeeded in discouraging them, but there may be others. If such a book should appear during your lifetime, and if I am not here to advise you, I hope you will take all necessary steps to bring about its suppression. My friend and attorney, Henry Partington, of Partington & Williamson, First National Bank Building, will know how to proceed. If it becomes necessary to enter suit for libel, a judicious selection from these papers may be very useful to our cause.

You will find that the thickest folder relates to a matter that has given me the most concern of all. I confess that I have sometimes been tempted to consign this entire file to the furnace. That I have not done so is the measure of my confidence in your good judgment. I have no wish to dictate the manner in which Father's biography shall be written. I should keenly regret it if he were depicted as a man without imperfections. Father had his faults, like all of us. He was, after all, one of the pioneers, and there is no denying that in certain respects the standards of his time were less strict than those of today. But on this one thing I am determined and, since I am providing the funds that will make the work possible, I believe any fair-minded man will agree that I have a right to make this single stipulation: Father's biography must contain no mention whatever of Christine Winton.

> Your loving brother,
> CLIFFORD WILKES HORTON

Chapter 5

THERE was a time when I considered making Chris Winton a character in a novel. I abandoned the idea only after it had grown clear that the qualities that made her interesting to me were of a sort that could not easily be got on paper. As every novel-reader knows, it was the fashion a few years ago to make heroines out of young women whose morals left a great deal to be desired. For a time the shelves of the circulating libraries were crowded with works of fiction the titles and jacket drawings of which hinted broadly that they were concerned with the exploits of maidens who would not have been eligible for membership in the Christian Endeavor Society.

I had no wish to add to that collection, yet I foresaw that unless my portrait of Chris Winton could be drawn with skill the result would be a very poor likeness indeed, and I should succeed only in picturing her as another bad girl with a heart of gold. It is nearly always a mistake to use real characters in fiction. The persons one finds so attractive in real life often seem commonplace once you put them on paper. On the other hand, if you try to point them up by exaggerating their pleasantly individual characteristics, all too frequently you discover that you have created, not a human being, but a caricature.

But I was a long time reaching that conclusion. Meantime, as opportunity presented, I picked up such facts as I could about her life. That was not very difficult. For a good many years she was " ignored " by the respectable ladies of San Francisco, which meant that her name was very often on their tongues. Although I felt it beneath my dignity to take part in such gossip, I frequently contrived to be within ear-shot when she was under discussion. Information I gathered in that way remained in my mind for years. Later I was able to piece out and complete her story.

Her maiden name was Christine West. She was born in Red Bluff, a town near the upper end of the Sacramento Valley, in 1866. Her father was Harry West, who once conducted a hay and provisions business there. Later he operated a group of freight-wagons between the valley and several mining and lumbering settlements on the west slope of the Sierra. Later still, after the railroad reached Red Bluff, he built a warehouse at the lower edge of town, with a spur track along its eastern side, and went into the business of buying and selling wheat and wool. He became one of the substantial citizens of the town. The town itself was more important than it is now.

When I passed through Red Bluff not long ago I was curious enough to stop and inquire if Harry West's warehouse were still standing. It was. I drove out and looked at it. It had been unused for years, and its roof and board-and-batting sides were warped and bleached by the hot valley sun. But the legend: " H. West, Wheat and Wool," painted in widely spaced fat letters along the side facing the railroad could be deciphered. Below the sign was a series of numbered doors. On the opposite side, fronting on the street, were a loading platform and a similar line of doors, most of them off their tracks.

That old building interested me, and I found myself reflecting that Casebolt could have written eloquently of its significance in the changing economy of California. Six decades ago it had been a very lively place indeed. Before its block-long loading platform were drawn up each August and September a series of great, dusty wagons, each pulled by six horses, bearing sacks of wheat from the huge ranches across the river. Each spring another line of wagons appeared, loaded high with bales of wool sheared from the immense herds that roved the plains to the west. Both are vanished caravans, living only in memory. The wheat ranches are of course no more, and if the sheepmen still send their wool to market at Red Bluff, Harry West is not there to receive it.

At the northern end of the warehouse, worn steps led to what used to be the office. One panel was out of the door; I looked inside. Piles of straw and empty cans were strewn about. I regarded the littered room with respect. There Harry West had played his part in the complicated processes by which bread had appeared on far-away tables, and men who spoke strange tongues had had clothes for their backs and blankets to warm them at night. There, too, Harry West had known a belated second flowering of romance. I told myself that when I wrote my novel about Chris this old warehouse should be good for an effective chapter. It should be, I decided, a little quaint and a little sad, this story of Harry West's courtship, touching in the way simple, far-off events sometimes are, and with a certain poetic charm. I sometimes did that sort of thing passably well.

I returned to the center of town and made further inquiries. The old West home, too, still stood. Changes come slowly in these quiet valley towns. I drove out Jefferson Street to its northern end, located the house, and stopped across the street. It was a rambling, two-story building, L-shaped, with a porch extending along the inside of the L. There were orange and magnolia trees in the yard and, along the sidewalk, a row of magnificent black walnuts. An iron fence enclosed the yard, and a driveway led back to a garage that had once been a stable. The lawn and flower-beds were carefully tended; the house itself was painted a cool green.

I let myself in the iron gate, walked up the steps, and rang. From inside came the sound of a woman singing, to an orchestral accompaniment, an aria from *Manon Lescaut*. I waited a few moments, then rang again. There was a mechanical click, followed by silence. A blonde young woman appeared and regarded me through the screen door. She wore blue slacks, a sleeveless waist of the same color, no stockings, and white sandals. A lighted cigarette in a holder depended from the fingers of her right hand; the fingers themselves had brightly painted nails. It was borne on me that the year was not 1870. I explained as best I could the sentimental errand on which

I had come. In the course of my explanation I mentioned my name and, to my gratification, she recognized it. She had read *The Uplands* and *Fortier's Landing*. She had a pleasant, intelligent face. She invited me in.

We sat in a cool, square room, with pale green walls and tan hangings. The furniture was a combination of old-fashioned walnut pieces and upholstered chairs covered with chintz. The room could not have much resembled that which Chris Winton had known as a child.

I learned that my hostess was the wife of one of the town's merchants. She had never heard of Christine Winton. Her husband had bought the house some years before from the widow of a Dr. Orson, who had gone to live in San Francisco with her son, who was also a doctor. It happened that I knew the San Francisco Dr. Orson. We commented on the coincidence and on the demonstrable fact that the world is a small place after all.

I mentioned that Christine Winton's maiden name was West and that her father's name was Harry West. She did not think she had ever heard either of them mentioned. The property used to be known as Dr. Orson's house, but now of course most people called it the Armstrong house. Dr. Orson had lived there many years. She had been under the impression that he had built it.

She asked if I were collecting material for a novel, and when I confessed that I had such an idea in mind she wanted to know if I planned to lay the scene of it in Red Bluff. I said yes, in part. In that very house? I admitted that that, too, was probable. She was far from displeased. When she expressed an intention of purchasing a copy I magnanimously offered to send her one. I wrote her name on the back of an envelope. We parted as old friends. I hope she is not still waiting to read my novel about Chris Winton.

I drove across town to the main highway and turned north. The afternoon was nearly gone and I had still many miles to go before I reached my friend's summer house in the Siskiyous, where I was spending the week-end. I decided to postpone further inquiries until I came south again. I was interested in Chris Winton's childhood, but I was also interested in my dinner.

I stopped at a gasoline station at the edge of the town. The young man filled the tank, checked the oil and water, polished the windshield, and took my money. When he brought the change he asked if there was anything further he could do for me. I asked if he knew anything about Harry West.

He shook his head. " Did you say he lives in town? "

" He did. About sixty years ago."

" Oh. You mean *that* Harry West? "

" I do."

" I've heard about him. In fact, my grandpa used to work for him. What d'you want to know? "

" Nothing right now. I'll be back in a few days and I'll look you up. Meantime, see if you can pick up some information about the old man. I'll make it worth your while."

" Sure," he said. " Fine. You can count on me."

He was as good as his word. When I returned he stated that he had been keeping an eye out for me, and he had got the dope on Harry West. He suggested that I let him drive me about town while we visited some of the old-

timers. I told him I was in his hands. He then suggested
that we go in his car and leave mine behind, and how
about giving it a grease job while we were gone? I agreed
to the grease job.

We talked with some elderly citizens who recalled
Harry West, and some others who had gone to school
with Christine. They remembered them both well, but
they remembered nothing of consequence. Christine was
a thin, leggy girl, tall for her years. She had dark eyes
and a good deal of light hair, which she wore in braids
down her back. No one recalled that she had been considered pretty, but she had a good disposition and a
cheerful smile. I asked about the flawless complexion
that was the glory of her after years. It stirred no memories. The Red Bluff girls seldom wore hats; their skins
were as brown as Indians'. They had freckles, not com-
plexions.

She had had one scholastic triumph. When her class
was graduated from high school she was one of two student orators. As a reward, her father gave her a Shetland
pony and a miniature buggy. It was the only outfit of its
kind in town and because of it she enjoyed a season of
fame. That summer Christine and her pony were to be
seen everywhere on the Red Bluff streets. Often she had
two girl friends on the seat beside her. When her father
took her down to the bay that fall and saw her enrolled
at Mills Seminary, the pony was put out to pasture and
the little buggy gathered dust in the West stable. Christine never saw either of them again.

The reason for that was her father's second marriage.
Soon after Christine's departure Harry West, who had

been ten years a widower, hired a young woman to keep books at his warehouse. She was the daughter of an east-side rancher, who had gone to Sacramento and taken a course in a business college. She was about twenty-five when she went to work for West, less than half his age. No one suspected that a romance was in the making, and when the pair one day drove to the neighboring village of Tehama and were married, the whole county was taken by surprise. They went to Chicago on their honeymoon; when they returned, the bride became the mistress of the house on Jefferson Street.

Christine never saw her stepmother. In Red Bluff it was said that the new Mrs. West objected to having a girl in the house who was only a few years younger than herself. Father and daughter met only when business took him to San Francisco. The town's sympathies were with Christine, but she never came back, and interest soon waned. About two years later Red Bluff learned that Christine had left school and eloped with a man named Winton. Six months later it had word that they had been divorced. Later still, after Harry West had died and his widow had moved to Sacramento, gossip connecting Christine with the San Francisco capitalist James Horton reached the town. That had caused a genuine sensation. Red Bluff remembered her as a gangling schoolgirl with her straw-colored hair in pigtails. In less than ten years she had been married and divorced, and now it was being said of her that she had captivated a multimillionaire. Some lives flowed evenly from beginning to end; others were destined for troubled waters. Impossible to guess what the future might hold for any of us!

As I drove down the main street toward the south I reflected on how little the town had changed since Christine's day. Time had softened the outlines of the double row of little stores, neon signs and gasoline pumps had sprouted here and there, and the sidewalk porches that had once sheltered pedestrians from the summer heat had disappeared. Where Concord stages and creaking freight-wagons had stirred up the dust, trucks and motor-cars now roll smoothly over the concrete. That was all. A little car, shining and new, glided past and swung smartly into a side street. Three young girls were crowded into its single seat, their hair blowing in the breeze. They were joyous and innocent and eager, heedless of what life might have stored up for them.

I thought of Christine and her friends driving her pony down that same street sixty years before.

i i

I must have seen Christine often when I was a child, but the first clear recollection I have of her was in the summer of 1886. It came about in this manner: It was then the custom for most San Francisco families to spend the months of July and August in the country. The exodus got under way immediately after the schools closed for the summer. For a few days transportation facilities were overtaxed, so great was our impatience to exchange comfortable homes in the city for the heat and noise and inconveniences of the resorts that dotted the landscape for a hundred miles to the north, east, and south. On every station platform in town, and at every hour of the day, husbands and fathers could be seen herding their families through the proper gates, repeating instructions as to trains and transfer points, planting hasty kisses on up-turned faces, and returning home to endure, not too un-happily, weeks of separation from their loved ones.

Except for the men who were left behind, I doubt if anyone much enjoyed these vacations. Most of the re-sorts were inland, far from the summer fogs and trade winds that made life in town delightful, but the force of custom was strong and few had the hardihood to op-pose it.

Most San Franciscans went to the same resort year after year, but our family tried a different one each sum-mer. That must have been my father's way of expressing his revolt against the monotony that ruled his life and that of his friends. If custom required that one be bored and uncomfortable for two months out of the twelve, he insisted that at least the scene of our boredom change from year to year. The consequence was that as a child I became familiar with most of the springs and beaches and lakeside hotels that flourished in northern California during the middle eighties.

Our search for variety brought us in due course to Schindler's Mineral Springs, in the foothills overlooking the Napa Valley. We lived in one of a double row of tiny cottages beneath a grove of oaks, and took our meals in the hotel dining-room. The hotel itself was a three-story wooden building of perhaps sixty rooms, with porches across its front at all three levels. From Monday to Sat-urday the place was manless. An air of listlessness hovered over it, broken three times a day by a greedy descent on the dining-room. Afternoons the women gathered on the porches, talking and doing " fancywork," the doors to their rooms open so they might hear the wails of their awakened infants. Children old enough to shift for themselves were under orders to play far enough away so the noise they made would not disturb their elders. At mealtimes they were summoned by the Chinese cook, who struck an iron triangle suspended from a post near the kitchen door.

Husbands and fathers arrived Saturday evenings, by the Vallejo boat and the railroad that extended up the valley as far as Calistoga. At dinner that night the dining-room was transformed. Bottles of Napa Valley claret appeared on the tables and the women wore their brightest summer dresses. The meal was prolonged far beyond the usual time. Male voices filled the room, and smoke spiraled upward from cigars produced from the upper pockets of vests and ceremoniously lighted. The Chinese waiters brought in bottles of brandy — with which the men spiked their final cups of coffee — and, grinning broadly, brushed crumbs from the red-and-white checked tablecloths and carried away the debris.

On Sundays there were picnics along the foothill streams, or visits, in buggies hired from the livery stables in town, to friends who had summer houses in the neighborhood, or to the stone wineries on the valley floor. Dinner was at six. At half past seven the bus left in a din of good-byes and rattled down the hill to meet the night train. When it was gone, women and children settled back for another manless week.

There were always a few women at the Springs who had no part in these noisy week-ends. Some were widows or elderly spinsters; their solitary Sundays (and Saturday nights) needed no apology. Others were on less solid ground. Their explanations: John has to work day and night at the factory this summer . . . George will be up as soon as he closes an important deal on which he is working . . . Frank is expecting to be called east — were accepted with reservations. The wives were not given the benefit of a reasonable doubt. The real cause of John's or George's or Frank's absence was usually known.

Christine Winton offered no explanation; none was possible. The Winton divorce had been in the newspapers two or three years earlier. The Springs was a family resort and a stronghold of respectability, and there was some resentment because Christine had been allowed to come at all. Yet I suspect that most of the women were well pleased to have her there. Few things so pleasantly ease the boredom of a summer hotel as the presence of a lady whom the other ladies can conscientiously snub.

We first saw Mrs. Winton in the dining-room the evening we arrived. During the next few weeks we saw a great deal more of her. Like us, she lived, not at the hotel, but in one of the cottages. The latter had names, painted on signs suspended from their ornate little porches. Ours was Daisy; Mrs. Winton's, across the street and a few doors north, was called Poppy. She was far more energetic than the other women guests, and we children encountered her often. She seemed elderly to us, as did all adults, but she was younger than most of the guests, and I know now that she was in her early twenties. Twice a day she took walks into the foothills behind the hotel. On our rambles we often met her, swinging past on her long legs at a pace that soon left us behind. That purposeful stride surprised us because it was so unlike the lagging gait then considered proper for strolling gentlewomen. Her hair was in tight braids about her head. Her face and arms were deeply tanned. By present standards her hips and breasts and arms were too full for beauty. The emaciated damsels of today would have dismissed her as cow-like. They would have been wrong. She was a fine physical specimen, healthy and strong and Junoesque. She should have had ten babies.

It is a mistake to imagine that children are as innocent of what goes on about them as they seem to be. Within a day or two even the dullest of us knew there was something about Mrs. Winton that merited our close attention. We were warned not to play on the porch of Poppy cottage. It was explained to us that Mrs. Winton liked to be alone. ("She doesn't understand children; she has none of her own, you know.") We must answer politely if she spoke to us, but we must volunteer no remarks. After these warnings she naturally received our undivided attention. When she appeared, all activity stopped. We watched her approach, doffed our caps when she came opposite, then turned and stared after her as long as she remained in sight. She never gave any sign that she considered such behavior unusual.

At mealtimes she sat at a corner table at the end of the room most remote from the door. She entered and left under our watchful eyes. She spoke to no one except the Chinese waiter. Yet she seemed perfectly at ease, and there was surely nothing wrong with her appetite. She was always among the first at table, and she devoted herself to her food with a gusto that did not fall very far short of greediness. Her long walks must have made her hungry.

Because she was usually so punctual, everyone was curious one Saturday night when her chair remained unoccupied until dinner was nearly over. She appeared at last, but not alone. She was followed by a tall, ungainly-looking man, whose hair and beard were streaked with gray. As they walked between the tables she turned and addressed him over her shoulder. " Look! It's almost seven. We're just in time! "

He regarded her soberly, but made no reply. Neither seemed to notice the silence that had fallen over the room. At her table he removed her cape — evenings at the Springs were sometimes chilly — and held back her chair. Her voice could be heard in every part of the room when she spoke to the waiter:

" Set another place, please, Wing. Mr. Horton is having dinner with me."

Jim Horton! A murmur rustled through the room. All activity was suspended as the significance of this joint appearance sunk in.

My mother leaned forward and whispered urgently: " I think it's outrageous. Imagine her bringing him here! "

Father seemed undisturbed. " This is the dining-room," he pointed out. " Where else would she bring him? "

" There's such a thing as decency," snapped my mother. " Come, Walter."

I had no wish to leave. "I want to finish my ice cream," I protested.

"You have finished it."

"I want some more."

"George, speak to Walter!" cried my mother.

Father regarded her tranquilly. "Let him have more if he wants it. There's no real danger of contamination." He produced a cigar and clipped off the end with the gold cutter Mother had given him for Christmas.

She subsided. But her manner said clearly: "Very well, I have taken a stand for the right and you have chosen to overrule me. I therefore remain. But the responsibility is yours." I was not a particularly observant child, but I realized that she was secretly glad to stay.

Jim Horton had driven down from Slaterock, only a few miles up the valley. We saw his light, yellow-wheeled buggy in front of Poppy cottage when we finally went outdoors again. But first we saw all that could be seen of Mrs. Winton and her guest.

Even to the eyes of a child they seemed a strange pair. It was not the difference in their ages, for at twelve there is little to choose between twenty and fifty; they were unalike in other respects. She was lively and talkative; he was slow of speech and motion. While she spoke she was seldom in repose; she tossed her head and made gestures with her hands; she smiled often. He slouched comfortably in his chair, one elbow on the table edge; the expression on his long face seldom changed; his eyes, beneath their bushy brows, regarded her gravely. She sat severely erect; his long body leaned and sprawled.

Horton ordered a bottle of champagne. (Everybody

in the room watched the waiter loosen the cork, waited expectantly for the pop.) He frequently refilled his glass, first adding a few drops to hers, which she hardly touched. He ate little. She applied herself to her food with her usual relish, keeping up a constant flow of talk. She may have been making up for her solitary days at the Springs. Sometimes she held her fork suspended between plate and lips while she rattled on, unable to find a pause.

They were among the last to leave the dining-room. As they left the hotel and walked down the little street, occasional snorts of disdain could be heard from the porches of the cottages. Neither paid any attention; they might have been strolling down a country lane. They paused before Horton's buggy and Christine rubbed the horse's nose and stroked its neck. The murmur of their voices could be heard; once Christine's laughter drifted across the summer twilight. Then Horton untied his horse, tossed the halter into the buggy and climbed into the seat.

Christine waited until he had passed out of sight round the turn in the road. Then she walked lightly up the steps of Poppy cottage and closed the door behind her.

iii

Seven or eight years after that summer at Schindler's Springs, I had what seemed to me a romantic adventure. I was then eighteen and in my second year at college. I was long since aware that Christine Winton was Horton's mistress, and that he had given her the house on

Sacramento Street where she lived, and the beautifully matched team behind which she daily drove over the red-rock roads of Golden Gate Park. She was by then a well-known figure in town, but it was not alone because of her notoriety that many turned and looked after her during her drives. She made an agreeable figure as she flashed past, sitting straight in her seat, her gloved hands holding the reins and whip, the wheels of her fragile Brewster trap spinning like polished disks as she faced the wind. Her lips were parted and her eyes bright with excitement. She drove too fast for safety, but even those who deplored her recklessness admired her skill. She had no accidents.

The Sacramento Street house is still standing. It and its history are well known to old-time San Franciscans. It is on the south side of the street, a few blocks beyond Van Ness Avenue, and unchanged in architecture, although it is not now so well kept as it was in Christine's day. It is a narrow frame building with a two-story bay window in front. White marble steps lead to a recessed entrance and a pair of tall walnut doors. When it was new, its severe lines and absence of " millwork " were regarded as too austere for the ornamental tastes of that generation, but it was well placed on its lot, and the lot itself was wide and attractively terraced. Like many of the houses of the period it was painted an unattractive putty color, a device that was thought to render invisible the soot from the soft Mount Diablo coal, then our staple domestic fuel. A stone retaining wall extended along the front of the lot, topped by a prim iron fence. At the upper end the wall gave way to a concrete driveway, ridged to prevent the horses' feet from slipping. The driveway led to the stable, a building almost as large as the house itself. It had three stalls and a carriage room on the ground floor, and a hayloft above. In the center of its roof was a graceful, six-sided cupola, surmounted by a weathervane: a racehorse in full stride, drawing a cart, the jockey bent low in its seat.

At that time there existed across the bay, a mile or two beyond Berkeley and near the county line, a place called San Pablo Park. It was a recreation park of the sort familiar all over California in the days before the automobile. There were benches and tables beneath a grove of trees where family parties came to eat picnic lunches brought in wicker baskets. Waiters hurried among the benches bearing trays of beer in glass mugs. At the edge of the grove was a baseball diamond, with a tiny grandstand behind the home plate. Other facilities for violent exercise were provided: a circular running track, dumb-bells and lifting weights, " acting bars," a boxing platform (with gloves for rent), an open-air bowling alley. There were also a bar, a restaurant, and — this was the central attraction — a dance floor.

On Sunday afternoons and evenings San Pablo Park was the liveliest place for miles around. Among the crowd were usually a sprinkling of youths from Berkeley, and I was sometimes among them. We regarded our visits to the park as slumming expeditions, I suppose because most of those we encountered there were workmen and their girls: mechanics and teamsters, clerks and domestic servants and factory hands. Many were foreigners, Spaniards and Portuguese and " bohunks," our collective name for middle-Europeans. The atmosphere was friendly; drinking was in moderation and there was never any serious disorder. This was in contrast to Shellmound Park, a few miles distant on the bay front in Emeryville, which was patronized by a rougher element and where drunkenness and fist fights were frequent. We steered clear of Shellmound; San Pablo Park was more to our taste. After a few glasses of beer we forgot our fancied superiority along with our shyness, and soon we were vying with the others for the privilege of dancing with the prettiest girls. To our minds an aura of sin hovered over the place, but that must have been imaginary. The girls we persuaded to stroll between dances into the remoter parts of the grounds proved to be veritable fortresses of decorum.

One Sunday afternoon I was dancing with a stolid Swedish girl — who worked in an Oakland bakery — when my attention was drawn to a party of three, two women and a man, who had just arrived at a table near the dance floor. Something in the posture of one of the women aroused my curiosity. Her back was toward me and I could see only that her light hair was in braids about her head and that her tan coat was thrown loosely across her shoulders. I kept an eye on her, certain I had seen her before, but unable to recall where. Then, as my partner and I circled nearer, she turned her head toward the man in her group, and I saw her face in profile. It was Christine Winton. I did not know her companions. The man was small and foreign-looking, with a singular, pointed mustache. He was certainly not Jim Horton.

My discovery strangely excited me. That Mrs. Winton,

one of the most talked-about women in San Francisco, should appear at this workmen's park on the edge of Berkeley seemed to me remarkable. It gave me a feeling of importance to reflect that, except for her two companions, I was perhaps the only one in all the park who knew who she was. I wondered what might happen if I were to approach her table and address her by name. I believed that my words might have some startling effect; she might even spring from her chair and flee in consternation. But there was nothing in her manner to indicate that anything so dramatic would ensue. If she considered her presence there extraordinary she gave no evidence of it. She sat relaxed and placid, a mug of beer before her, gazing about with a pleased sort of interest. She looked exactly as she had during her solitary meals at the Napa County resort years before.

Perhaps I had had too many glasses of beer, or it may have been that my knowledge of who she was gave me courage I would not otherwise have had. At any rate, when the music started again and her two friends joined the crowd on the dance floor, I marched boldly to her table and asked if I might have the honor of waltzing with her.

Her eyes rested on me with a mild sort of curiosity. She shook her head. "Thank you for asking me just the same," she added.

The smile that accompanied her words was so friendly that I was encouraged to make a further suggestion. Might I sit out the dance with her?

"Of course, if you like," she said. She nodded toward the chair opposite. I sat down.

I could not at once think of anything to say. I had fully expected that she would recognize me, and her failure to do so left me temporarily at a loss. But before I could feel embarrassed, she spoke:

" I was just about to order a sandwich. I've been horseback riding all day and I'm starved. D'you think you can catch that waiter's eye? "

I grandly summoned the man. But having accomplished the miracle of speaking to her, of sitting across the table from her, my courage ebbed away. I was a shy youth, solemn and humorless and, for all my belief to the contrary, innocent and naïve. How could I hope to carry off this situation? I had read my share of romantic novels and I well knew what role I wished to play. I had brought myself to the attention of a beautiful woman (I thought she was beautiful); we were seated tête-à-tête in festive surroundings, and the strains of a romantic waltz filled the air. It was my cue to be amusing in a careless way and toss off epigrams in a gay, bantering tone. But there should be an undercurrent of cynicism in my gaiety, a suggestion of weariness that would show that here, beneath the mask of playfulness, sat a lonely man who had known disillusionment. There should have been, too, a touch of gray at my temples, a pointed Vandyke (jet black), and in my tanned, lean face a pair of steel-gray eyes with the look of far places in their depths. My ambition, in short, was to be a dead ringer for one of Laura Jean Libbey's heroes.

Christine slid her beer mug across the table.

" Have a sip," she invited. " It's a shame to let it go to waste. I've hardly touched it."

Mrs. Libbey's hero would have known how to cope with that remark, but it was beyond me.

"Thank you," I said politely. "I don't mind if I do."

I took a long and bitter swallow. At least I would make it clear to her that alcohol and I were not strangers.

When I put down the mug she smiled approvingly. "That's sensible. Some people just won't drink out of people's glasses. What nonsense!"

"I don't see why not," I said, a trifle indignantly. I took another swallow.

I was aware that I was creating the impression that I made a practice of going about finishing others' drinks. I didn't mind. Her smile was so friendly, her interest so warm, that my shyness slipped away. It was impossible to feel constraint in her presence. She was completely natural. It was as though she had never lost the enjoyment of simple pleasures — that gift we are all born with, but which most of us get rid of as soon as we can. The world was ever a pleasant place to her, to be accepted with gratitude and enjoyed to the full. She lived in the present. The past was worth recalling only for its happy memories, and if she gave a thought to the future it was to anticipate how much fun she was going to have.

That is not, of course, the sort of philosophy prudent men approve. Most of us find such irresponsibility outrageous. We recognize that life is grim and the future uncertain and probably dark, and that if we don't look out for number one, no one else will. Christine never bothered her head about number one. She was confident that so pleasant a world would not fail to take excellent care of her. And so it proved. So far as anyone knew, she never had a worry in her life. Her career confounded the moralists and earned her the censure of the just, but that caused her little concern. Her interest in people bore not much relation to what they thought of her. If they were kind she accepted their kindness as her due; if they were hostile that idiosyncrasy interested her fully as much. I don't believe there was anything conscious about all that. Chris was not given to self-analysis. It was merely that the behavior of human beings interested her immensely.

She seemed to find even me interesting. My confidence returned.

iv

" I used to know you a long time ago," I said. " It was that summer at Schindler's Springs."

Immediately she was all interest. The coincidence delighted her. We had met before and I had recognized her after all those years. She began to ask questions, leaning across the table, not stopping until she had identified me among the group of children at the Springs that summer, and the house where I had lived. Daisy cottage! And hers had been called the Poppy! The waiter brought her sandwich. She ate it with gusto, keeping up her cross-examination.

" I can't get over the way you've grown. You're almost a man. And so intellectual-looking! "

That is not the sort of compliment I would much enjoy today, but I had great respect for learning in those days and I flushed with pleasure. My embarrassment made me bold. " I thought you were beautiful," I said. " I still think so."

She smiled at my compliment, but made no comment. She regarded me with friendly eyes. I found her expression extremely attractive. It seemed to say: " We two understand each other, and what's more, we understand that the world's a fine place, made especially for our enjoyment." Many have commented, not always approvingly, on the peculiarly personal quality of her gaze. A woman of my acquaintance once remarked that the way Chris Winton looked at a man reminded her of a cocker spaniel puppy begging for its dinner. That was not a very apt comparison. There was a certain warmth in her glance, but no self-interest, and of course she never had to beg for anything. People said that she might have got a great deal more out of Jim Horton, and no doubt they were right. She lived comfortably, but in no great luxury. Her Sacramento Street establishment was unpretentious. It was about the sort of house one would expect, say, of a wholesale butcher or a reasonably honest public official. Her next-door neighbor was a retired Episcopal clergyman with whom, by the way, she was on excellent terms. Horses were her one extravagance. Clothes, jewelry, the theater, these held no consuming interest for her. She took them as she took everything else, never permitting the wish for more to spoil her pleasure in what she had. There were dozens of women in her position in San Francisco, and of course hundreds of wives, who made a greater display with money wheedled from men far poorer than Jim Horton.

I was not a talkative youth, and when I was with persons I did not know well, it was usually an effort to keep up my end of the conversation. I had no such trouble with Chris Winton. Talk flowed from her lips as effortlessly as water in a brook, and made no more demand on the listener. One could understand why Horton, who was a reticent man, so much enjoyed her company.

Without my asking, she explained her presence at San Pablo Park. She had gone by train that morning to Port Costa, a town some miles farther up the bay. Horton owned a manufacturing plant there, the California Clay Products Company, which made sewer pipe. She kept a riding horse on the property — it was hundreds of acres in extent — and she went up several times a month. She liked to ride over the windy hills; besides, she explained, if she stayed away, her pony would eat his head off in idleness.

" I'll tell you something funny," she said. " Mr. Horton tells me that the plant is losing money and that the only reason he keeps it running is so I can go up there and ride. ' That pony of yours costs me twenty-five thousand dollars a year,' he says. That's all nonsense. He'd shut the plant down fast enough if he thought it didn't pay. He likes his little joke."

She must have found the memory of this entertaining, for she gave an amused chuckle.

" Tony says the plant is doing well and that Mr. Horton can easily afford to keep my pony out of his profits. Tony's the manager at the plant, and that's his wife with him. Did you notice her? — she's pretty as a picture.

They've only been married two months. His name is Pedrini and hers was Schoenfelt, but they get along beautifully. They're on their way to Oakland now to a dance at his lodge, and they asked me to ride in with them. They'll let me off at the Sixteenth Street station. Can you imagine them driving all that way for a dance? And home again afterwards! It will be daylight when they get back. But that's not all. When we were passing just now, Tony heard the music. Nothing would do but he had to stop and have a dance or two, just to get warmed up for tonight. I never knew anyone who liked dancing the way he does, although Rose is almost as bad. There they are now! "

Tony's waxed mustache and flashing white teeth rotated into view and disappeared again.

" Are you sure you don't want to dance? " I asked.

" I'd rather just sit and look on. But I mustn't keep you. I see lots of pretty girls about. I'm sure they'd all be glad to dance with a handsome college boy. D'you know many of the girls? I suppose you've got a special favorite? "

" Oh, no," I said airily. " It's lots more fun taking them as they come. One meets all kinds here, you know."

That mildly cynical remark was lost on her. " It seems such a jolly crowd. Everyone is having a good time. Do you come often? "

" Not very." I was a little ashamed of frequenting so plebeian a resort. " This is the third time."

" But you ought to come oftener. You know that saying about all work and no play. I suppose they make you study hard at the university? I went to Mills, you know; there was always a great deal for us to do. We had dancing on Saturday nights, from eight to ten thirty, but it wasn't so much fun as this. I can see the university from the train whenever I go to Port Costa. Now that I know you're there, I'll think of you. I'll try to picture you sitting in the classroom, answering all the professor's questions and getting high marks."

I do not know if I have been able to suggest the easy charm of her inconsequential flow of talk. It was impossible not to be pleased with her. It was never what she said, for she dealt entirely in trivialities. I doubt if she consciously made a profound remark in all her life. She spoke her mind, and her mind was frank and artless and with a childlike sense of fun. Her most severe note was a sort of gentle raillery. Perhaps the secret of the pleasure one got from listening to her lay in the fact that she talked for her own mild amusement and because she assumed you would be mildly amused too. You always were. Time passed unheeded and presently Tony and his wife were standing beside the table.

I sprang up as Mrs. Winton introduced us. " Mr. Doane has been keeping me entertained. Did you wonder who he was? He's an old friend. He goes to the University. His father is editor of the *Herald*."

Tony's teeth flashed as we shook hands. They had, he vowed, had a marvelous dance. The music was divine and the floor, although a bit bumpy in that far corner, was superb. But they had stayed too long and now they must drive like mad to get Mrs. Winton to her train.

Christine gave my hand a reassuring squeeze.

"It's been so nice having a little talk," she said.

I watched them thread their way through the crowd and disappear among the trees.

v

It is hard to explain the reticences of youth. To this day I do not know why I kept that, to me, dramatic meeting to myself. Although I mentioned the incident to no one, it was often in my thoughts. When Christine Winton's name was mentioned, which was often, I pretended indifference, but little of the gossip about her escaped me. I had no trouble keeping tab on her movements, her appearance, or her behavior. If she spent an afternoon shopping, or went to a matinee, or took her usual drive through the Park, the fact was reported over hundreds of dinner tables that evening. "I saw that Mrs. Winton in the Lace House, at the glove counter. She bought three pairs of pigskin driving gloves and charged them. I'd like to see the bills Jim Horton pays every month!" "She was sitting across the aisle, big as life, eating a bag of peanuts and dropping the shells on the floor." "If Roberts hadn't pulled over to the right, she would have crashed right into us. I wonder the authorities allow it."

The city's curiosity about Chris Winton was not to be explained wholly by the fact that she was what was called a notorious woman. The San Francisco of the eighties was less puritanical than most cities. Ladies who earned their livelihood by going to bed with gentlemen not their husbands were far from rare. Not many years earlier, a man who wanted a mistress, and who could afford the considerable expense of supporting one, was more often envied than censured. Far from keeping his lady in the background, he missed no opportunity to exhibit her in public as evidence of his prosperity, his initiative, and his standing in the community. Thirty years later such frankness was no longer condoned; the man who did not preserve a nominal secrecy in such matters was made to feel the public's disapproval. He was likely to be snubbed by decent citizens, especially by those who did no business with him and didn't expect to.

Horton's case was a little different. He had a finger in so many pies that to disapprove publicly of his behavior required a high degree of moral courage. But there were a few who met that test. In 1891 the Reverend Henry Starkweather frankly told his friends that if Horton sent a contribution to the building fund of his church (which Mrs. Horton had once attended) he would return it forthwith. Horton sent no check and the preacher was spared the necessity of carrying out his threat. None the less his courage was widely applauded and for several months he preached to a noticeably enlarged congregation. A few years earlier Horton's name was absent from the list of patrons of a fair held at the Mechanics Pavilion for the benefit of the Children's Hospital, and in 1898 Ned Greenway is said to have seriously considered withholding Clifford's card to the Friday Night Cotillions. That about exhausts the list, so it would not be accurate to state that Horton's friendship with Mrs. Winton made him a social pariah. One heard, of course, a good deal of reproving comment, but it was usually under circumstances where there was small likelihood of its ever reaching Horton's ears. In general, our citizens took the stand that secret condemnation was better than none at all, and the pious had the further comfort of knowing what fate was eventually in store for sinners.

Chapter 6

CHRISTINE WINTON entered Mills Seminary in the fall of 1881. She spent the Christmas holidays at the school. During the long vacation the following summer she visited a classmate who had become a close friend. The friend was Juliet Horton. They spent July and most of August at Slaterock.

In her garrulous later years Aunt Julie often speaks of Christine and when she does I listen with attention. Their friendship began when their German music teacher selected them to sing a duet at a Sunday evening musicale. These were weekly functions at the seminary, the times when parents and selected guests were permitted to share the social life of the students. Both girls were thoroughly unmusical and remained so all their lives. (Aunt Julie could never understand her brother's contributions to our Symphony Orchestra or to the Opera Association.) Juliet went to Herr Berner and asked to be excused. She did not mind the singing lessons, for they were required of all the girls, but she objected to making a spectacle of herself in public. The man of music was inflexible. Each of his girls must once a year perform at a musicale. The musicales were a tradition at the seminary; they were known far and wide, and they had sometimes been artistic triumphs. Emmy Wixom had been happy to sing before Mrs. Mills and her guests, and Emmy Wixom was now Emma Nevada of the Metropolitan Opera Company, and the entire West was proud of her. Juliet, who knew all about Emmy Wixom and who had no wish to sing at the Metropolitan, continued to object. Herr Berner put his small foot down. All the girls had performed that year except Miss Horton and Miss West. Miss Horton and Miss West would therefore perform the following Sunday evening. He had selected two simple *Lieder* for them, suited to their voices and without difficult passages. From Monday until Saturday they must practice their songs one hour daily, and on Sunday evening they must entertain their guests, their teachers, and their classmates.

Juliet left with fire in her eye and hunted up Christine. She proved to have as little taste for the ordeal as Juliet herself. They talked over their bad luck and tried to think of something they might do about it. The next day they appeared at Herr Berner's studio and sang their parts at the top of their young lungs, resolutely refusing to keep in key. The little German struggled with them for five days, made no progress, and on Saturday morning pronounced them hopeless and canceled their appearance. Thereupon the girls professed to be disappointed. They had worked hard with their songs and they thought it only fair that they be allowed to make a public appearance. Would Herr Berner permit them to sing just one

song? Herr Berner would not. They must not be allowed to disgrace themselves and their teacher. Positively, they could have no part in the musicale. Outside
his door the conspirators shook hands triumphantly. A
lifelong friendship was born.

Slaterock was newly completed that summer. The cli-
mate of the Napa Valley was then much admired and
many San Francisco families went there to escape the
foggy months about the bay. It was an ostentatious age
and few of the summer homes were simple. Slaterock
takes its name from an outcropping of stratified stone
behind the stables — which, by the way, Casebolt states
is not slate but something quite different. It occupies a
shelf on the west side of the valley. An early photograph
of the house appears in Casebolt's *Life*: it is a big, square
building with dormer windows and a tower. The wooden
siding is grooved to give the illusion of stone blocks.
There were, and still are, folding wooden shutters inside
the tall windows. When the photograph was taken, the
garden was newly laid out; the acacias and magnolias that
now surround the structure and hide its ugliness were only
a few feet high.

The photograph is one of the family groups popular
a generation ago. On the gravel driveway to the left of the
porch stands a handsome horse hitched to a buggy. In the
buggy lounges a bearded figure wrapped in a linen duster.
A number of other figures are visible. A servant holds the
horse's head. A woman wearing a skirt with broad, hori-
zontal stripes is at the top of the steps, one hand against a
fluted column of the porch. Below her, two girls are
seated side by side; two pairs of pointed shoes show de-

murely beneath the folds of their skirts. A small boy in a tight jacket poses on the lower step, his crooked elbow resting on the balustrade. The caption reads: " Summer at Slaterock, 1882." Below, in small type, some of the group are identified. The man in the buggy is Horton. His wife stands beside the pillar of the porch, and the small boy is Clifford, aged about ten. The two girls are stated to be " Juliet Horton (left) and friend." The friend is Chris West. Aunt Julie, using her magnifying glass, recently made a positive identification. She professed to recall even the dress Christine was wearing. It was of sea-green silk, a product of the sewing class at the seminary. The photograph, Aunt Julie avers, was made on a Sunday. Only thus could their formal attire be explained. Besides, her father was rarely there on weekdays.

Her examination of the photograph stirred Aunt Julie to reminiscences of that summer. She recalled that Christine celebrated her sixteenth birthday there, with a party under the oaks behind the house, and with refreshments served and eaten by the light of Japanese lanterns hung from tree to tree. About twenty of Juliet's friends were there, young people whose families had summer houses in the valley. She was able to recall many of them; they bore names still well known in San Francisco: Fuller, Spreckels, Woodward, Brannan. Some had brought guests. One of the latter was Clyde Winton, a tall youth with a poetic face, who was then preparing for the ministry. He was fascinated by Christine. He contrived to be her partner at croquet, to see that she did not lack lemonade, to propel her in the swing, and to sit beside her at supper under the lanterns. It was Christine's first grown-up party and her first beau. She was flattered by his attentions, and far from displeased.

But the next day when Juliet teased her about her conquest and predicted that she was destined to become a minister's wife, Chris shrugged and dismissed the matter. She had three more years at the seminary and she intended to study hard. She had no time for beaux. If Clyde Winton called on her at Mills (young men were permitted, under proper restrictions, on Sunday afternoons), she would send him about his business. Her good sense was applauded. She was pronounced a well-balanced girl, prudent beyond her years.

Only a few months later she climbed out of her dormitory window one rainy night and eloped with Clyde Winton. They were married at San Jose on February 6, 1883.

ii

The bride and groom spent several days at the St. James Hotel in San Jose, then moved to San Francisco to the Pleasanton, a family hotel on Sutter Street. Clyde Winton was nineteen, his wife was three years younger. His father had been a partner in the firm of Schular, Winton & Briggs, a well-known law firm of the seventies and eighties. He had died a few years earlier, leaving his widow and only child a comfortable home on Jones Street and large holdings of land in the San Joaquin Valley. Judge Winton had married late in life. When he died his wife was still a comparatively young woman; within a year, the minimum period then permitted by convention, she married Dr. Horace Allbright, the physician who had attended the Judge during his last illness.

Clyde Winton's elopement with the pretty Mills Seminary girl delighted thousands, but his mother was not among those who applauded. When the news from San Jose reached her she placed herself under the care of her new husband, took to her bed, and remained there for days. But she aroused herself long enough to shut off Clyde's allowance and to inform him, by letter, that henceforth he was on his own. This change in a hitherto compliant parent must have astonished young Winton, but he behaved admirably. He and Christine moved out of the Pleasanton into a Pine Street boarding-house while he set off to find a job suitable to a young married man intent on carving out a fortune. But business was in one of its slack periods and none of the firms to which he applied had a desirable opening. Their cash dwindled. Christine had received her quarterly allowance a few days before their elopement and this tided them over the first weeks. When it was gone her pride would not allow her to ask for more. She had not told her father of her plan to marry, and he had failed to answer the telegram she had sent him from San Jose. Their last dollar was presently spent.

Juliet and Chris had been roommates at the seminary that year, and Juliet was the only one who had shared the secret of the impending elopement. She had done nothing to discourage it; even then Christine was not one who took advice easily. For all her amiability, her air of

accepting whatever life might offer, she had an inner core
of stubbornness. Once she had taken a stand she was as
solid as a rock. Julie did not try to talk her out of the
elopement; instead, she asked her to write fully and often.
The promise was fulfilled. Letters came regularly back to
the seminary, from San Jose, from the Pleasanton, from
Pine Street. Juliet read them closely. She was not deceived by their serene tone.

Juliet tells of crossing the bay one Sunday and spending an afternoon with Chris. She found her packing her
belongings and preparing to move again. They had rented
a room south of Market Street. This, Chris explained,
was a temporary measure. When Clyde found a job — he
had several in prospect; one would surely materialize in
a day or two — they would find more suitable quarters.
Perhaps they would buy one of the attractive cottages
they had admired one day in a new district called Hayes
Valley. Juliet offered her the few dollars she had in her
purse. Chris refused, good-naturedly but with finality.
Clyde did not put in an appearance. Defeated, Juliet
went back across the bay.

She did not hear from Chris for some time. Then she
had a letter telling her the news she had been expecting.
Chris had not written sooner because she had a job and
it had kept her busy. She had been working two weeks
and had earned ten dollars. The job had come about in
this way: One day she was passing the shoe factory on
Valencia Street and had noticed a sign in the window of
the office: " Girls Wanted." She had started at seven
the next morning. She checked the sizes of shoes and
packed them in cardboard boxes and then in wooden

cases. The work was hard, but she had no intention of doing it forever. She had rented a room near by; there she slept and cooked her meals. Clyde had gone back to Jones Street, to his mother's house. She had not heard from him for nearly a month.

iii

What happened to Chris during the next few years and how she accepted it make it clear that she was never one to cry over spilt milk. Having got herself into trouble, she made the best of the situation, with no signs of regret. Then and later she faced adversity with a fortitude that some thought was due to an unconquerable self-reliance and others put down to plain lack of imagination. I doubt if Chris gave the matter any particular thought. With her the past was the past, the future was still to come, and the present was never half so bad as it might be.

Her job at the shoe factory ended after a few weeks. It was some time before she found anything else. She answered ads in the newspapers and made the rounds of the employment agencies. She did not pick and choose. Her money was nearly gone and she had a healthy appetite that needed to be satisfied. She became a waitress in a Sansome Street restaurant and was discharged at the end of the first day for general incompetence. She crossed the bay and became nursemaid to the children of a Berkeley physician and regretfully left when the widowed father of her charges nightly made determined attempts to get into bed with her. She worked as a cash-girl in a Market Street department store and had to quit after a few days because nine hours of hurrying through the aisles caused her feet to swell so badly that she had trouble getting her shoes on in the morning. Her wages for the four days were not quite enough to pay for the uniform she had been obliged to buy. In later years she gave that store a wide berth. Each morning she got up soon after daylight, bought the *Chronicle* and the *Morning Call*, and read the help-wanted ads while she drank a cup of coffee in a Howard Street restaurant. Then she hurried off to the address that looked most promising, intent on getting a place near the head of the line.

One morning she lined up on the third floor of a South of Market loft building. When the door opened, a little before seven, she was one of five girls admitted. The firm was Bridgeman & Company, which manufactured novelty garments for women: cotton shirtwaists and dresses and aprons. The girls were paid by the piece, which meant that until they acquired speed they earned very little. Christine acquitted herself well. She was naturally quick with her fingers and she had operated a sewing machine at home and at the seminary. Within a few weeks she could hold her own with women who had been following the trade for years. The competitive spirit of the place fasci-nated her; she enjoyed the excitement that came from pressing to increase her production. Because her work-manship was neat and her hand and eye accurate she man-aged to hold her job when the slack season came and all but a few of the girls were dismissed.

She remained at Bridgeman's six years. During much of that time she was a supervisor; in addition to operating her own machine she kept an eye on a group of other girls. She had a housekeeping room in a big, dilapidated house on Rincon Hill, once the residence of an early-day banker, the windows of which looked out on the big brick warehouse of James Horton & Company, two blocks distant. She did not lead an austere life. She was hardly twenty, and she liked a good time. Her surroundings were unlike those she had known at home or at the seminary, but Christine never had trouble adapting herself to new environments. Neither the long hours, her small earnings, nor the unfamiliar background of her new companions prevented her from enjoying herself. With other girls from the factory she went to dances at the public halls or at lodges or neighborhood clubs. She fell easily into the pattern of a new life. She developed an interest in the theater and week by week followed from seats in the gallery the fortunes of her favorite stock-company actors and minstrel teams. On fine evenings she joined the noisy groups that danced and flirted and drank beer at Woodward's Gardens, or made the long trip by cable and steam car to the beach and watched the sea lions climb over the rocks below the Cliff House. During the long, golden summers she was among the throngs of mechanics and clerks and salesgirls who streamed aboard the ferries on Sunday mornings and spent the day at picnic grounds on the Alameda or Marin shores.

It was because of these Sunday jaunts that she and Juliet renewed their friendship after the lapse of several years. They had lost touch with each other when Juliet, after two years at Mills, had gone east to complete her schooling. During her absence Juliet had heard of Christine only once, and that indirectly. It was the news of her divorce. Juliet learned none of the details until she returned to California, but when she heard them she was not surprised at how her old friend had behaved. Chris's attitude had been one of entire indifference. She did not appear at the hearing. She waived alimony or other settlement. So far as she was concerned, her marriage had ended two years before; this legal hocus-pocus had no bearing on a situation that had already resolved itself. To expect Clyde Winton to pay for the freedom he already had seemed to her too foolish to discuss. Besides, she had a job, she earned enough to support herself and to permit an occasional good time. What would she do with more? The divorce action, being uncontested, was awarded to young Winton. He remarried a few years later. There is no evidence that Chris was even mildly interested.

One evening Juliet, who was returning from Slaterock, boarded the ferry at Vallejo for the trip down the bay to San Francisco. As always on Sunday nights in summer, the boat was jammed with a holiday throng returning from a day at the town's amusement park. It was a far from decorous crowd. Juliet sat on the lower deck and watched it stream aboard. There were family groups, gangs of young toughs from the Potrero, noisy with wine and high spirits, stolid Teutons in caps and corduroy coats, members of rifle teams, their weapons swung over their shoulders, and — far in the majority — groups of young men and girls, disheveled from a day of activity under the hot sun.

The benches were presently filled, then the forward

deck; finally even the aisles were packed with late-comers. From somewhere forward an accordion struck a few bars, then swung into " Mary Ann McCarthy." Two hundred voices took up this perennial favorite of picnickers on the bay, singing the verses at the top of their lungs.

Juliet presently found herself looking into the face of her old schoolmate. Christine was singing lustily, her body swaying to the rhythms of the song. She was hatless. Her face was flushed and her eyes bright; her yellow hair was piled on her head in an unruly mass. Two young men had their arms about her waist; her own were thrown across their shoulders. Juliet declares that those sitting near could not keep their eyes off her. I can well believe it. When Chris was having a good time her face was transfigured. Her eyes sparkled with amusement, her smile invited the world to share her pleasure; she became the embodiment of the spirit of joy.

The accordion blared forth the final bars and the music expired. Christine looked out over the crowd. Her eyes fastened on Juliet and an exclamation of surprise and pleasure escaped her. She disengaged herself and shouldered her way to Julie's side. The two greeted each other with delight. On Chris's part there was no embarrassment at having been seen by her old friend in this plebeian group of picnickers. Juliet made room for her on the crowded bench. They devoted the ride down the bay to learning what had happened since they had last met.

iv

The interrupted friendship was resumed.

Chris was presently climbing the Vallejo Street Hill two or three times a week. She became a familiar figure at the Hortons'. When there were guests in for the evening, she was usually among them. Those who met her there once invariably looked forward to seeing her when they went again.

She made a lasting impression on strangers, and it is not altogether easy to explain why. She was a striking girl but hardly a beauty. Her complexion was fine and I have always thought that her eyes, brown and warm and clear, were uncommonly attractive, but her other features were ordinary. Her greatest asset was her smile. It was friendly and full of good humor. It was at once naïve and wise, childlike and comprehending, and its effect was delightful. Her voice was low and a trifle husky, and when she spoke she did not expect one to listen very closely. One seldom did. It was more pleasant to watch for the appearance of her smile, which was half innocence and half the distillation of wisdom. Her lips were wide and full.

On Juliet's part this reappearance of her old school-mate must have been welcome. Juliet had then been back in San Francisco only a few weeks and she had not yet embarked on the business career that was later to bring her a good deal of attention. Time hung heavily on her hands. She had no taste for the routine to which, as Horton's daughter, she was eligible. Her scorn of our local society was real enough, but it was not wholly due to what she considered its pretentious emptiness. Her renunciation of its pleasures was made easier by the fact that nature had never intended her to shine in such surroundings. Even as a young girl she missed beauty by a wide margin. She had the beak-like nose, the deep-set eyes and equine face of the Hortons. It was a face that a warm friend might pronounce intelligent, but no young woman intent on popularity and beaux could have considered it an asset. To that handicap, perhaps because of it, Juliet added another: a sharp and malicious tongue. That combination proved too much for San Francisco's eligible swains of the eighties. Even the fact that she would presently come into a large fortune could not overcome their fear of this homely, clever girl who was more interested in exposing their stupidities than in flattering them with glances of maidenly admiration. They gave her a wide berth.

I have always considered Juliet the most interesting of the Horton clan. She has character. She has never failed to do and say exactly what she pleases. She was not ashamed to remain unmarried at a time when to be an old maid was at least as serious a crime as grand larceny, and far harder to live down. She is a model of consistency. Her enemies are more numerous than her friends, but most of those in both categories are of many years' standing. Whatever else may be said of her, one always knows where Juliet stands.

She has long had an excellent head for business. When she came back from the East her father put her in charge of the management of the Russian Hill house. Her parents had separated during her absence and Anita had gone to live in New York. Juliet was not long in discovering that during her mother's easy-going regime the functioning of the domestic machinery had grown lax and wasteful. She confronted Horton with evidence that his servants were incompetent and lazy and in collusion with the merchants who supplied his kitchen. Horton tossed the problem back in her lap. The house was her bailiwick; it was her job to clean it up. This she proceeded to do, and with thoroughness. She began by discharging every servant in the place, including the coachman, Elmer Heymes, who had been a hero of her childhood. Horton said nothing. He must have been secretly pleased at this appearance of a vein of iron in his eldest child. It was perhaps his first intimation that Julie, who had been a self-centered child, had phases of her character that he could understand and applaud. The ruthlessness of her reforms may have seemed to him an assurance that she was capable of coping with the world.

Juliet established herself in the second-floor corner suite that had been her mother's and moved a desk into an alcove of the sitting-room. There for an hour or two each morning she interviewed the hired help, issued orders, and planned the day's routine. The result was soon evident. Returning home at night, Horton found order and efficiency in sharp contrast to the days when his wife had exercised her easy-going sway. Meals were bountiful and well prepared, and they were served properly and on time. Inside and out the house was orderly, carefully tended, and neat as a pin. It remains so to this day. Juliet is a notoriously good housekeeper.

About a year after she accomplished this domestic re-organization, Horton one evening announced that he had taken over a North Beach planing mill, the owner of which had failed, owing him several thousand dollars. He planned to hold the property until the building industry, then in one of its slack periods, picked up again, whereupon he hoped to sell it for enough to get his money back and a reasonable profit besides. Juliet was highly interested. She asked Horton to tell her all he knew about the property, what products it made and who bought them. The next day she went down and looked it over for herself. It was a sprawling frame building with a tin roof, its windows opaque with grime and its interior full of lumber, sawdust, and idle machinery. That evening she proposed a business deal to her father. She had time on her hands and some hundreds of dollars of idle savings. She wanted to take over the operation of the mill. The two discussed the possibilities of the arrangement until past midnight.

As a result of that conversation San Franciscans began to pay much closer attention to Juliet. She has since had more spectacular feats to her credit, but few created such widespread curiosity. In 1892 it was unusual for the daughters of prominent citizens to take over the operation of planing mills. Juliet was far too interested to care what the town thought. Once Horton had granted her request, he left her strictly alone. Juliet signed a lease to the property, with an option to buy it at the end of two years, and at a price that would enable Horton to get his investment back, plus eight-per-cent interest. It was the sort of agreement he would have made with any responsible stranger.

It was understood that if she failed she would get no special consideration.

Juliet embarked on her venture at a particularly inauspicious time. The depression of 1892, the severest the town had known since the seventies, was under way. Building was at a standstill. Many contractors, caught with rows of newly finished residences on their hands, no buyers, and pressing bills for materials and labor, went broke. This in turn threw into bankruptcy a group of business firms that had extended the contractors credit: lumber merchants, building-supply houses, planing mills. Horton did not escape entirely. Only his native caution and the fact that he had correctly read the portents and so had curtailed credit to builders kept him out of serious difficulties. He was denounced for having helped precipitate the crisis, but in the end his judgment was proved sound. His was among the few building-supply businesses in San Francisco that rode out the storm.

Juliet met the emergency with energy and good sense. Her aim during the first months was not to make a profit but to keep her mill in operation. There were then a score of similar plants in San Francisco and not enough business for a third as many. It was a question of which could hang on. In her eagerness for a share of the limited business she used whatever advantages came to hand. She undersold her competitors. She extended more liberal credit. She cut wages. When her father refused to sell lumber at the prices she offered, she bought from his rivals, who, close to bankruptcy, proved willing to supply her at less than the cost of production. She drove tirelessly about town in one of Horton's buggies, striving to convince skeptical contractors and builders that the public was again about to begin buying houses. A contractor who lived far out on Jackson Street was persuaded to put up a row of cottages on an adjacent hillside. They were completed, stood idle for several months, then miraculously began to sell. It was an omen, the first intimation that the tide was turning. The city's long-stagnant building industry began to stir again. Juliet, near the end of her rope, continued her efforts. The volume of her business began to grow; she was able to make judicious increases in the prices of her doors and window-sash and moldings. In a few weeks more the North Beach plant, one of the few mills that had operated through the stagnant period, was working at full capacity.

By the summer of 1894 Juliet was out of debt and her business was returning her a modest profit. When her lease expired, she took up her option and assumed ownership. She continued to operate the mill for several years longer. Then, having become involved in more lucrative enterprises, she in turn leased it. It was burned in the fire of 1906.

v

For a number of years both Horton and Juliet confined their social activities to one weekly function, their Thursday evening dinners on the hill. The gatherings were usually a bit on the dull side, but there were sometimes exceptions. Both Horton and Juliet invited their friends — more often they were business acquaintances whom

they were currently cultivating — and the two groups seldom had much in common. Horton's guests were likely to
be from out of town: an Eastern manufacturer on a business tour, the superintendent of one of his Humboldt
County sawmills, the captain of a tramp steamer. Juliet's
new acquaintances in the building industry were much
in evidence. It was not uncommon after dinner to see one
of her guests, a former carpenter graduated into contract-
ing, wandering through the downstairs rooms while he
closely examined the design of paneling or moldings,
the treatment of a stairway or the mechanism of a sliding
door. The democratic functions included, too, friends
with whom Juliet had grown up, or long-standing acquaintances of her father.

Chris Winton became one of the fixtures of the Thursday evening functions; I have often thought that her presence was what saved them from being completely dull.
There must have been many who, like me, would hardly
have gone so often had they not known that she too would
be there. For Chris had all the qualities of a satisfactory
diner-out. She was easy and undemanding, and positively
everything (and everyone) interested her. I have often
seen her spend the better part of an evening listening with
rapt attention to the monologue of some guest whom
everyone else regarded as a shocking bore. It is yet to be
disproved that a man can sit beside a young woman at
dinner, discover that she is interested in him, his work,
his opinions, and his prejudices, and get up at the end
without the conviction that here is a girl of sense and
good judgment, well worth cultivating.

Those who wanted to see more of her frequently had

their wish. If some fellow guest, in town temporarily, asked her to share his unoccupied evenings she was usually glad to accommodate him. There was generally a show she had not seen or, if there was not, a drive to the Cliff House or an evening at Woodward's Gardens was a satisfactory substitute. She presently had a wide acquaintance among Horton's out-of-town friends. Many of them were older than she; they not only enjoyed her companionship but were pleased to be seen in public with a young and attractive girl. Her appearances at the theaters, or at supper at the Maison Riche or the Palace grill, became frequent enough to attract attention. She carried herself well, with a sort of natural distinction, and she made an agreeable impression as she walked down the aisle of a theater or entered a restaurant.

I did not believe she gave these casual admirers any particular thought. If she could do a lonely man a good turn and at the same time see an amusing play or enjoy a good supper, that must have seemed to her a satisfactory arrangement all around. I used to wonder if these acquaintances did not sometimes try to make love to her when they took her home and said good-by in the doorway of her Rincon Hill boarding-house. I should have liked to know by what firm but tactful methods she repulsed their advances. I was convinced that none of them was permitted any familiarity.

Christine's crowded calendar did not prevent her from spending an occasional quiet evening with Juliet or, in summer, from frequent week-ends at Slaterock. These two, unlike in most ways, had their common interests. Both were part of the business world, at a period when that was far from the rule, and both were fascinated by its demands and stresses.

When he was home, Horton sometimes joined them in Juliet's sitting-room and spent the evening listening to their solemn discussions with tolerant interest. He could seldom be prevailed on to give them the benefit of his seasoned judgment. He answered their appeals with a favorite wise saw: "The only advice worth taking is: Don't take advice." For the most part he lolled in one of Juliet's big chairs, puffed on his cigar, listened with lazy interest and said nothing.

It may have been that, for all the activity of his crowded days, he was often lonely, and these young women gave him the human companionship he needed. He treated Christine very much as he treated Juliet, with a good-humored and patronizing irony.

vi

One summer Bridgeman & Company shut down temporarily, and during Christine's enforced vacation she and Juliet made a trip up the coast in one of Horton's lumber schooners. It was an experience Juliet never repeated. Although the weather was fine and the sea calmer than it usually is off the north coast, she became seasick while the ship was still passing through the Gate. She spent the twenty-hour voyage huddled in a bunk in the mate's cabin (which had been given up to the two passengers), rejecting with horror the meals Chris brought her. She was

helped down to the dock at Carrick, a shaken and disheveled figure and — like all bad sailors — vowing never
again to put foot off dry land. They spent the night at
the Carrick hotel and the next day returned to town by
stage and railroad.

The trip gave Juliet a lasting aversion to lumber schooners, but it had an opposite effect on Chris. She discovered
a lasting new enthusiasm. A born sailor, she was delighted
with the cramped cabins, steep companionways, and
compact galley of the grimy little schooner. With Juliet
asking only to be left to her misery, Chris had time to
explore the ship from stem to stern. She descended oily
ladders to the engine room and listened with excitement
while dials and moving pistons were pointed out to her
and unintelligible information was shouted in her ear.
She watched sweating stokers shovel coal into a glowing
inferno visible through the open furnace doors. She ate
the heavy meals with gusto — the salt air gave one an appetite — and delighted her messmates by her engaging
smile, her enthusiasm, and her ignorance of all things
nautical. Against regulations, she was allowed on the
bridge and permitted to grasp the vibrating wheel and
hold the ship on her course. She made her way into the
bow and, with the wind roaring in her ears, felt the deck
rise and fall and looked out across blue-green swells at
the surf foaming against the cliffs of the northern coast.

Back in town, Chris could talk of nothing else. Horton,
at whose suggestion they had made the outing, was entertained by her enthusiasm. He, too, enjoyed traveling
on the schooners; he made the trip to the north as often
as his affairs permitted. Juliet's aversion to salt water

amused them both. Some weeks later Horton announced that he was leaving the following day for Carrick. Would Juliet and Chris like to go along? Juliet rejected the suggestion with horror, but Chris accepted at once. Bridgeman's was still closed and she had nothing to keep her in town.

The schooner stayed two days at Carrick. That little settlement is still listed on many California maps, but there is nothing about it today to suggest that half a century ago it annually produced more millions of feet of lumber than any other town in California. Those who drive over the coast road that skirts the shore north of Fort Bragg will recall that every few miles small rivers break through to the ocean, forming a breach in the cliffs and a few dozen acres of sandy delta. On the floor of the Carrick gap may still be seen traces of the log dam that once impounded the river and formed a shallow lake. At the base of the northern cliff remains a line of rotting piles, part of a trestle over which narrow-gauge locomotives once pulled strings of trucks from the camps in the hills. To the left, beyond the level space that was once the drying yards, a few massive timbers projecting above the beach mark the site of the pier, long since demolished by winter surfs.

Of the town that covered the steep northern promontory, only a few wind-swept buildings remain: a combination store and post office, with a gasoline pump — sole touch of modernity — in front; a two-story clapboard hotel, now patronized by infrequent parties of hunters or fishermen; several cottages once occupied by officials of the mill and, clinging to the steep slopes above, a few workingmen's shacks, gray and dilapidated.

But Carrick was at its zenith when Christine first began to visit it. The raw energy of the place, its hustle and noise and activity, stimulated and excited her. She tramped over the wooden sidewalks of its windy street, past the line of saloons, pool halls, and barber shops. She explored the company store, a big, unpainted emporium that supplied the town's fifteen hundred inhabitants and other hundreds in the logging camps in the back country. She walked along the dusty road to the spot where it curved about the cliff, and from that vantage point regarded the plain below, filled from edge to edge with activity: the big sprawling mill, black smoke pouring from its stacks; the procession of logs drawn from the lake and fed to the saws; the cars of lumber moving over trestles into the yard; the huge bonfire fed with tailings and sawdust from the mill; beyond, the schooners moored to the pier while, to the noisy put-putting of hoisting engines, loads of lumber were lifted up, swung outward, and deposited on the decks.

In these surroundings a new Horton emerged. At Carrick he took on added stature. In San Francisco he was immersed in the routine of business; his life there did not differ from that of thousands of others. But in the din of the mill town something of the power he wielded became manifest. Against the background he had himself created he must have seemed to Chris, if not a romantic figure, at least a consequential one. He was in his early fifties. His hair and beard were beginning to gray, but his observant blue eyes remained youthful. He moved deliberately — Chris had to shorten her long strides when she walked beside him — and all his movements reflected a disinclination for physical effort. He was not a ready talker, but he was skillful at drawing out others. On their walks he constantly stopped to exchange greetings with employees. He would ask a question, listen while it was answered, find a place to sit down, ask another question, and in the end get reluctantly to his feet and proceed.

At Carrick Horton had the air of a man in a subdued holiday mood. He enjoyed tramping about, aimlessly watching the functioning of the big plant and exchanging views with those he met, quite content to waste an unproductive half-day in casual conversations. Chris, walking beside him on these rambling excursions, stopping at the hotel bar for a glass of beer, leaning over the rail above the log-filled lake, found him far more communicative than he had ever been in town. It was clear that he was proud of the active, ugly settlement he had caused to rise in this remote inlet. From the cliff above the mill he pointed out the spot where, six years earlier, he and one of his engineers and a party of surveyors had camped when he had first visited the spot. No one then lived within miles of the inlet. When they awoke the next morning they discovered a dozen deer drinking at the edge of the stream. Eighteen months later the first lumber schooner had tied up at the new dock. Since then the mill had been twice enlarged, scores of miles of logging railroad had been built through the canyons, and lumber cut at Carrick had been used, millions of feet of it, all over the West. Some had been shipped to the Orient and round the Horn to the east coast, some even to Europe.

That Chris encouraged these revelations one may well guess; she had a faculty for sharing the enthusiasms of her friends. This was a fundamental part of her, as instinctive as the narrowing of her eyes when she was amused or the attraction of her easy, slow smile. Horton had known few women well. This active girl with the clear complexion and straw-colored hair must have seemed to him an uncommonly pleasant companion. He could not have been unaware of the admiring glances that followed her on their rambles about the town. There were not many women at Carrick; none at all like her.

Back in San Francisco, Chris returned to work, and her life fell into its normal routine. Evenings when she was not on Russian Hill she went to dances or the theater, often with acquaintances she had met at the Hortons'. Several weeks later Horton made another trip north, and again Chris went along. This time she had to be absent from her job, but Horton had promised to take her on a tour of the logging camps; they would travel in the cab of one of the logging locomotives. It was far too exciting an adventure to miss.

They were gone ten days. The week-end following their return Chris spent at Slaterock. Early on Sunday morning Juliet was awakened by the flapping of a shutter in one of the ground-floor windows. She slipped downstairs and fastened it. On her way back she heard a door open cautiously and the sound of laughter, quickly stifled. She continued to the top of the stairs and waited. Her father, in bathrobe and slippers, left Chris's bedroom and with unhurried strides walked down the hall to his own.

Juliet went back to her room and quietly closed the door.

Chapter 7

THE FACT that so many persons consider Dr. Casebolt a distinguished ornament of California letters is, I am convinced, mainly because he neither looks nor acts like a literary man. There is about him none of the hallmarks of the professional scribbler. When one encounters him in public — which is often, for he bobs up practically everywhere — one cannot help contrasting his vigorous handclasp, his hearty voice and rollicking laugh with the subdued and apologetic demeanor of the usual run of authors, and concluding that it might be worth while to look into whatever of Casebolt's books is currently in the public eye.

Those who meet him for the first time are frequently heard to remark, with an air of pleased surprise, that he is not at all like a writer. Casebolt does what he can to further that impression. If he is invited to speak at a luncheon club or a banquet, or to take part in a radio discussion of some pressing national problem, he is likely to begin by modestly disclaiming any pretensions to literature. This is a process known to the profession as lathering up an audience, and its purpose is to make it clear that the speaker is just one of the boys.

A few weeks ago Casebolt addressed a convention of Pacific Coast manufacturers. The proceedings were broadcast over one of our local stations, and I, who had turned on my radio intending to listen to the nine o'clock news, heard his voice come booming through the loud-speaker. His opening remarks were so ingenious that I refrained from turning him off again. Casebolt began by stating that although he didn't mind being introduced as an author, he disliked to give his listeners a wrong impression and he therefore felt that he had better qualify the term. He went on to say that while he had never pretended to know much about art he had always tried to be a conscientious workman. He hoped his manufacturing friends didn't expect him to deliver a literary speech, because if such was their expectations he would have to disappoint them. After all, he told them, he too operated a factory, and what he had prepared was just an unpretentious little shop talk. Applause. Casebolt went on to say that, compared to the complex organizations over which his listeners presided, his own factory was small potatoes. He conducted his business in his home, in a one-room plant he called his library. His output was limited; it was a good year when he turned out so much as a single unit. But that didn't disturb him, because his overhead was small and the boss himself did all the work. Moreover, he believed he had one advantage over other manufacturers, and that lay in the fact that his raw materials cost him nothing. He got them out of his head and, although the critics sometimes hinted that the supply was running low, he thought he might continue to operate for several years longer. Laughter and applause. Casebolt was off to his accustomed flying start. I turned on the news.

Like other good businessmen, manufacturer Casebolt never ignores what is happening in the literary factories of his rivals. He keeps close tab on what other local writers are doing. So I was not surprised when, not long ago, he called me by telephone, to learn that he had got wind of how I had been occupying my time.

After some preliminary inquiries about friends in common, including Aunt Julie, and his usual regret that he had so few opportunities to enjoy my company, he said: " I hear you're doing a book about Jim Horton."

I admitted the charge.

" I'm delighted to hear it," he exclaimed. " You've got a grand subject."

" Thank you," I said. " I think so too."

" When I was working on my biography I couldn't help thinking what a stunning novel the old man would make. A real epic of San Francisco! He had a hand in everything that went on for fifty years. I often regretted that I had to confine myself to things that really happened. It would have been easy to dramatize him, to point up his story by tossing in some imaginary incidents here and there. But of course we historians have to suppress such impulses; we deal only in facts."

I admitted that must be a severe handicap.

" Of course I recognize that you novelists have your troubles too," Casebolt added. " Take Horton. He's an ideal subject for a novel, but you naturally can't use him as he was. You've got to take some liberties. I imagine you've had to do something about adding a strong romantic interest to the old man's story. To please the ladies, you know."

"I think Horton's career was very romantic," I said.

"I suppose it was, from one standpoint," Casebolt granted. "A man who starts from scratch and dies worth five or six millions is a romantic figure all right. But that's not the sort of romance that sells novels. You've got to have a love interest."

"Horton had a love interest."

Casebolt's hearty laugh came over the wire. "Well, Walter, you've done a lot of that sort of thing; you know more about it than I do. I bow to authority. But, frankly, doesn't Horton's romance strike you as a bit on the dull side? No doubt it was a love match in the beginning, but there's no denying his home life was unhappy. Mrs. Horton went east in the early eighties. They lived apart for nearly thirty years. He left her nothing in his will. I'd hardly call that a very satisfactory love story."

"There was Chris Winton," I pointed out.

Casebolt was silent for a moment. Then he said: "Naturally I know all about Mrs. Winton. D'you mean you're putting her in your novel?"

"I'm not writing a novel."

"No? What are you writing?"

"I don't know."

"Now look here, Walter. I'm not trying to pry into your affairs. You don't have to tell me if you don't want to."

"I understand that."

"Well, do you resent my curiosity?"

"Not in the least."

"Then why not tell me what sort of a book you're doing?"

"Because I don't know," I replied. "It's not fiction and it's certainly not biography. You've already done that, and done it very well. I've found your book a great help. In fact, it's been indispensable."

Casebolt ignored the compliment. "You're not writing fiction and you're not writing biography. What is it — a narrative poem? Or perhaps a ballet?"

"I'm not trying to do another biography of Horton," I explained. "He doesn't interest me enough for that, and besides you've already done the job. What I've been trying to do is to tell, not who he was, but what; not what he did, but why. It struck me it might be amusing to tell a man's story by gathering up the scraps that the conventional biographer would reject for one reason or another — because he thinks them unimportant, or indiscreet, or because they don't fit into the picture he's trying to present — and to put them together and see what results. I've an idea such a method might be effective. The picture of the man would differ from that of his formal biography, but it might be closer to the mark."

"I doubt it," said Casebolt.

"You may be right."

"I don't see how digging up that affair with Mrs. Winton changes the picture of Horton as I presented it. That sort of approach is more likely to distort the man than mine."

"They both distort him, naturally. But one method serves to correct the other. It's too bad all biographies haven't such supplements, or footnotes, or whatever you care to call them. It might then become possible to understand our eminent men."

"Phooey," said Casebolt.

"I'm quite serious," I insisted. "Consider Horton. I've read your book. It has six hundred pages. You go in detail into many matters: business deals, speculations, trades, mergers, and the like. And what's the result? Merely to confirm what we already know, that Horton was an accomplished trader. You devote a chapter to the growth of the California lumber industry and to what effect it had on Horton's pocketbook, but you don't mention Chris Winton, who lived with him eight years. Didn't she have any influence on his career?"

"Perhaps she did," Casebolt admitted. "But it happens I'm not interested in that sort of thing. I've never believed in airing a man's dirty linen in public."

"Even a capitalist doesn't spend all his time presiding over board meetings and getting the best of his competitors," I pointed out.

"I don't think any reader of my *Life* will get the impression that Horton was a stuffed shirt. I gave plenty of informal views of him; times when he took off his coat and relaxed."

"He also took off his pants."

There was a cold silence at the other end of the wire; I supposed Casebolt was reproving me for my bad taste.

He said, stiffly: "I'd hardly call it dignified for a biographer to invade his subject's bedroom."

" I don't mind being undignified."

" That's becoming obvious," said he. " None the less, I'll continue to believe my book's a good job, even though it may be a bit old-fashioned for some tastes, including those of the Literary Foundation jury."

Casebolt's reference to the Literary Foundation amused me, for the Foundation award (it was established under the will of our enlightened Mæcenas, the late Senator Trappan) is on its way to becoming the California equivalent of the Nobel Prize. The fact that the jury had never seen fit to award the Foundation's handsome medal to one of Casebolt's books must have annoyed him a great deal, judging from his frequent tart references to the matter.

I tried to comfort him. " Don't let that worry you," I said. " You've done a very creditable job. No one who wants to know who Horton was or what he did need look further."

" Then why write more about him? "

" I can't think of a reason in the world. Except that I've become interested in the old man. Your book recalled a great many things that I'd forgotten. I've got to wondering what sort of human being he really was. You didn't throw much light on that, you know."

" No doubt you'll do better," said he.

" I hope to find out what made him tick."

" Well, I wish you luck. It's been pleasant having this little chat, Walter. We must have lunch together soon."

" I'd like to," I said. " Give me a ring any time."

❖❖❖❖❖❖❖❖❖❖❖❖❖❖❖❖❖❖❖

ii

About 1885 my father bought a house on Pine Street, three or four blocks west of Van Ness Avenue. We moved from the cottage on the Washington Street hill, which we had rented, and which was only a few blocks from the big Horton residence at the other end of the hill. The fact that we had moved out of Horton's neighborhood did not mean that I saw less of Horton himself. Soon after we settled in the Western Addition, Chris Winton came to live in her new house on Sacramento Street, less than a quarter of a mile away. I frequently saw Jim Horton drive up of an evening and tie his horse to the iron hitching-post in front.

Our move into a house of our own was a result of my father's having been made managing editor of a new paper, the *Herald*, and that had persuaded him the time had come to settle down as a substantial citizen of the town. This showed a good deal of optimism on his part. Journalism is at best an unstable profession and it was uncommonly so in San Francisco fifty years ago, when new dailies were launched with no more thought than one gave the opening of a grocery store, and were killed again without compunction when their usefulness ended. Of course a few of these ventures gained a measure of popular support, or proved consistently useful to the men who were putting up the money, and these remained in the overcrowded field for years.

Of such was the *Herald*. Many San Franciscans still recall that truculent little journal. It lasted fourteen years, from '85 to '99. It had its greatest following during the early nineties and it declined when the interests of its readers were diverted from local reforms (which were the Herald's stock in trade) by two external events: the Klondike stampede and the Spanish War.

It has since become known that Jim Horton owned the Herald, but the secret was well kept during the paper's lifetime. Ostensibly the owner and publisher was William Hinchman, of the California pioneer family, who had formerly been known chiefly for his interest in amateur theatricals and for his proficiency on the flute. His office in the Herald Building on Sixth Street, where he spent not more than two hours a day, had on its walls a considerable collection of flutes, both old and new. He often entertained chance visitors by demonstrating their tone and range. My father, who occupied a connecting office, sometimes composed editorials on such sober subjects as the award of a sewer contract or the extension of a street-car franchise to the accompaniment of " After the Ball is Over " rendered plaintively on the flageolet.

Hinchman exercised only casual supervision over the affairs of the paper. He went about a great deal socially, and he was sometimes useful to the society editor by supplying her with advance word of engagements, of the comings and goings of the elite, and occasional bits of gossip. He fancied himself a music critic and sometimes composed notes on concerts and recitals. These he signed, for what reason I know not, " Betsy Boggs." That whimsy earned him the unofficial office title of Betsy. Because of the Herald's stand for reform and the atmosphere of indignation in which it conducted its campaigns,

Betsy Hinchman was often in bad odor with the leading families on whose toes his paper was treading. But although he was looked on as a renegade by those with whom he had grown up, Betsy became a shining knight to the humble citizens from whom the paper drew its support. Finding this situation beyond him, he found solace in his flutes and left the management of the *Herald* to others.

The fact that Horton encouraged the paper in its fight against the plutocrats would have astonished the town, had it been known. Horton had none of the reformer's zeal. He was indifferent to politics except when his interests were involved. He was a Republican and a high-tariff man because he wanted to keep Puget Sound lumber and Australian wool out of the California markets. On the other hand, he advocated low duty on machinery and metals and leather belting, for he imported such materials in quantity from abroad. In the local field he favored the extension of street-car lines and the maintenance of low fares because they encouraged the development of new districts and new construction, and so stimulated the sale of building materials. As a large owner of real estate he was a staunch supporter of low assessments and low taxes. He not only favored these things; whenever the opportunity presented, he did what he could to bring them about. He disliked politicians, but if the man in office was reasonable Horton could get along with him. It was only the militantly incorruptible official that he found intolerable.

There was nothing haphazard about Horton's entry into the newspaper business. He knew what result he wanted and he knew what kind of paper would get it with the least expense and delay. Like others before him he recognized that skulduggery can best be concealed by an elaborate show of virtue. At one point in his *Memoir* he made some mildly cynical remarks on this subject:

" As long as I can remember," he stated, " we've been having reform movements of one kind or another. Nothing pleases us so much as a good campaign to clean up something and to send somebody to San Quentin. We don't much care what we clean up or who goes to jail so long as it gives us a chance to feel that we're being upright, virtuous citizens. And the more virtuous we feel, the more anxious we are to make somebody pay through the nose. I've had some experience along those lines myself. Well, every time one of these campaigns gets started I ask myself what's happening in the background, while everybody's busy looking the other way. I won't go so far as to say that all such movements are started with the idea of drawing the public's attention away from something else, but a good many of them are. I've got a little saying I've found useful in that connection. I always say when the dogs are all barking down by the barn that's the time to wander over and see what's happening at the hen house."

How many of the *Herald's* reform campaigns were designed to divert attention from Horton's raids on the municipal hen houses is not known, but their number must have been large. In the early nineties the *Herald* launched an exposé of inefficiency in the conduct of the county poorhouse. During the ensuing uproar the tax board quietly reduced the assessments on several dozen pieces of property owned by Horton, including the Russian Hill house and his Market Street office building. The *Herald* supported a carmen's strike against one of the street-car companies and succeeded in arousing so much feeling against the corporation that the supervisors rejected its pending application for a new franchise. They awarded it instead to a rival company, controlled by Horton, that had recently given its employees a handsome increase in wages. The strikers were subsequently defeated (after the *Herald* had lost interest in their fight), and Horton's company thereupon reduced wages to conform to that of the other line. A year or two later the *Herald* launched a moral crusade that not only drove the prostitutes from the downtown streets and alleys (where they had been ensconced for years), but prevented them from following their usual custom of moving back again a few weeks later. After the houses along Maiden Lane and its environs had remained untenanted for months and Horton had quietly bought up two thirds of them at bargain prices, the *Herald* relaxed its vigilance and business was presently flourishing again. A competing paper promptly called attention to the fact that the downtown tenderloin was again booming, but by then the public had temporarily grown tired of reading about prostitutes and it refused to be interested. Besides, the *Herald* had provided a counter-attraction by uncovering irregularities in the office of the inspector of weights and measures. Housewives were daily told how they were being swindled by improper scales in their butcher shops and corner groceries.

Horton's hand was never seen in these exploits. He

never visited the *Herald* office or, so far as anyone knew, exercised any control over its routine affairs. It used to be said that the *Herald* came closer to being an independent paper than any of its rivals. What was meant was that its owner gave the management a free hand in all matters that did not affect him financially. Its virtue above its competitors was that it served only one master. That was a distinction in San Francisco journalism of the nineties. No doubt it would be less of a distinction today.

i i i

I have already remarked that an enthusiasm for the details of business operations is one of Casebolt's most striking characteristics. He is never so happy as when he is setting forth, for the benefit of those who can follow him, the steps by which two corporations are merged, a new bond issue is floated, or a bankrupt railroad or steamship line is rehabilitated. The gusto with which he tackles such problems and the pleasure he takes in describing operations involving large sums of money have always aroused my admiration. I never encounter, and skip, such passages without the feeling that perhaps I have placed too low an estimate on his capabilities. No man who can toss millions about with so much ease can be, I tell myself, so complete an ass as he sometimes seems to be when he is dealing with less complicated matters.

Yet I am never quite sure. Having no grasp of those matters myself, it is possible that I overestimate Case-

bolt's talents. Any financial transaction beyond such ele-
mentary exercises as balancing a checking account and
adding up a dinner check is likely to have me stumped.
In my own work I have given such subjects a wide berth.
I doubt if anywhere in the far too many words I have
written there is so much as a paragraph devoted to pure
finance. To be sure, my novels often have businessmen
in them, and some of these men, if I say so who shouldn't,
have been uncommonly successful. But I haven't an idea
how they did it. My businessmen have offices, to which
they retire during those periods when I have no need of
them, and it is while they are absent downtown that they
earn the large sums necessary to support their homes, to
clothe their wives and daughters, and to pay their admirable cooks. On the whole I have found that this arrangement works well. If a novelist has a businessman character who is a good provider, that should be enough for
his purpose. For his creator to follow him to his office
and there attempt to interfere with matters of which he
knows nothing would be only to invite disaster.

In view of the foregoing it will be clear that I have
no taste for what is to follow. For it is necessary now for
me to say something about Horton's fight with the lumber trust. I shall make it as brief as possible; those who
want the whole story will find it in Casebolt. This is an
outline, rough and incomplete, but without, I think, anything essential omitted. I did not dash it off in five
minutes.

There must be many who recall the series of sanguinary labor strikes that kept the town in turmoil during the
middle and late nineties. It was the time when capital

and labor first embraced the theory that their interests were mutually antagonistic and that the only way one could attain the well-being it desired was to wipe the other off the map. That is, of course, the theory on which they continue to operate today, but the first bloom of enthusiasm has long since worn off, and the business of polishing off an adversary has become a routine assignment. Our early strikes were conducted in no such humdrum spirit. Half a century ago the contending factions threw cobblestones and swung the handles of pickaxes with a fresh enthusiasm that would put their present-day successors to shame. When the teamsters or street-car operators or bricklayers walked off the job and the strike-breakers walked on, it was a signal, not for conferences, but for carnage.

A good example of what might be termed the golden age of California strikes was that of the loggers and mill-hands in the middle nineties, which first slowed up and then completely stopped the production of the Simmons-Wheeler Lumber Company, the largest concern of its kind on the Coast, and Horton's chief competitor. That corporation, which became known to the *Herald* and other opposition newspapers as the "lumber trust," owned millions of acres of timberland and half a dozen mill towns spaced along the coast of northern California and southern Oregon. It employed fifteen thousand men and operated a large fleet of schooners. Its yards and planing mills were to be found in scores of Pacific Coast cities and towns.

The trouble began when the crew of one of the company's schooners walked off the ship in San Francisco in protest against the quality of the meals supplied them. Specifically they objected to certain servings of salt pork tendered them on the trip south from Coos Bay. The captain signed on a new crew, unloaded his cargo, and sailed again on schedule. Members of the former crew told their story up and down the waterfront, gathered adherents, and met other company schooners with pleas that their crews join the walkout. In this they were uniformly successful, although in most cases it proved necessary for them to resort to other than verbal arguments. But the waterfront was then swarming with idle seamen and the company had no trouble keeping its schooners operating. In a few weeks the ex-crews of a dozen ships were tramping the sidewalks of East Street with empty pockets and appetites sharpened to a point where the meals against which they had revolted would have been welcome indeed.

The next step was not long delayed. One afternoon ambulances were heard clattering over the pierside cobbles, and the town learned that rioting had broken out on the waterfront. Several hundred striking seamen and their friends had gathered at the dock where a company schooner was moored and forcibly prevented its crew from returning to their ship. The crew had withdrawn. But an hour later they had returned, supported by company guards armed with pick-handles. Forming themselves into a flying wedge, they attempted to run the strikers' blockade. In the melee skulls were cracked and noses broken. The strikers' lines held, however, and the attackers withdrew, dragging their casualties with them into the street. The process was repeated as other schooners arrived. Soon half the company's fleet was lying idle at the local docks.

The entire city was presently following these water-front riots with mounting indignation. This was mainly due to the *Herald*, which supported the strikers' cause with all its usual energy. In news columns and on the editorial page it daily informed the public of the privations of the striking sailors and their families, and denounced the unprovoked assaults of the hired thugs of the lumber trust. When the company conceded defeat in San Francisco and routed their ships to Oakland, the strikers sent forces across the bay and continued their triumphs on the Estuary docks. Soon not a foot of Simmons-Wheeler lumber was being sent into the bay. The *Herald* announced proudly that the lumber trust's hold on California had been broken.

The strikers did not rest on their laurels. Supporters of the cause went north to enlist the aid of the loggers and millhands. There they were met by company employees and driven off its property. The workers responded by presenting demands for higher wages and improved living-conditions. When these were rejected the leaders called a strike and the company retaliated by bringing in strike-breakers. The arrival of the latter was actively opposed; for a few days bloody warfare raged under the redwoods. Logging trains were derailed and wrecked. Fire swept one of the big mills. Doctors and nurses were sent north to treat the injured when the traditional axe-handles and cant-hooks gave way to knives and shotguns. Citizens urged the Governor to call out the National Guard.

iv

It was during the strike in the northern camps that San Franciscans first began to hear about Fred Foschay. I have known Foschay for many years. He is now well past seventy and I have been told that today the rank and file of union men regard him as a bit on the conservative side. That only shows how far we have traveled.

Foschay is an unlettered Swede who left a Wisconsin farm some time in the middle eighties. He came up the hard way. Before he was twenty he had worked in the Idaho copper mines, in the wheat fields of eastern Washington and the Puget Sound lumber camps. He drifted south to California about 1890 and went to work in one of Horton's lumber camps. Within a few months he was boss of a logging crew.

I do not know by what steps he advanced, but within a year or two his importance was such that he frequently came down to San Francisco to consult Horton on matters connected with operations in the north. Horton sometimes invited him to dinner and it was during one such visit that I first made his acquaintance. I remember walking into the Russian Hill parlor one evening and seeing a short, heavy-set stranger standing in front of the fireplace. I guessed at once that he was one of Horton's lumberjacks. He looked uncomfortable in his tight city clothes; his big hands — one of which gingerly held a wineglass — and his thick, straight hair, which he wore plastered down on his skull, shouted of the outdoors. He had small blue eyes, a broad nose, prominent ears, and a wide grin that was frequently in evidence. He didn't seem at all abashed by what must have been unfamiliar surroundings. There were seven or eight others in the room: Horton, Chris Winton, Mr. and Mrs. Pepper, old friends of Horton, a local builder and his wife — Juliet's guests — and Juliet herself.

When I arrived Foschay was describing an accident that had happened in the woods a few days earlier. Juliet introduced us — I knew all the others — and the stranger extended a huge hand, gave mine a grasp that made me wince, and went on with his story. I poured myself a glass of sherry and sat down beside Chris. She gave me an abstracted smile and returned her attention to the stranger.

Like most shy persons, I then had a lively sense of my importance, and I kept an eye alert for possible affronts to my dignity. I could not but reflect that my arrival had been something the others were glad to get over quickly so they might again give their attention to this newcomer. I subjected him to a hostile gaze and, naturally enough under the circumstances, I put him down as an uncouth fellow, not likely to say anything worth listening to. I restricted my attention to my sherry.

But I could not help hearing what he was saying (it would have been ungentlemanly to stuff my fingers in my ears) and presently I began to be interested in spite of myself. Even then Foschay was an effective talker, with a certain rough eloquence that captured attention. A string of loaded trucks had broken loose from the end of a logging train, had coasted several miles down a grade and crashed, at high speed, into an ascending work train. A very spectacular wreck had resulted. Wreckage was strewn over the tracks for half a mile; five men had been killed and a dozen injured.

Foschay had been among the first to reach the scene. He had helped remove the victims. His story omitted no details. In his blunt way he told of bodies so horribly mangled that identification was impossible, of heads crushed by hurtling logs, and of the rough-and-ready methods of the rescuers.

I listened with unwilling fascination, strongly tempered with disapproval. I thought his recital of these realistic details very reprehensible. Was it possible the fellow had forgotten there were ladies present? Did he not know that a description of such happenings, familiar enough in the crude environment of the lumber camps, was in bad taste in the Horton parlor? I glanced with concern at the ladies, half expecting them to fall from their chairs in merciful unconsciousness. But they seemed to be bearing up very well. If I had not known that gentlewomen were instinctively revolted by the mention of bloodshed I should have had to conclude that they were enjoying Foschay's grisly narrative. He spoke of the dead and maimed with an unconcern that struck me as both brutal and callous, but the ladies, far from being revolted, hung on his words with an interest that could hardly be distinguished from pleasure. It was all too much for me.

Foschay was the lion of the evening. At dinner I sat between Chris and Mrs. Pepper, but they were so taken with this loquacious lumberjack that I could hardly get in a word edgewise. I lapsed into a disapproving and dignified silence. I half expected that Chris would notice my reserve and accuse me of sulking, and I was prepared to deny the charge with amused surprise. But she never noticed my austerity. No one noticed it. Foschay related his experiences in the wide-open gambling houses of Boise, and after that he had some tales to tell about a French chef who had strayed into eastern Washington and tried to exercise his skill on the threshing crew at a wheat ranch. I considered his remarks pointless and dull. It occurred to me that Horton's dinners were singularly tiresome gatherings and I wondered why I had considered them entertaining. We returned to the parlor and, as soon as I suitably could, I excused myself and prepared to leave.

To my dismay Foschay said he must be going too. The protests of the others at this announcement — which, I reflected bitterly, were less perfunctory than had greeted my own impending departure — fell on deaf ears. He had to be getting on. He wasn't used to late hours. Up in the woods everybody went to bed with the chickens.

V

We walked down the hill together and turned south on Taylor Street. A number of the big houses beyond Jackson Street aroused his curiosity. He asked who lived in each. I told him. He looked them over carefully. He wanted to know how their owners made their living. I told him that too: mining, railroads, grain, real estate.

" There's certainly lots of money in this town," he observed.

I didn't think that required an answer.

" How much do you suppose Horton's worth? "

" I don't know."

" Well, what's your guess? Five millions? "

" I haven't any idea," I said shortly. As a matter of fact, I had often wondered about that myself (my estimate was seven millions and a half), but I was not going to discuss the subject with one of Horton's employees. The fellow didn't know his place.

" I'd say at least five million," he went on. " Maybe more. That house of his, now, that must have cost a pile of money. It's certainly a beautiful place."

He liked Horton's house! I felt a soothing sense of superiority. I remarked: " Most persons think it's in very bad taste."

" The hell you say! " he ejaculated. " Why? "

I considered myself something of an authority on architecture. I could not pass up an opportunity to air my views.

" For one thing, it's much too elaborate. All those meaningless towers and steeples and gingerbread decorations! That sort of thing's not being done any more. People of taste are returning to the traditional styles, Georgian or Classical or Italian Renaissance. They're building some very artistic homes in the Western Addition."

" Well, Horton's house suits me. I'd be satisfied with it. Or that place across the street. Who lives there? "

We had reached the California Street corner, where I was to turn west. I held out my hand. " Here's where I leave you."

" I think I'll tag along," he announced. " I want to ask some questions."

" You've been asking some."

He grinned. " I've got plenty left."

We walked up the slight rise to Jones Street, then down the hill toward Polk. The fog had rolled in from the ocean and the wind was sharp. I turned up the collar of my overcoat and shoved my hands into its pockets. The California Street cars slid by, their dummies deserted and their oil-lamps throwing dim shadows on the fog. An occasional carriage rattled past, the horses' hoofs clop-clopping on the wet cobbles. Foschay seemed in no hurry to begin his questions.

When we approached Polk Street he took my arm and headed across the street toward the saloon on the far corner. " What we need is a drink," he announced.

I had no desire for a drink, certainly not for a drink in that saloon (it was a squalid place frequented by laborers and cabbies and by gripmen from the near-by car-barns), and I resented Foschay's familiarity. But his big hand was clutching my arm with a grasp that seemed to mean business. To try to break away would have meant an un-dignified scuffle. I allowed myself to be propelled through the swinging doors.

The bar was crowded, and hazy with smoke. We went through to the back room, which had tables in alcoves about its walls. The floor was streaked with sawdust trailed in from the bar, and the only illumination came from a gas-jet suspended from the ceiling. Two sailors, both quite drunk, sat with their girls in one of the booths. The place reeked of stale cigar smoke and stale beer.

Foschay found nothing wrong with it. He made himself at home, banged his fist on the table to summon the waiter, and stared with interest at the group in the opposite booth. One of the girls caught his eye and, over the shoulder of her befuddled companion, smiled invitingly. He turned to me, grinning.

"That's a woman for you," he observed. "Always anxious to shake one sucker when another one comes along."

I looked at the two girls. They were quite young, probably not more than seventeen or eighteen. They were dressed in cheap finery with flower-bedecked hats and showy jewelry. The one who had smiled had a feather boa thrown over her shoulders. Both had mascara on their eyelashes, and their cheeks were rouged.

"If those drunks have got any money they can kiss it good-by," observed Foschay. "They'll wake up in the morning flat broke."

"I'm not so sure about that," I replied. I was not going to let Foschay think I knew less than he about the seamy side of life. "These girls are seldom as bad as they're painted. They're human beings too, you know."

"That pair?" asked Foschay scornfully. "They're out for the cash. Those sailors won't have time to get their pants off before their friends will be going through their pockets."

"Suppose they do?" I retorted. "If they're like that it's because society made them that way. They lead a sordid life any way you look at it. And you needn't think they make a fortune."

"Some of them do all right. The smart ones."

"That's where you're wrong," I replied. I had strong views on what we then termed, rather quaintly, the social evil. One of the things I firmly believed was that no girl ever willingly embarked on a career of prostitution. I was also convinced that few of them were so far gone in evil that they couldn't be regenerated by an appeal to their better instincts and the offer of an honest job (at five dollars a week) as a servant girl or a waitress. Foschay's remark that some of these unhappy creatures found the life remunerative was more than I could stomach. "The smart ones, as you call them, get out of the life as fast as they can."

"Sometimes yes and sometimes no," said Foschay. "It's like anything else. It all depends on how they play their cards."

I became instructive again. "In the long run they can't win, no matter how they play their cards. Sooner or later they end up in the gutter."

"All of them?"

"All of them," I replied.

Foschay's grin widened. "How about Horton's girl?" he demanded.

I stared at him. For a moment I was too surprised to speak. All I could manage was an astonished: "Who?"

"Horton's girl. That Mrs. — what's her name? — Winton. She's doing all right."

I said, weakly: "You're not comparing her with *them!*" I glanced at the two prostitutes in the booth. "She's not like that at all."

I was profoundly shocked. I had thought a good deal about Chris Winton's morals and I had formed my opin-

ion of her conduct. Of course I disapproved of her relations with Horton, who was her senior by so many years.
I had even faced the fact that she was not a moral young
woman. But I also admired her very much. I could not
bring myself to think harshly of her. The whole situation
was baffling, not to be explained by ordinary standards.
I used sometimes to sit in Horton's house and reflect on
the strangeness of their relationship. They did not behave
at all like guilty lovers. In public she always addressed him
as Mr. Horton. (I did not know what terms she used when
they were alone, but it was impossible to imagine her
calling him endearing names, a man of his age!) Her
manner when she spoke to him had the slight deference
proper in a girl addressing the father of her best friend,
who was also her host. Horton replied with the good-
humored condescension usually adopted by members of
an older generation when they speak to well-meaning but
rather foolish youngsters.

In point of fact, they seldom had much to say to each
other during the Thursday evenings on the hill. Immediately after dinner the guests divided into groups, the
older members collecting about the fireplace and talking
business while the others gravitated to the other end of
the room and considered more frivolous topics. Chris
was invariably in the latter group, while Juliet, already
captured by the world of commerce, shuttled between the
two. As for Chris, it was clear that she hadn't a care in
the world. She never permitted Horton's presence to
spoil her fun. She was full of high spirits and enthusiasm
and a childlike sense of mischief. The young men who

chanced to be present — and the older ones too — were delighted with her. She was far from discouraging their attentions. She liked admiration and welcomed a mild flirtation. This was often embarrassing to the men — it was, of course, also flattering — who sometimes had an uneasy feeling that Horton might be keeping an eye on them. They might have spared themselves any uneasiness; Horton was not in the least jealous. It was one of the things about him that I neither understood nor approved. Had I been in his place, I told myself, Chris would have enjoyed no such freedom. I would have kept a far tighter hold on the reins.

I had no precise idea how two persons who were carrying on a clandestine love affair ought to behave in public, but I was sure their method was not the correct one. One had a right to expect some outward intimation of their secret passion, an occasional tender glance or a surreptitious word in passing. Or, on the other hand, a studied indifference designed to further the impression that they were virtually strangers. They adopted neither role. They were friendly and casual and natural. They neither pointedly ignored each other nor obviously sought each other out. I considered their behavior both baffling and reprehensible. I should have felt more kindly toward them had they sometimes behaved like conspirators. I could not quite forgive them for not having guilty consciences.

But it was impossible to say anything of this to Foschay. For him to bring up the subject at all seemed outrageous, and I cast about for some means of expressing my indignation. Nothing would have pleased me more than to have been able to put the fellow in his place. But how? A scornful silence would have been wasted on him. To have got to my feet, bowed coldly, and stalked from the room would have been only to make myself ridiculous. A gentleman would have recognized the correctness of such a procedure, but not Foschay. I might indeed have invited him outside, ordered him to put up his hands, and on the foggy Polk Street sidewalk, avenged the insult man to man. But Foschay must have weighed two hundred pounds (to my hundred and forty) and his big hands looked as hard as cobblestones. I concluded that a vulgar saloon brawl would only draw Chris's name deeper in the mire. I repeated, with dignity:

" She's not like that at all."

" Who said she was? " demanded Foschay. He didn't seem to notice my agitation. " That's what I was saying. She's a smart girl and she's doing all right. I hear the old man gave her a twenty-thousand-dollar house and her own carriage and riding horse. That's not bad for a factory girl."

" She wasn't a factory girl," I replied indignantly. " She was a forelady. I happen to know that she was looked on as practically one of the managers. She made a very good salary."

" Could she afford to keep a carriage? "

" She doesn't care a snap of her fingers about that. She has very simple tastes. If you think she's friendly with Horton because of what she gets out of him, then you're mistaken. She's very fond of him. She wasn't someone he picked up off the street, you know. She comes from a very good family. She went to Mills Seminary."

" Sure. I'm not arguing with you. That's what I'm try-ing to tell you. She's got brains and she's using them. She's getting along fine."

" Horton would marry her tomorrow if his wife would give him a divorce."

" He might do worse," Foschay granted. " She's not bad-looking."

" She's got more than good looks," I said warmly. " She's got character and charm and refinement. She'd fit in anywhere."

" What does Horton's daughter think about the lay-out? "

" Juliet? She likes her very much. They've been friends for years."

" So I hear. It's a damned funny situation."

" I don't see anything funny about it."

" Don't you? "

A certain smugness in his tone rekindled my indigna-tion. " I suppose the whole thing shocks you," I said, and my lip curled.

" Not especially. Only where I come from we keep our lady friends one place and our families some place else. We don't bring our mistresses home and introduce them to our daughters."

" It's too bad Horton didn't consult your wishes in the matter," I said with heavy sarcasm.

Foschay looked at me and grinned. " Are you trying to tell me it's none of my business? "

" I am."

He thought this over for a moment. " I don't know but that you're right," he admitted.

Our drinks came. He held up his glass and regarded me good-naturedly. " Well, here's wishing them luck! "

I didn't feel happy about it, but I drank.

Chapter 8

THE NEXT time I saw Chris she asked me what I thought of Fred Foschay.

I said, indifferently: "He's all right, I suppose. I didn't pay much attention to him. He seems to think very well of himself."

She smiled. "You don't like him at all, do you?"

"I didn't say so."

"But it's true, isn't it?" she persisted.

"Since you ask, I don't think he's the sort of person I'd care to be friendly with. He struck me as rather commonplace. But I only saw him once."

"He says you stopped and had a drink."

I looked at her. "So you've seen him since I did," I said.

Her smile was that of a child who has been caught with his hand in the cookie jar. "He took me to Morosco's last night. We saw *The Bride's Dilemma*."

"Oh. I see."

"He asked me if I'd like to go to Morosco's. I hadn't seen the show, so I said I'd love to."

"You didn't lose much time."

She regarded me curiously. Her face broke into a pleased smile. "Why, I do believe you're angry!" she exclaimed. "Is it because Mr. Foschay took me to the show? What's wrong with that?"

"I'm not in the least angry," I returned coldly. "Why should I be?"

I was perfectly furious. I was sure I could never forgive her. It was useless to tell myself that Chris had no knowledge of Foschay's real character. She had no means of knowing about his conversation with me, when he had shown clearly what he thought of her. He had called her a smart girl who played her cards well, a factory worker who had snared a millionaire and got herself a fine house and a carriage. Naturally, she knew nothing about that. But I was surprised that she had been taken in so completely. I was angry at her for being so gullible. She was as pleased as Punch because she had gone out with him. I blamed her for being so bad a judge of character. For my part I had not been deceived an instant. I had disliked this brash stranger the moment I had clapped eyes on him. There was something gross about him, a sort of cocksure arrogance that did not sit well with me. He had pronounced her a smart girl with an eye to the main chance. And now, I thought bitterly, she had proved him right. She had been taken in by this backwoods Lothario, this swaggering, lumber-camp Don Juan. I could not forgive her for having so cheapened herself. I thought of

Foschay's complacent pleasure in his little triumph. He had gone out with Horton's girl, right under the old man's nose. What a sensation that must have made in the bunkhouses up north!

A new thought struck me and I couldn't forbear confronting her with it.

" I suppose you let him kiss you," I said.

She was far from displeased at the charge. She turned on me what I suppose would be described as an arch look.

" Wouldn't you like to know! "

She accompanied the words with a singular motion of her shoulders, a sort of flirtatious wiggle. My heart sank. There were times when Chris's behavior grievously disappointed me, and this was one of them. I hated to admit it even to myself, but there was something vulgar about her, a strain of earthiness that cropped out when it was least expected. I put it down to the life she had lived since her foolish elopement with Clyde Winton. She had been married, deserted, and divorced before she was twenty. She had worked hard and her pleasures had been those of the unlettered girls and youths whose lot she had shared. It was too much to expect that she should continue to observe the admirable rules of conduct laid down for the young ladies at Mills Seminary. Chris had frequented the public dance halls and amusement parks and other gathering-places of young job-holders on pleasure bent, and that had induced a certain laxness in her behavior. She had had her share of flirtations. She had met young men without the formality of an introduction and had danced and drank beer and gone on buggy rides with them. No doubt she had submitted willingly enough to their embraces when they had left her at the door of her boarding-house. I did not consider that particularly reprehensible of her. But now that she had left that phase of her life behind, now that she was moving again in the sphere to which her background entitled her, I felt it only fair that she should have been more circumspect. Besides, there was Horton. One would think that in her position she would realize the necessity of watching her step. The gossips would be only too glad of an opportunity to link her name with those of other men. It was her failure to recognize so real a danger that provoked me to renewed anger.

I said: "I think you might have picked out somebody besides Foschay. He works for Mr. Horton, you know. You met him in this house."

My tone must have been venomous, for her eyes widened in surprise. "Why, you're simply furious! You're as pale as a ghost." She looked at me with real concern. "What on earth has got into you?"

"You haven't answered my question," I said. "Well, you don't have to. It's none of my business. Besides, I know the answer."

We were sitting at a domino table in the recess of one of the windows, well removed from the others. Chris reached across and took my hand. I tried to draw it away, but her grasp was firm and I subsided. I avoided her glance.

"Look at me," she said. I looked at her. It is hard to describe her expression. Her eyes were comprehending and compassionate. They were all sympathy and understanding, with just a trace of severity in their depths. I thought she had never looked so beautiful.

She said quietly: " Don't you think we've had enough of this nonsense? "

I regarded her resentfully for a moment and my anger melted away. It was impossible to withstand the kindness and friendliness of her gaze. I would gladly have forgiven her anything.

" Yes," I said.

She smiled and gave my hand a little squeeze. Her fingers were strong and capable; the pressure of her cool skin was singularly pleasant. An odd thing happened. We remained for a few moments without motion, and into her eyes came an expression I had never seen before. It had a sort of enveloping warmth and tenderness. Her lips were parted. Her fingers tightened over mine and, as though an electric current had passed between us, my heart gave a great thump and began pounding in my ears. I was suddenly on fire with desire. She relaxed her hand and drew it slowly away, her fingers sliding over mine. A grave smile played about her lips.

" You're not mad at me now, are you, dear? " she asked.

" No."

" If you don't like him I won't go out with him again."

I had forgotten Foschay. " Oh, him," I said. " That's all right. I don't care."

She started arranging her dominoes. In her usual tone she added: " Well, let's get on with our game."

" All right," I said.

I glanced surreptitiously at Horton. He was sprawled in his chair beside the fire, his long legs crossed. He was studying the end of his cigar while he listened to one of his guests, a short, dark man who hailed from Denver. They had talked all through dinner about the price of silver and about some speeches by a young politician, whose name was Bryan.

ii

Whether or not Chris kept her promise not to go out with Foschay again I had no means of knowing, but they continued to see each other on the hill. Foschay spent a great deal of time at the Hortons'. One rarely dropped in without finding him there, and behaving, so it seemed to me, as if he owned the place. It did not take him long to claim the privileges of an old friend, to address Juliet and Chris by their first names, to monopolize the conversation, and to talk familiarly with the servants. Horton alone he treated with a certain deference. He invariably addressed him as " the Chief." The old man in turn was uncommonly civil to his brash visitor, a sure sign that Foschay had become important in whatever plans he currently had under way. I had long since learned that when Horton exerted himself to be attentive to a caller it was because he wanted something from him in a business way. The other guests were permitted to shift for themselves, as they were glad enough to do. In general they were there because they had enjoyed favors from him and because they hoped for more in the future.

There were always a few, of whom I was one, who did not belong in this category. We were guests of Juliet, and Juliet invited us because an evening spent in the exclusive company of business people was likely to bore her. I understood that perfectly. I liked to believe that in her eyes I stood for something more than mere money-grubbing. I could not have been very entertaining, but I cared nothing about the lumber or shipping business, or about real estate or taxes or the tariff. The consequence was that we got off by ourselves and played cards or dominoes or talked about actors or lecturers, and sometimes even about literature. I enjoyed myself. Because I was working on a paper and was considering what I loftily termed a career of authorship, I had a slight standing with Juliet and Chris. My opinion on art and letters and the drama was listened to with interest and some degree of respect. When Julie or Chris saw a show or read a novel they made a point of discussing it with me afterwards. Thus it was often my pleasure to inform them that the books or plays they had enjoyed were trash and that those that bored them to distraction were in reality sound and significant.

All that was flattering to my ego and I should probably have continued to spend an evening a week at the Hortons' with entire content had it not been for Foschay. I liked him less each time I saw him. It would have been possible to tolerate him had he recognized that his place was at the far end of the room where prosaic matters of trade were under discussion. But that was never Foschay's way. He felt equally at home with us youngsters (he was in fact not yet thirty) and of course it never occurred to him that he was not completely welcome. Sooner or later he would stride down upon us and pull up a chair. It made no difference what we chanced to be talking about; Foschay had opinions on all subjects and he assumed that we would be delighted to hear them. My resentment at these interruptions was not lessened by the knowledge that no one else shared it. The others, even Juliet, and certainly Chris, welcomed his coming with every sign of pleasure. When he seemed about to exhaust a subject, they were ever ready to toss in a word that would start him off again. Sometimes I caught Chris's eye during these monologues and she gave me a glance of amused understanding; for the rest, my disapproving silences were wasted.

I adopted a more drastic means of showing my resentment. I stopped going to the Hortons'. When, after I had been absent several weeks, Juliet telephoned to ask why, I pleaded the pressure of work. My paper had been giving me night assignments and I had finally made the plunge and started a novel.

" Well, you can't work all the time," she pointed out.

" It's only temporary," I said, in a harassed tone. " I'll be free again soon."

" Chris thinks you're staying away because you don't like Fred Foschay."

" That's ridiculous! "

" I hope so. I didn't think you were that foolish. Besides, he's gone."

" What do you mean, gone? "

" Just what I say. He's quit his job."

I was astonished. " But I thought he was doing so well.

To hear him talk, he was practically running things up north."

" They'll have to get along without him. He quit last week."

It was some time before I learned what was behind all that. It is an odd story, but in keeping with the times, and I don't think it has been told before. Foschay had not left Horton's employ; he only seemed to have done so. He had gone up the coast and got a job as a logger in one of the Simmons-Wheeler camps. I have mentioned that he was a convincing talker. The story he told was that he had seen too much of the greed of the mill-owners and their exploitation of their employees. He had been a worker all his life and he was going to remain one. But he was eager to do what he could to see that they got better treatment: better wages, better living-conditions, and better hours. He drifted from camp to camp and from mill to mill, talking to individuals, then to groups, arousing them to a sense of their wrongs. The strike of the lumber-schooner crews was in progress in San Francisco and its success lent point to his arguments. Before the owners realized what he was about, he had laid the foundation of an active organization of workers. He was fired, ordered off company property, and told not to return. He made the most of that piece of bad judgment. He stole back, set himself up as a martyr in the workers' cause, and brought his campaign into the open. The workers crowded to hear his speeches and shouted approval when he denounced the crimes of their capitalistic oppressors. He became the chairman of a committee that was formed to present the workers' grievances and to formulate their demands. His name began to appear in San Francisco papers in stories of labor unrest in the lumber towns. When negotiations between employer and employees broke down, Foschay called the workers out on strike. The company countered by bringing in strike-breakers. The battle of the lumber camps, one of the most sanguinary in California's labor history, got under way.

i i i

About fifteen years ago there was published, by a labor organization with headquarters in Chicago, a small paperbound book entitled *Labor's Battles and My Part in Them,* by Fred Foschay. A great many copies must have been printed, for one still sees a copy or two on the Californiana shelves of most of the second-hand-book shops. It sold for twenty-five cents. The story is told in the first person, either by Foschay himself or by someone who was a close student of his speeches.

I have sometimes wondered if Casebolt, during his investigations into the career of James Horton, ever examined a copy of *Labor's Battles.* If he did so, he must have concluded that its author was an unreliable historian. In the final chapters of his book Casebolt makes many references to Foschay, but nowhere does he indicate that the labor leader and Horton were ever anything but enemies. Foschay, indeed, is the villain of Casebolt's final chapters. That is understandable, for many of Horton's troubles during his last years were labor troubles and on the whole he came off second best.

I was interested in the way Casebolt handled that phase of Horton's story. It was a difficult assignment and he did it well. I do not think it is clearly understood that here in California writers who touch on the relations between capital and labor must be prepared to endure a considerable amount of abuse. The wisest of them try to steer clear of the subject entirely. But that is not always possible, and the next best thing is for the unfortunate scribbler to follow the dictates of his conscience — or, if you will, his prejudices — and boldly espouse the cause he thinks just. This course brings down on him the wrath of the other side, but it brings too the compensating praise of those whose game he is accommodatingly playing. But for the man who from expediency, or from a sense of scholarly detachment, or merely because he can't make up his mind, attempts to apportion the blame and praise between the two, there is no silver lining. He is roundly damned by everyone.

This oddity on the part of our reading public has caused Casebolt some bad hours. For on this question circumstances force him to be a fence-straddler. As a man of property he naturally inclines to the side of capital. He is a professor in a conservative university that has a large endowment and hopes to increase it. He likes the company of men of wealth and influence. No one more enjoys the privilege of breaking bread in the spacious dining-rooms of Pacific Avenue and Broadway, or a luxurious week-end at Lake Tahoe. Besides, who but a capitalist can afford to put out seven dollars and a half for one of his handsome two-volume works of scholarship?

On the other hand Casebolt sincerely believes himself

to be a liberal. He campaigned for Roosevelt and Johnson in 1912, and until recently he continued to register as a Progressive. In the classroom he denounces the Tories quite as roundly as a few years ago he denounced the I.W.W.'s and as he denounces the Reds and the Fifth Columnists today. But beyond that, Casebolt has political ambitions, and in California no man gets elected to office who doesn't continuously and vocally love the laboring man. It was because of doubt as to the quality of his affection that he was defeated — by the narrowest of margins — when he ran for lieutenant governor some years ago. Casebolt will hardly allow that to happen again. So, while he continues to enjoy the hospitality of the well-heeled, he neglects no opportunity to extend a helping hand to the under-privileged in their fight for a larger share of the good things of life. Carrying water on both shoulders is a difficult feat at best; one can but sympathize with Casebolt in his dilemma and admire the dexterity of his performance. But if he had lacked the aptitude for such gymnastics he would hardly have gone as far as he has.

An early chapter of *Labor's Battles* contains an account of Horton's part in the strike against the Simmons-Wheeler Lumber Company, and of Foschay's use against Horton himself of the power Horton put into his hands. The story has elements of irony. Horton's chief competitor on the Coast was, as I have said, the Simmons-Wheeler Company. The strike of the crews of its lumber schooners, which decreased its sales and increased Horton's, had suggested to Horton that labor troubles in the mills of his rival would have a further stimulating effect on his own business. He called in Foschay, then the boss of a logging crew at Howell's Landing, and sounded him out. Foschay believed the plan feasible; more, he proved willing, for a reasonable consideration, to try to bring it about. His success exceeded Horton's most sanguine hopes. Within two months after Foschay had gone into the woods the Simmons-Wheeler mills were idle and Horton's sales had grown so brisk that he was able to make substantial increases in the prices of all grades of lumber.

But his triumph was brief. The Simmons-Wheeler strike was presently ended, after the loss of five lives, and the employees were granted pay increases and most of their other demands. In his book Foschay relates that while negotiations were in progress in San Francisco, Horton sent him an urgent message asking for an appointment. They met secretly one evening on the darkened upper deck of an Oakland ferryboat. Foschay states that Horton insisted that the strikers scale down their demands. He had by then foreseen that whatever concessions were wrested from his competitor would inevitably be forced from him. Foschay refused to entertain any such proposal. When Horton threatened to make public the fact that Foschay had all along been in Horton's pay, Foschay urged him to do so. But evidently Horton decided to allow his part in the scheme to remain secret; no word of it was given out until Foschay told the story in his book.

It is a curious episode for many reasons. As Foschay recalled it, years after the event, he had all along been using Horton as a dupe. He had, he stated, intended to part company with Horton whenever the latter's interests came in conflict with those of the workers. Readers will have to draw their own conclusions on that point. My feeling is that when he made his deal with Horton, Foschay did not expect to change sides. I believe it was only after he had organized his loggers and millhands and found himself heading a movement powerful enough to bring the owners to terms that he cast his lot permanently with the workers. My guess is that he found the role of labor leader exactly to his taste. One does not have the experience of organizing hundreds of laborers and leading them through a violent strike to a successful conclusion and then willingly return to a routine job.

During that campaign Foschay must have made some pleasant discoveries about himself and his capabilities. He found that he could deliver from the steps of a bunkhouse or the topside of a flatcar the kind of speech that stirred men to a sense of their power and to an eagerness to put their adversaries to flight. He learned that slipping through enemy territory to plan strategy at secret meetings was exciting, but not more so than to wait in ambush and fall on gangs of scabs with axe-handles, or later to sit at a conference table and politely reject, one by one, the enemy's attempts to soften the terms of capitulation. It is easy to understand why Foschay chose to remain under labor's banner.

After the successful Simmons-Wheeler campaign, his victory over Horton was easy. Horton recognized the inevitable and agreed to sign the same contract that had been wrested from his competitor. He made one reservation: that every company that shipped lumber into San Francisco Bay be forced to pay the same wages and to abide by the same rules as to hours and food and housing. This was to the advantage of labor; Foschay readily agreed. The meetings at which these matters were thrashed out were held at Horton's Market Street office. Horton's assistant, Charles Pettit, who was present, once told me that Foschay and the old man parted on friendly terms.

i v

I had long since resumed my visits to Russian Hill. The unexampled treachery of Fred Foschay was mentioned from time to time, but presently even that was forgotten under the pressure of other problems. There were changes. Clifford was graduated from college in 1897 — he had left Berkeley and spent his final two years at Yale — and after six months in Europe he entered his father's office to prepare for the responsibility of some day managing a large fortune. Juliet, her homely, shrewd face relentlessly taking on the cast of an old maid's, grew more tart in her manner, her tongue sharper, steadily finding new stupidities on which to heap her scorn. Horton himself changed least of all. His hair and beard grew thinner and his clothes hung more loosely over his bony frame, but otherwise he remained as before.

Now that Casebolt's *Life* has been published, Horton's place as one of the city's leaders is secure. I've no doubt that in due course our local authorities will name a street after him, or perhaps a school, and so pay official homage to another adopted son who started from scratch and died rich. It will then be hard to convince anyone that those of us who knew him well never considered him particularly important, or that the real source of such contemporary fame as he enjoyed was due to his association with Chris Winton. But, as has frequently been pointed out, posterity often remembers the wrong men, and remembers even them for the wrong reasons.

Throughout the winter I visited the Hortons as often as I could get away from my job. The dinners were heavy and overlong, and everyone ate too much rich food and seemed none the worse for it. Even in that day of lavish cuisines Juliet was known for the variety of her table. Meals under the gas-lamps in the redwood-paneled dining-room lasted from seven until after nine. Horton himself did the carving and the portions were placed before the guests by the Chinese butler, Wong. Later Wong and a serving maid passed a succession of platters, and we helped ourselves until our plates were fairly groaning with food. I have memories of an endless succession of provender: thick soups, oysters, steamed clams, rainbow trout, roast wild ducks, quail, chickens, squabs, roast beef, lamb, venison, platters of chops, fragrant, clove-studded hams, biscuits, honey, jam, spiced peaches, pie, layer cake, ice cream, plum pudding, coffee, cigars, brandy. . . .

Later in the warm parlor the semi-drugged groups talked and smoked while the younger and more energetic played dominoes or euchre for standard stakes of five cents a game. In those days Juliet had a passion for games; she would gladly have continued until after midnight had not Chris, who had little card sense, insisted on stopping on the stroke of eleven. We collected our winnings, paid our losses, and left. On evenings when I did not have to go back to the office, Chris gave me a lift home.

I do not know why so unimportant a circumstance should stand out in my memory, but I clearly remember those chilly drives. I remember even the mild physical shock that came when, leaving the hot rooms, the sharp breeze off the ocean swept my face as we hurried down the steps and along the marble-flagged path to the stable yard. There Chris's horse was waiting, blanketed against the chill. My hand was on Chris's arm, but she needed neither guidance nor support. The cold exhilarated her. She actively enjoyed the opposition of the elements. If the wind was strong — it often was — she put her head down and forged into the teeth of it, delighted to pit her strength against its force. She was full of solicitude for her horse while I removed his blanket and halter, forced the cold bit into his mouth and cramped the wheels of the buggy for her to climb in. I then sat down beside her and threw the robe over our legs, tucking it in securely.

During these drives we talked over the games, the hands we had held, and our good or bad luck. Chris sat erect and watchful, holding a taut rein on the horse, which, impatient after his long wait, pressed forward over the wet cobbles. Wrapped in her sealskin coat, with a small round turban on her head, she made a pleasant picture. I glanced with admiration at her profile, lips parted, chin up, eyes alertly ahead. Except when it was actually raining, the top of her smart little buggy remained down the year around. When she was driving, her normal placidity gave way to animation. She turned frequently and smiled at me as though sharing her pleasure in our exploit. To hurry through the dark streets into the teeth of the wind or a damp swirl of fog became in her eyes a major adventure. We huddled close on the narrow seat, the robe close about our legs, our shoulders touching.

On these rides I was never unaware of the physical fact of her nearness. I recall that once, out of a sense of delicacy (and with a thought of Horton in the back of my mind), I drew away slightly and so relaxed the pressure of my knee and shoulder against hers. My exemplary behavior won no praise from Chris. "Move closer," she commanded. "You're letting a draft in." I moved closer. "That's much better," she commented. I thought so too. Thereafter I sat as close as it was possible to sit, and no further drafts disturbed us. Later, also in the interest of warmth (so I told myself), I removed my arm from its cramped position and slipped it about her waist. I accomplished this in a casual way, as though it were a perfectly natural maneuver and quite without significance. But if I expected Chris to ignore my action I was disappointed. She turned and regarded me curiously. I feared she was about to reprove my boldness and I resisted an impulse to withdraw my arm. But she didn't seem displeased.

I said, lightly: "That's better, don't you think? My arm got cramped."

She gave me an amused glance. "That's a funny excuse," she said. "Is that why you put your arm around girls?"

She was laughing at me, but I didn't mind. I increased the pressure of my arm and she settled closer. "There's no harm in being friendly," she announced.

We drove on in silence.

When we reached the Sacramento Street house the horse turned in the driveway, trotted briskly up the incline, and stopped in the yard. The stable-boy came out (he lived in a tiny cell behind the carriage room) and took the bridle. I climbed down, took Chris's arm as she stepped lightly to the ground, then stood by while she searched through her purse for the key to the back door. She passed it to me and I opened the door, then removed the key and reinserted it on the inside, tipped my hat, and left. A gaslight was kept burning for her in the kitchen. Through the window I could see her face in profile as she turned it off, the sleeve of her coat falling back from her arm. I then continued down the driveway, walked two blocks south and half a block west, and was home. I was always in high spirits during those brief walks. The sound of my steps echoed sharply back and forth between the dark houses.

I became more faithful than ever in my attendance at the Hortons' Thursday evenings. It would have taken a great deal to make me miss one, and the reason was the chilly, late evening drives across town with Chris. I looked forward to them with eagerness and impatience. The days from Thursday to Thursday seemed interminable. I revolved in my mind everything that had happened on our last ride and anticipated the enjoyment of the next. I had shunted off my early shyness. We hardly left Horton's yard (the carriage entrance is in the rear of the house, through an alley cut into the rocky hillside) before I slipped my arm about her and drew her close. At best our drives were far too short; I did not want to lose any time.

One evening as we were turning in the driveway Chris announced that the stable-boy was away for the night, and would I give her a hand at unhitching the horse and putting the carriage away? I was more than willing. At once the task assumed importance in her eyes. It was as though we were to perform a complicated tactical maneuver and she was the commanding general. I was ordered to open the doors of the stable and the carriage room. Meanwhile she unfastened the tugs, drew the horse forward until he was free of the shafts, lopped the reins through the saddle terrets, and gave him a slap on the rump. The well-trained animal disappeared through the stable door and clattered over the plank floor to his stall. While I backed the buggy into the carriage room and drew the big door shut, Chris removed the harness and hung it on its pegs, then snapped the halter about the horse's neck. When I returned she was vigorously pitching back the clean straw bedding from the front of the stall.

She leaned the fork against the wall and regarded me in triumph. Her face was flushed from her exertions.

"There," she announced. "That didn't take long, did it?"

Her tone implied that we had jointly performed a heroic feat. I smiled at her enthusiasm, yet I was strangely exhilarated. Standing in the dim stable (it was lighted by a single oil-lamp with a tin reflector, on a bracket above the door), the outer world seemed remote. We were like two spies, deep in the territory of the enemy, who had just completed a desperate secret mission. A few minutes before, we had been driving through the sleeping city. My arm had been about her waist and she had allowed herself to be drawn close. Once she had turned and regarded me with a tranquil, unhurried glance. A grave smile had played about her lips. An unaccustomed silence had fallen then, and we had driven on without words through the dark streets.

But when she spoke now, her tone was brisk and matter-of-fact.

" I think I'll give Chief some more feed. There's no telling when that boy will get back."

That meant climbing up to the loft and pitching hay into the rack above the horse's manger.

" I'll go," I volunteered. I started up the steep stairs.

" Wait," cried Chris. " I'm coming too."

" But that's foolish," I protested. It was quite unnecessary for us both to go.

She laughed. " Of course it's foolish. But I'm coming just the same. Give me a hand."

She was still wearing her long fur coat and it impeded her progress. I turned and grasped her extended hand.

It was dark on this elevated platform, for the light of the lamp did not reach it. We moved cautiously forward, still hand in hand. Her grip on mine tightened.

" Frightened? "

" Not a bit. It's fun." Her low laugh told me she was pleased and excited.

We edged forward until our feet touched the loosely piled hay. Its sweet autumnal odor permeated the loft. We stopped. Chris had turned and faced me. I could see the outline of her head and shoulders between me and the light. Her fur turban (it was like the visorless caps one saw in pictures of dashing Russian Cossacks) was drawn close over her head. Below it her hair spread out in two small waves above her ears; in silhouette it gave her a saucy look that was strangely moving. I stared at her entranced; I was sure I had never seen anyone so beautiful. Of a sudden I felt a dryness in my throat and my pulses were pounding.

"You're so lovely," I said.

She made no reply. She released her hand and stood motionless. I put my hands on her shoulders and then she moved slowly toward me until I felt her breath on my cheek. Her lips touched mine, drew back, and with a sort of finality presented themselves again, full and moist and clinging. I slid my arms under her coat. I could feel the play of the muscles of her back as her arms tightened about my neck. Her head was tilted upward as she gave me her mouth. I was astonished at the warmth and urgency of her caresses. There was no hesitancy about her, no maidenly acceptance of love. She was electric with passion, yielding herself eagerly. Her thighs pressed against mine. She put my hands on her breasts and held her own above them.

We drew apart and she slipped out of her coat.

"Spread it on the hay," she whispered.

I groped forward, found a level spot, and guided her toward it. In the darkness we lay down together on our springy couch. In the distance I heard the bell of a Sacramento Street cable-car as it coasted down the hill toward Van Ness Avenue.

ν

When the next Thursday evening approached I was half inclined to forgo my usual visit to the hill. But I was afraid my absence would cause comment and I concluded that the best concealment was to behave as though I had nothing to conceal. Besides, I was eager to see Chris again.

I gave a great deal of thought to what attitude I should adopt toward her at our next meeting. I decided that a dignified bearing and a sober, sad smile would be about right under the circumstances. I intended that she should read in my face and manner evidence that what had happened between us had not left me unchanged. I imagined her saying to herself, not without a touch of pride: " He's graver and more mature, more self-reliant. He has not taken our love lightly." The others too, I was sure, would notice a change in me and wonder about it. Perhaps they would discuss the matter among themselves. " I can't for the life of me make out what's come over Walter. Only yesterday he seemed a mere boy, but now! Why, he's quite the man of the world, so grave, so distingué! I must say it's very becoming to him."

I did not much doubt my ability to carry off this difficult first meeting, but I was less sure about Chris. My admiration of her was great and my affection deep, but I had little confidence in her judgment or even in her common sense. I believed her quite capable, when we met again in Horton's parlor, of betraying our secret from sheer thoughtlessness. In particular I feared Juliet. She

had an observing eye; she could not be easily hood-
winked. Very little that went on in her presence escaped
her. It would be easy for Chris to let the cat out of the
bag; a sigh or a too ardent glance would do the trick. She
might even let slip some telltale term of endearment that
would startle the room into silence. " Walter darling,
pass the salt." Or: " Is that your ace, my pet? " I lay in
bed at night and pictured the effect of such a catastrophe:
the immediate suspension of all activity, Chris's confusion
when she realized what she had done, my own horrid
embarrassment, the alarmed, covert glances we would all
steal at Horton.

And Horton himself? It is hard to imagine him behaving violently in any situation — his was not a volatile
temperament — but on the other hand the circumstances
were far from usual. I had no idea how one was expected
to react to the discovery that one's mistress was sharing
her favors with another, but I felt that this was a time
when even a phlegmatic man might be capable of sur-
prises. In my imaginings I conjured up all manner of possibilities, each more appalling than the one before. Horton unfolding his long legs, rising to his full height while
he fixed me with an icy gaze and pointed a scornful finger
at the door. Horton begging the indulgence of his guests,
then drawing a revolver and — before Chris could throw
herself between us — dispatching me with an accurately
aimed bullet through the heart. Horton pretending he
had heard nothing, pointedly breaking the electric silence
with some careless remark, then as I was leaving, saying
gravely: " Walter, I shall expect you at my office tomorrow morning at nine." I imagined myself confronting

him in his Market Street lair, coldly rejecting his attempt
to buy me off (the bribe, in shining double-eagles, was
stacked on his desk before me), and reminding him nobly
that a love such as ours was not for sale.

If the foregoing seems to imply that my feeling toward
Horton was entirely one of apprehension as to what he
might do if he found us out, I can only state that I recall
nothing more. Perhaps I was also troubled by the stir-
rings of a guilty conscience, but if that was the case all
memory of the fact has vanished. But then it has been
my observation that of all the crimes man commits against
his fellows, this one of which I have been speaking is
among those we most readily forgive ourselves and from
which we make the most rapid recovery.

I climbed the hill with lagging steps. Once inside,
however, all my uneasiness slipped away. Everything was
as it had been before. It was evident that the convulsion
that had shaken my world and, so I believed, changed the
entire course of my life had had no reverberations here.

"Here's Walter," observed Juliet when I walked into
the parlor and joined the group for our before-dinner
glass of sherry. "You haven't met the Hansons, have
you?"

She introduced me to the Hansons, a smiling little man
in the building business and his tall, dour wife. I exchanged greetings with the others. Wong, in his white
coat and baggy silk trousers, was moving about with his
tray of small glasses. The others were regular guests whom
one met week after week: Mr. and Mrs. Peters; Juliet's
bachelor friend, Dr. Haywood, who was on the staff at
St. Luke's Hospital and who periodically told us how he

had once proposed marriage to Juliet and had been flatly turned down; Helene Richards (the former Mrs. Lafavre), French and fat and flirtatious, and her husband, Hervey Richards. Horton glanced at me as I passed, said: " Good evening, Walter," and continued his conversation with Richards. I approached Chris. She was sitting on a sofa with Mrs. Peters. I gave them both a slight, formal nod and was passing on when Chris reached out and grasped my hand.

" Here, come sit with us," she commanded. " We've been wanting a man to talk to." She made room for me on the sofa. I sat down between them.

I did not feel altogether at ease — I had hoped Chris would follow my cue and adopt an air of respectful but distant friendliness — but I tried to behave with nonchalance.

Mrs. Peters, an ardent playgoer, claimed my attention. Two new plays had opened that week; she asked me which one I thought the more entertaining. I was obliged to admit that I had seen neither.

" Oh," she exclaimed, " I thought you never missed a show. I was telling Harry I'd ask you tonight before I got the tickets."

I said I was sorry to disappoint her, but that I hadn't felt in the mood for the theater. That struck me as a perfectly simple statement, but Mrs. Peters seemed to find it baffling.

" But I always thought you wanted to write plays yourself. You shouldn't miss a single show. You can never tell when you'll get an idea for a play of your own. Besides, I hear Mr. Goodwin's as funny as ever, and they say the Elliott girls are pretty as pictures."

I said lamely that I hoped to see them soon.

" Walter has had a good deal on his mind lately," said Chris.

I looked at her suspiciously. She was the picture of innocence.

" Yes," I admitted. " I've been thinking about things quite a bit."

" I can think just as well at a show as I can at home," said Mrs. Peters. " I always find the theater so stimulating. I never feel so keen mentally as I do after I've seen a good comedy."

" Walter adores the theater," observed Chris. " Don't you, my pet? "

She did not lower her voice. Her words seemed to reverberate through the room, and I felt the blood rising to my face. I raised my glass and drained off what remained of the wine. Chris had never before so addressed me in public (we had used many terms of endearment in the hayloft); I fully expected that the walls would come tumbling about our ears. Nothing happened. No one had paid any attention. Even Mrs. Peters, who had surely heard the incriminating words clearly, showed no sign of amazement.

" I think I'll choose Mr. Goodwin," she remarked. " As I say to Harry, you'll never be disappointed if you pick out a good comedy."

Wong announced dinner. As we stood up I shot an accusing glance at Chris. Her gaze was untroubled and serene, but I thought I could see a flicker of amusement in her eyes.

"I'm glad dinner's on time," she announced. "I'm hungry as a wolf."

As for myself, I doubted whether I should be able to eat a morsel. But when we were seated and the others had fallen to, for politeness' sake I permitted myself to take a sip of soup. Its aroma was appetizing and its flavor delightful. Soon I was plying my spoon industriously. My confidence returned and I began to enjoy myself. It gave me a secret pleasure to look about at these familiar faces and reflect that had I chosen I could have tossed a bombshell into their midst. I was seated between Helene Richards and the wife of Juliet's contractor. Both were garrulous ladies, not accustomed to receiving undivided attention. I was at liberty to give rein to my imagination. I subjected Horton to a searching scrutiny; it was perhaps the first time I had ever looked at him with close attention. I had to admit that despite his advanced age (he was then almost sixty) he looked quite well preserved. In the past I had sometimes wondered what Chris saw in him. I had never subscribed to the theory that on her part theirs was a purely mercenary connection by which she gave him her favors in return for a life of ease. I had always contended that she had a genuine regard for him, an admiration for his accomplishments, and indeed a sort of respectful affection. That she had ever cared for him in the passionate sense of the word I would have dismissed as preposterous. The fact that Horton was twice her age seemed to me to dispose of that possibility; besides, I had always thought her cold by nature. But I was now in possession of evidence that rendered this belief untenable, and I no longer knew what to believe. It was all very confusing. I transferred my troubled gaze to Chris. She was seated up near Horton's end of the table. The conversation was general there and she was taking a lively part in it, though not, I observed, to the point of neglecting her food. Her expression was calm and untroubled. She was the picture of serenity; it was obvious that she didn't have a care in the world. She happened to glance down the table and our eyes met. She gave me a little smile. It was spontaneous and innocent and delightful, without a shade of reserve. It seemed to say: " What a nice, friendly group this is! And aren't we all having a nice time! " I sighed and focused my attention on what Mrs. Richards was saying.

Chris drove me home as usual that evening. When we reached the alley I put my arms about her and kissed her. She leaned toward me and remained passive. Then she withdrew her lips, regarded me with a slow, half-mischievous smile, and resumed her driving. We clattered on through the dark streets. Nothing was said until we turned in her driveway.

" Yin's home tonight," she remarked then. " We won't have to unhitch the horse."

" Oh." I had hoped Yin would take every Thursday night off.

She gave me her key and I unlocked the back door. Then, as I had often done before, I removed the key and inserted it in the inner side of the lock. I stood regarding her uncertainly. The stable-boy was only a few yards away. I didn't dare kiss her good-night.

I removed my hat. "Good-by," I said. "Thank you for the ride."

She looked at me in surprise. "You're not going, are you?"

I was sure the Chinese boy was listening.

"I — I suppose so," I said. In a lower tone I added: "I don't want to."

She gave me a smile. "You may come in for a little while if you like."

It was almost daylight when I let myself out the door and hurried through the sleeping streets toward home.

Chapter 9

 YEAR passed.

One afternoon in the fall of 1901 I returned to the office and found a note on my desk stating that Miss Horton had telephoned and that it was important, and would I call right back? I called. Juliet herself answered. She responded so promptly that it occurred to me that she must have been sitting beside the phone.

She said: " Oh, it's you. I've been trying to get you all afternoon."

" I just got in. Is something wrong? "

" I want you to come up right away," she said.

" I'm leaving now," I replied, and hung up.

Juliet was in her upstairs sitting-room. She greeted me calmly enough, but there was a sardonic gleam in her eye.

" What's up? " I asked. I couldn't imagine what had happened.

" You'll find out soon enough. Cliff will be back in a minute. He went up to his room. He wants to break the news himself; he says it's a man's place."

◇◇◇◇◇◇◇◇◇◇◇◇◇◇◇◇◇◇◇

I had to smile at that. The idea that Juliet was not capable of telling me what had happened (whatever it was) would have occurred only to Cliff. I gave her an understanding glance. "Don't you think you had better leave the room?" I asked.

"I wouldn't miss it for the world," said she.

Cliff entered. He closed the door behind him and strode over and shook hands. He had the demeanor of an undertaker. His tanned, wholesome face wore a tragic expression. I was more mystified than ever.

"We had better all sit down," he said in a stricken tone. We sat down. There was a considerable pause.

Juliet broke in. "Well, go ahead and tell him," she said, with asperity. "What are you waiting for?"

Cliff cleared his throat. From the pocket of his tweed coat he produced a small bulldog pipe he smoked in those days, regarded it a moment, then put it away again. He straightened up and pulled himself together.

"There's no point in beating about the bush," he began. "You're an old friend of the family. We feel sure we can trust you. It's not like telling our troubles to a stranger."

"If I can be of any help I'll be only too glad," I replied.

"We're both sure of that," said Cliff. Then he added: "We're anxious to keep something out of the newspapers. You can arrange that, can't you?"

I looked at him in surprise. That was not at all the sort of remark I had expected him to make.

"That all depends," I said cautiously. I had no exaggerated regard for the integrity of the local press. I knew that stories were sometimes suppressed, but the word to suppress them came from above and not from the likes of me. " What's it all about? "

Cliff looked at Juliet. She returned his glance stonily, an ironical smile on her face. She gave him no help.

He blurted out: " Christine has run off with that fellow Foschay. They were married this morning at Sacramento. She sent Juliet a telegram."

I said the first thing that came into my head:

" What did your father say? "

Cliff looked harassed. " We haven't told him yet. Juliet called him when she got the wire, but he wasn't in. So she read it to me. I promised her I'd tell the governor when he came in, but I couldn't do it. I just couldn't bring myself to the point. I came home instead to talk things over with Juliet. We decided to call you."

" I don't think I can help," I said. " Foschay is pretty well known. The papers will print the news of his wedding."

" We don't care about that," returned Cliff. " Let them go ahead and print it. We're not disturbed about this marriage. It's the best thing that could have happened. We just don't want the governor's name dragged into it."

I smiled. The public's idea of what a newspaper will or will not print has always entertained me.

" You needn't worry about that," I assured him. " No editor would think of mentioning your father's name in that connection."

" Are you sure? "

" Positive. When the papers run a story about a wedding they're very careful about one thing. It's not considered good form to say that the bride has been sleeping with somebody else."

Cliff winced, but he looked relieved. "You don't think, then, there'll be any scandal?"

"Not in the papers. You can expect a great deal of talk, though."

"We realize that," Cliff acknowledged. "We'll just have to bear it as best we can."

This was said in a tone of manly resolution, but it brought a disdainful snort from Juliet. I looked at her. I wondered what was going on behind the contemptuous mask she was wearing. Chris Winton had been her best and oldest friend. Their friendship had survived even the years when Chris had been her father's mistress. With what emotions had she learned of this latest treachery, for surely Chris's elopement could only be regarded as an act of callous ingratitude. The entire affair was inexplicable. I couldn't reconcile it with anything I knew about Chris, whose kind heart was proverbial and whose affection for Juliet had never been questioned. I was then too little acquainted with life to realize that it is seldom the out and out scoundrels who deal the cruelest blows; most often of all it is the friends who are thoughtless or vain or weakly selfish. For the first time (but not the last) I thought of Juliet, who was always so self-reliant, as a tragic figure.

She may have seen a hint of this in my face, for she got up abruptly. "There's no sense keeping Walter any longer," she snapped. "He's got his work to do."

Cliff came downstairs and helped me on with my overcoat. We shook hands gloomily.

"D'you know," he remarked, "I can't help feeling sorry for the governor. Of course it's his own fault for getting himself into this jam. But," he lowered his voice, "you know how men are, once they get on in years. A clever woman can wrap them around her finger, especially if she's young and good-looking."

I nodded. "It happens all the time," I said sagely. "The strange thing is they often think the girls are in love with them."

"That's the odd part of it," returned Cliff. "The governor must have been nearly fifty when this thing began."

"It hardly seems decent," I said.

"Of course, I can't mention that phase of the matter to Juliet," added Cliff.

"Naturally not," I agreed. "She wouldn't understand."

I walked back downtown.

ii

Thereafter I saw much less of the Hortons.

I learned that the Thursday evening gatherings were continuing as before, but I could not bring myself to go. I was afraid my presence might be embarrassing; it could hardly fail to recall Chris Winton, who had been, like me, one of the faithful who showed up regularly. In the past if I, as sometimes happened, had to be absent several times running, Juliet would telephone and order me to return. I felt that if she wanted me now, she would not fail to let me know. The call never came, and I was not disappointed. I felt that an evening on the hill would be different now, and far less enjoyable. Until the months just prior to her desertion of our group, I had never consciously admitted that it was Chris who had drawn me to the Hortons' so faithfully. But I recognized now that she had been the attraction from the beginning, and I was sure the others shared my feeling. Now that she was gone, I wondered if they too were unwilling to face the heavy dinners and the hours of dull talk afterwards.

Had anyone asked me why her presence made so much difference I could have found no logical answer. She was the least obtrusive of guests. Although she had a ready flow of small talk, one thought of her as rather silent than otherwise. She was so mild and undemanding that one would have thought her presence would have been ignored. The opposite was true. We were conscious of her every minute. When she spoke, a dozen ears were cocked to listen. We considered our *bons mots* a success only if they brought an appreciative gleam to her eyes. If someone told a story, when he reached the end he glanced first of all at her to see if she was amused. Sometimes she failed to see the point and it had to be explained to her. Her delayed laughter was then so infectious that we all joined in and the joke was doubly enjoyed.

Of this there is no explanation. One can only say that some persons are like that. Through no effort of her own her presence lent a sparkle and an odd sort of exhilaration to our gatherings, and we all felt it and reacted to it. I had no longer a desire to frequent the hill.

Our brief romance had run its course. For two or three months I had driven home with her each Thursday evening and spent the rest of the night at the Sacramento Street house. I imagined myself in love, and I made secret plans to run away with her, to offer her the protection of my name in marriage, and to begin life anew in some distant land. I rather fancied the South Seas as the setting for our idyllic adventure. I said nothing of my plan to Chris; something told me her practical mind would find fatal flaws in such a program. She would be sure to ask what I proposed to use for money. So I kept my daydreams to myself, and presently my hours on the paper were changed. I was assigned to the night police beat, which meant that I had to be on duty from nine at night until seven the following morning. Of course I decided to quit. But when I showed Chris the letter of resignation I had composed (but had prudently refrained from mailing), she wouldn't hear of it. She pointed out that I was getting along splendidly at the paper — the new job meant a raise of two dollars a week — and that she would never forgive herself if she permitted me to give it up for her sake. It was noble of me to want to make so great a sacrifice, but we must be practical. I must think of my future. Surely I wanted her to be proud of me, and wasn't that worth the renunciation of our present happiness? Moreover, we would remain friends and meet each week at the Hortons', and, besides, nothing could rob us of our memories. We kissed tenderly and parted. For a week I considered myself a broken man.

Within a month I was rather glad the affair was over.

Every now and then I encountered Cliff on the downtown streets. He was working hard in his father's office, and he had gradually taken over many of the tasks that Horton had once performed himself. One of his jobs was collecting rents; when we met he usually had a leather satchel suspended from a strap over his shoulder. It was through these meetings that I kept in touch with the family. Cliff never had much news. Juliet was well. Horton had gone to Honolulu soon after Chris's marriage. Cliff and Juliet had hoped his trip would extend over several months, but Horton had transacted his business promptly and returned on the next boat. He spent long hours in his office. Times were not what they had been; Cliff asserted that the number of problems that constantly came up was past believing.

Although I was curious to know how Horton had taken Chris's elopement, I refrained from asking questions. Cliff was a very gentlemanly young man; he was born with a high regard for the conventions. I felt he would resent any attempt on my part to reopen what must be an extremely distasteful subject. Therefore, when he himself one day brought up the matter, I had difficulty concealing my surprise.

" I suppose you've heard that the governor has sold the Sacramento Street property," he announced.

" What property? " I asked. I didn't at once know what he was talking about. Horton owned a great deal of real estate all over town.

" Christine's house. You know the place."

I nodded. I didn't tell him how well I knew it.

"But I thought it was hers," I said. "I understood he gave it to her."

"That was the general impression," stated Cliff. "I always thought so myself."

I tried to think of some non-committal remark. I said, lamely: "It's a very pleasant place. I've always considered it one of the most attractive houses in town."

"Others seem to think so too," returned Cliff. "The governor got a good many offers. People seemed to think the place had unpleasant memories for him and that he'd let it go for a song." Cliff regarded me a shade grimly. "They were wrong," he added. "He made a nice profit on the deal."

I didn't say anything.

"There was one complication," continued Cliff. "The new owner doesn't want the furniture and it's going to be sold separately. It's to be auctioned off next week."

"Auctioned?"

Cliff nodded. "At the house. The public's invited."

"I don't think that's a very wise plan," I said. "Won't it cause a lot of talk?"

"It wasn't my idea," said he. "Juliet suggested it in the first place. She says people have been wanting to get inside that house for years. She said they'll pay good prices to get something that used to belong to Christine. The governor thought it was shrewd of Juliet to think of that." He added: "The worst of it is, she's right. There'll be a terrible mob."

I knew how galling all this was to Cliff, and I suddenly felt sorry for him.

"It's too bad, old man," I sympathized.

He managed a pained grin. " It's not important. It will blow over." Then he added: " You understand, of course, why the governor's doing this? Most people will think it's because of the extra cash he'll get from an auction. He doesn't care about that. It's his way of telling the town to go to hell."

" Of course," I agreed. It seemed a typical gesture, on both Horton's part and Juliet's.

Cliff strode off down the street and I looked after him with respect. He had his share of the Horton fortitude. He had need of it, too, for the auction created a sensation. I didn't attend, but I heard the details. During the three days of the sale, crowds milled through the rooms and gathered in queues on the porch and trampled the lawn and the flower-beds. It was a memorable demonstration of morbid curiosity. But the event that caused the biggest stir was the presence at all three sessions of Juliet, and her bland explanation that she had come to pick up a remembrance or two of her old friend Christine. If such was her purpose she had her trouble for nothing, for, although she bid on dozens of articles, she got none of them. In every case they went for more than she was willing to pay. There were those who claimed that her real purpose was to bid the prices up. In any event the auction was a great success. Chris's furniture brought at least three times what it was worth.

From long experience San Francisco has grown used to the eccentricities of its millionaires. Horton's auctioning off the furnishings of the nest from which the bird had flown was regarded as an entertaining episode, but no one remembered it long. It would certainly have made a bigger stir had it happened elsewhere. I venture to say that in most cities Horton himself would have been regarded as a picturesque character, yet I don't recall that any of us paid much attention to him.

I think I have made it plain that Horton was not personally a spectacular figure. He was far less known than dozens of men whose accomplishments were inferior to his. For many years he was seen daily on San Francisco's streets, stalking along the sidewalks of the financial district with his peculiar, unhurried tread, or driving by in the high seat of his buggy, staring moodily at the rump of his horse. Probably not one citizen in ten realized that this spare, bearded man who went about wrapped in a sort of perpetual reverie was the Jim Horton of the lumber mills and shipping lines, of the wholesale establishment on Rincon Hill, or the office block on lower Market and of the big ugly mansion on the western height. Even among those who knew him by name, few realized how large a stake he held in the industrial and commercial life of the city. Over the years he had extended his holdings, using his surplus funds to buy, at bargain prices, whatever promised a safe investment and a large profit: business houses, residential property, industrial plants, mines and timber and ranches. He put his money into nothing that he himself did not control. He would invest in a corporation only if he could acquire a majority of the stock. The inventory of his estate was peculiar in one respect: he had few holdings in the standard investments of the period: traction lines, gas or water companies, banks, railroads. He refused to allow his dollars to be handled by other hands than his.

It is unfortunate that the term " rugged individualist " was not in use in his day. It would have suited him to a T.

iii

After Christine's marriage I saw little of Horton or Juliet; of Chris herself I saw nothing at all. I learned that she was living in the Mission district. Occasionally someone reported having met her downtown, shopping in one of the Market Street stores or emerging from the gallery of the Orpheum after a matinee. It was said that she looked unchanged (though less handsomely dressed), that she seemed pleased to see old acquaintances and chatted with them with pleasure and without embarrassment. It was clear that she had accepted her altered status with philosophical good nature. I sometimes wondered what I should find to say to her if we met, but that contingency never came to pass, and gradually I thought of her less often.

In 1903, the settlement of my father's estate having brought me a small inheritance, I set off for Europe, intent on applying myself to literature in the, I hoped, favorable environment of the Left Bank. I remained in Paris three and a half years. I well remember, one spring day toward the end of my stay, sitting at a sidewalk table on the boulevard Raspail and reading in the black type of a newspaper that an earthquake, followed by a tidal wave, had completely destroyed San Francisco. Later reports modified the extent of the catastrophe and I think it was this reassuring word that at least a part of the town had been spared that started me thinking about returning.

Meantime I had had some small success.

During the early 1900's the public's taste in fiction ran to romantic adventures laid in distant and picturesque lands, and I, who have never believed in cutting across popular trends, tried to be as romantic and remote as the best of them. Any admirer of *Graustark* or *Zenda* or *Monsieur Beaucaire* who chanced on one of my early novels was assured of getting some more of the same. My imaginary Balkan castles were guaranteed to be as moss-grown and intrigue-ridden as those of my betters, my princesses were at least as statuesque and lovely, and my American heroes all looked remarkably handsome in the uniform of the captain of the guard. If I entered literature clinging to the coat-tails of Anthony Hope and George Barr McCutcheon my conscience was not troubled. At least they had got me inside, and I had plenty of company on the trip.

It would be pleasant to state that my decision to return to California and to write about persons and places I knew was inspired by an awakened artistic conscience. Such, however, was not the case. The fact is that the third (and least bad) of my Balkan romances had sold less than three thousand copies, and it was suggested to me by my publisher that if I wanted to stay on his list I had better learn to play a new tune. He was a practical man with a habit of speaking his mind; it was his letters, following closely on news of the earthquake, that sent me scurrying back across the Atlantic.

I returned to San Francisco in the fall of 1906, rented a room in a building beyond the burned area on Mont-

gomery Street, and started a novel about the clear-eyed
daughter of a Comstock millionaire. I worked hard all
that fall and winter, doing my research at the university
library across the bay and living the life of a recluse. I
renewed few of my old acquaintances. I seldom read the
newspapers. I knew as little about what was going on
about me as if I had remained in Paris. Then, one evening on Columbus Avenue, when I was returning from
the Italian restaurant where I sometimes ate my dinner,
I came face to face with Chris.

We stopped and stared at each other. I felt a glow
of pleasure at the sight of her. At the moment she looked
exactly as I remembered her, although I discovered later
that she had put on weight (her magnificent figure was
now definitely on the plump side), and her corn-colored
hair, which she had worn close to her skull, was done in
a stylish pompadour. We stood on the sidewalk while
we expressed our mutual astonishment at this meeting.
She told me she lived only a block or two away, on the
slope of Telegraph Hill, and that she had stepped out
for a breath of air and to give her dog his exercise. The
animal, a surly-looking English bull, which she had on a
leash, sniffed noisily at my legs while we talked.

We were only a few yards from Montgomery Street.
I invited her to come up and have a glass of wine. She
hesitated; she had thrown her cape over her shoulders
and she was not dressed for calling. Then she laughed
and took my arm.

" I don't have to dress up for you," she announced.

" Certainly not! " I was absurdly glad to see her.

While I closed the windows and lighted the gas heater

(my stay in Paris had inured me to cold rooms) she wandered about, examining my domestic arrangements. They were not elaborate. My work-desk, a kitchen table bought in a second-hand shop, stood between the windows, and the couch where I slept — which in daytime I concealed with a tapestry spread and two hard sofa-pillows covered with leather — was against one wall. The floor was covered with Chinese matting. I had two chairs, a comfortable rocker in which I did my reading and one with a straight back and hard wooden seat, where I sat while I struggled with my Comstock heiress. The glare of the white plaster walls I had tried to soften by putting up some drawings I had brought from Paris. They were watercolors and charcoal sketches that had been presented to me, because I had politely admired them, by artist friends; most of them were nudes. Chris went from one to another, giving each a placid scrutiny. From her expression I could gain no hint of what she might think of them. By the time she had finished I had poured the wine. I had her take the comfortable chair and I sat down on the edge of the couch.

She held up her glass, looked at me over its rim, and smiled.

" Here's to old times! " she said.

She had always been easy to talk to. She wanted to know all about what I had been doing since we had lost touch with each other. Yes, she had heard I had gone to Paris, but she had had no idea I was back again. When she had started out for her walk that evening, I was positively the last person she had expected to meet. I had been away how long? Nearly four years? She supposed I

had had a great many adventures. I said no, that I had
lived a very humdrum life. She smiled knowingly and
glanced at the drawings. At any rate I had got on well
with the French girls. Chris was a close reader of the
magazine sections of the Sunday papers and she knew all
about what went on in the artists' studios in Paris. I said
nothing. If she chose to regard me as a gay blade, that
was all right with me. She asked if I had been writing all
the time I was gone and if, now that I was back, I was
going to work for the papers again.

It grew clear to me that she had not heard about my
books, that she had no idea of how I had come up in the
world. There are few darker moments in an author's life
than this. The fledgling littérateur meets a friend he has
not seen since his literary triumphs. He approaches the
latter with outstretched hand, prepared to see a gleam
of admiration and perhaps of suppressed envy in his eye,
and ready to turn aside his words of congratulation with
a modest shrug. But your friend looks puzzled at your
exuberant greeting, gives your hand a flaccid grasp, and
you realize with chagrin that he thinks you still sell life
insurance for a living.

But I felt no such disappointment now. I didn't care
a rap whether Chris knew that I had written three novels;
it would not have made any difference to her in any case.
She took you for what you were; no nonsense about what
the world thought about you concerned her in the least.

All the while she rattled on I was asking myself how
life had been treating her. I had already guessed that she
was still married to Foschay — she called him just that,
" Foschay " — and still living with him. She told me that

by way of explaining the dog. Foschay was often away evenings, attending meetings and such, and he thought she needed the dog for protection, particularly because she was frequently on the streets after dark and because this was a tough neighborhood. The neighborhood was indeed tough. The Barbary Coast, eclipsed by the fire but again going full blast, was at the base of her hill, and a block or two to the west and south was Bartlett Alley with its rows of cribs and parlor houses, the center of our booming red-light district.

"I must say I was a little nervous at first," she said. "The streets are full of drunks every night of the year. If they see a lady walking about at night, they think she's trying to drum up trade. I wouldn't dare go around the way I do if it wasn't for Sport. If some fellow gets familiar all I've got to say is 'Sic 'em,' and Sport's after him like a flash. I've often wondered what would happen if his leash ever broke; sometimes it's all I can do to hold him. Anyhow, the drunks can't get out of the way fast enough."

She reached down and rubbed the dog's head. At the sound of his name he had sprung to his feet. He was eyeing me alertly. "You see!" Chris exclaimed. "He's right on the job! Besides, he's company around the house. I've always been crazy about animals."

"I remember you used to like horses."

She sighed reminiscently. "Didn't I, though! D'you remember how I used to go driving in the Park? I never missed a day. And how I went all the way to Port Costa to ride my pony? That's one thing I miss now, having to go without a horse and carriage."

"You'll be getting an auto soon," I said. "Horses are passé."

Chris sniffed. "Not I. I can't stand the smelly things. Besides, they'll never take the place of horses; not in San Francisco. The hills are too steep."

"I suppose you're right," I admitted. "But if you want a horse and carriage, why don't you get them?"

She shrugged good-naturedly. "Did you ever hear of a workingman's wife riding around in a carriage?"

"I don't see why not. Your husband's an important union official. He must make a good salary."

"That's just the way you used to talk. Always getting excited over things you knew nothing about." Then she added, and there was in her eyes a mischievous gleam I remembered: "I suppose you were upset when I married Foschay."

"I was perfectly furious."

She seemed delighted. "I thought you would be. While we were on our honeymoon — did you know we went to Portland to visit Foschay's sister? — we often talked about how we'd surprised everybody. We used to wonder how they were taking it."

"So far as I know, they took it very well." I must have spoken a bit stiffly, for her smile broadened.

"I'd like to have seen Juliet's face when she got my wire!"

It struck me that this was a bit too much. Juliet had been her loyal friend. Yet Chris seemed to take delight in recalling her discomfiture. It was contrary to all I knew about her.

"I thought you treated us very badly," I said. "I was disappointed in you."

"Why should you have been? I wanted a home of my own and Foschay offered me one. It's no crime to get married."

"Foschay and Jim Horton were enemies," I pointed out. "It wasn't very pleasant for him when you ran off with the one man who'd ever got the best of him. You must have realized that."

"I didn't owe old Horton anything," said Chris.

"Perhaps not," I granted. "But you'll admit he was kind to you. And liberal."

She regarded me with tranquil good nature. "For a man who wants to be a writer," she observed, "you don't know much about women."

"I'm always anxious to learn."

"I suppose you think I was perfectly contented all that time."

"I don't know," I said. "You seemed happy enough."

"That just shows how much you know about it," returned Chris. "Well, I can tell you it didn't take me long to find out one thing: that being an old man's darling was no picnic." She eyed me ironically. "Do I shock you, talking like that?"

"I can stand it," I said. "Besides, it might have occurred to you to look before you leaped."

"It's easy to say that. I thought I knew what I was about. I'd been earning my living for seven years and I was sick of it. I thought I'd take things easy for a change. I thought having horses and a house and money to spend would make up for everything. Well, it didn't, not for long. D'you know what made me tired of the whole business? "

" Maybe your conscience began to trouble you," I suggested.

" My conscience never gave me any trouble at all. And I didn't mind what people thought. It only amused me when men tried to make love to me behind old Horton's back or when the women used to point me out in the stores and turn up their noses. D'you know what finally got on my nerves? "

" No."

" It was having to act so damned pleasant all the time."

I looked at her and smiled. " I shouldn't think that would have worried you. You had a naturally sweet disposition."

" People used to tell me that. I often said to myself: ' That's all very well, my friend, but how would you like to have to be sweet twenty-four hours a day? You'd see then how long your nice disposition would last.' Other people could blow off steam now and then, but I had to watch myself every minute. If I showed any sign of being out of sorts, people would say: ' What did I tell you? She's sorry for her bargain, just as I expected. I could have told her not to be such a fool.' Of course I couldn't give them that satisfaction, so I pretended to be happy as a lark. It got so I couldn't stand it another minute."

" Is that why you married Foschay? " I asked, smiling.

" As a matter of fact, it was. He asked me one night when I was feeling so mad I wanted to scream. I said: ' All right, let's get married right away.' "

I looked at her. " You don't expect me to swallow that," I said.

" It's true, just the same," she insisted. Then she added: " Of course I wouldn't have consented if I hadn't respected him."

" I give you up."

" It's turned out very well," she continued. " Foschay works hard and he needs somebody to look after him. I see that he gets good wholesome food, and clean shirts and socks. I've made him a good wife."

" Do you love him? "

She smiled. " I expected you'd ask that. You always did have romantic ideas."

" You needn't answer me if you don't want to."

" I don't mind answering. No, I don't love him, but I don't think that's important. I admire him and I was grateful when he asked me to marry him. My reputation wasn't any too good, you know. I respect him for being so generous, and I help him with his work. It's a satisfaction to know I'm doing something for the cause."

" What cause? The labor movement? "

She nodded. " It's become very close to my heart."

" Nonsense," I protested. " You know very well you don't care a damn about labor."

She gave me an injured look. " That's where you're mistaken," she asserted. " I devote a great deal of my time to it. I'm always busy with some committee, or going to meetings, or marching in the parades. I worked night and day last year when they were organizing the sewing girls. You know, that used to be my trade."

I regarded her thoughtfully. " Isn't it possible," I asked,

" that you've got yourself in the same fix you were in before? "

" What d'you mean by that? "

" You left Horton because you didn't want people to know you sometimes got tired of your bargain. And now you're married to Foschay you have to pretend to be happy so no one will guess you miss the luxuries you used to have. D'you think you've bettered yourself? "

She regarded me closely for a moment, then she shrugged. Her face broke into a smile. " You think you're clever, don't you? Well, what makes you think I'm going to let you question me? Besides, I've got to fly. Foschay will be home any minute. Come, Sport, we're going."

I got her cape and slipped it over her shoulders. She leaned down and fastened the dog's leash, then turned and regarded me. A strand of hair had fallen over her eyes and she smoothed it back. I was struck by the grace of the gesture, by the soft bloom of her cheeks and her fine eyes. She was still an uncommonly attractive woman. She must have seen the admiration in my gaze, for some of the old mocking pleasure came into her eyes. When she gave me her hand it felt warm and pleasant. I was in no hurry to release it.

" It's been nice talking about old times," she said. " Now that we're neighbors, we must see each other often."

" Drop in again soon, by all means. You'll always find me at home."

" I will, if you're sure I won't bother you." She glanced at my littered work-table.

At the door I took her in my arms and kissed her. She returned the pressure of my lips quite frankly. Her eyes were closed. After a moment her dog began to bark furiously. She disengaged herself and slipped into the hall.

She looked back over her shoulder; there was a mischievous glint in her eye.

" Foschay will be so pleased to know you're back," she said.

She disappeared round the turn of the hall.

iv

During the months I remained on Montgomery Street she dropped in two or three evenings a week. She was almost my only caller. Her coming was announced by her dog, which soon became used to the visits. She would unfasten his leash when she stepped off the street and he would bound up the stairs and make a bee-line for my room. I would hear a flurry of feet as he catapulted himself down the hall, then a series of throaty snorts while he pressed his nose against the crack of the door. Chris's rapid stride would follow a few seconds later and I would put aside the book I was reading and let them in. Both were breathless from their game and highly entertained.

I guessed that Chris was bored by the humdrum life she was leading. Foschay was seldom home evenings (union officials, like night-club entertainers, seem to do most of their work after dark) and Chris had a great deal of time on her hands. I suspected that, notwithstanding her boast to the contrary, she did not take her household duties very seriously. They lived in a flat on the steep lower side of Vallejo Street; it was reached by a series of wooden steps that zigzagged down the cliff.

" It's quite a come-down from Sacramento Street," she observed one evening, with her placid smile.

I soon discovered that she liked to talk about the old days. She would lean back in my big chair and clasp her hands behind her head and recall persons and events I had almost forgotten: men and women we had met at the Hortons', week-ends at Slaterock, her horses and servants and her charge accounts at the stores.

" I'll say one thing for old Horton," she remarked. " He never once made a row about the bills. When they came in I used to put them in a drawer in the hall. Once a month he got them out and spread them on the table and added them up. Then he'd take his wallet out of his pocket and begin stacking up the twenties until he had the right amount. He'd tell me to fetch my purse and I'd hold it open while he slid the stacks over the edge of the table. He'd say: ' Now you'd better run down first thing in the morning and pay these.' He didn't believe in keeping money in the house. That was all there was to it. He never cared what I'd been buying. Even when the amount was much larger than usual — like the time I bought my sealskin coat — he didn't seem to notice. Of course," she added, " I was never extravagant. I didn't go about buying things just for the fun of it. Still, I didn't feel that I should deprive myself of anything I really needed."

Occasionally she let slip a bit of information that surprised me. One evening I admired a pin she was wearing, a gold fleur-de-lis, outlined in pearls. She unfastened it and passed it over. " Pretty, isn't it? I've never cared much about jewelry, but I've always liked this. Jack Haley gave it to me one year for Christmas. I scolded him for being so extravagant, although I knew he could well afford it. It must have cost him plenty."

I remembered Jackson Haley very well. He was a mining engineer, middle-aged and jolly and a little stout. He sometimes appeared at the Hortons' when he chanced to be in town, perhaps three or four times a year. It had never occurred to me that his acquaintance with Chris was more than casual.

I said: " Did Haley ever come to see you at Sacramento Street? "

She regarded me thoughtfully. From her expression I could see that she was secretly amused. " What difference does it make now? " she asked.

" None at all. But there was a time when I would have cared a great deal."

" Ah, but you didn't know about it then."

I had to laugh. Just the same, I felt that she had behaved outrageously. " Suppose Horton had found out about Haley. There'd have been a terrific row."

She said a peculiar thing. " Perhaps old Horton knew more than you think he did. He wasn't a fool, you know."

I didn't pursue the subject further.

It was from Chris that I learned the news of the Horton family. Not much had happened during the years I had been away. Chris had had no direct contact with the clan since her marriage, but other channels of information had not been lacking. She was a careful reader of the daily newspapers and she had, besides, discovered that the woman who lived in the flat above her, a Mrs. Morrish, was a sister of Katherine Ringe, who had long been a maid in the Horton household.

"You can imagine my surprise," said Chris, "when I walked in on Mrs. Morrish one day and saw Kathie sitting with her in the kitchen having a cup of coffee."

Between Kathie and our daily journals Chris kept herself informed of what had been happening at the Hortons'. In the public prints she had followed Clifford's rise from obscurity to a place of prominence among the young businessmen of the town. He did nothing spectacular, but he was active and civic-minded, and those who read the papers closely encountered his name often. He became a member of the board of directors of a boys' club in the Potrero; for several years, as chairman of its finance committee, he conducted successful fund-raising campaigns. He warmly supported the City Beautiful movement, one of the lively civic activities of the early 1900's. On its behalf he wrote letters to the *Chronicle* and the *Morning Call* urging that the celebrated Dr. Burnham, of Chicago, be brought out to survey the situation and to work up a suitable program. I do not know to what extent Clifford's letters influenced the issue, but the fact remains that Dr. Burnham did indeed come out and that Cliff's name was on the committee that welcomed him. After the fire he seems really to have put his shoulder to the wheel. Chris states that she was always coming across his name on committees for the relief of the needy, the succor of the destitute, or the cheering up of the down-hearted.

" I was surprised to find that he had become so prominent," said she. " I always considered him such a stupid boy."

I pointed out to her that many of those whose names appear frequently in the newspapers are less than brilliant. Chris was unimpressed. She had a great deal of respect for the printed word.

" He must amount to something or he wouldn't be mentioned so often," she maintained. " I misjudged him when he was younger and I admit it. I believe in giving credit where credit is due."

Toward Juliet her attitude was definitely hostile and I could not understand why. Once or twice when, my curiosity having got the better of me, I questioned her on the subject, she shrugged and grew silent. But I observed a stiffening of her spine and I could see a scornful curve to her upper lip.

" But you must have heard something about her," I once insisted. " She's been right here in town, hasn't she? "

" I'm sure I've no idea. I haven't been keeping track of her movements."

" Well, what does Kathie say about her? "

" You might ask her."

" I don't see Kathie and you do," I pointed out.

" If you think I've got nothing better to do than to encourage servants to talk about their employers, then you're mistaken."

" I doubt if Kathie needs much encouragement."

" It may interest you to know," said Chris, " that I've forbidden her to mention Juliet's name in my presence."

" But why? " I asked.

" Because she's an evil-minded old maid. That's why."

I regarded her in astonishment. It was the first time I had ever seen her angry. Hers was a singularly placid temperament, but, like many of that disposition, when she was aroused she went to the opposite extreme. Her face was flushed. Her lips were fixed in a scornful line. Her eyes, in the old phrase, flashed fire.

I was conscience-stricken. " I'd no idea you felt so strongly on the subject," I said. " I should have minded my own business."

She looked at me, then she shrugged and grinned. " You needn't apologize. It's just that when I think about some things I can't help getting mad, even now."

It was clear that she was eager to tell me all about her grievance against Juliet. I did not urge her. It is seldom wise to encourage such confidences. In the first place they are rarely as entertaining as the narrator believes them to be, and when he has finished one has to either pretend an interest one does not feel or be branded as an unsympathetic fellow with a callous lack of feeling. But this time I didn't protest very strongly. I had a considerable curiosity.

She told me a singular tale.

v

After the far-off night at Slaterock when Juliet saw her father steal out of Chris's bedroom, an odd change took place in Juliet's behavior toward her friend.

Chris asserted that it was some time before she grew aware of precisely what was going on. When she paid her next visit to Slaterock she was surprised to discover that Juliet wanted her to occupy the large bedroom across the hall. Chris protested that she was quite comfortable in the little north room where she had always stayed, but Juliet refused to listen. The other room was far more pleasant. The morning sun streamed into it. It had a bay window and a fireplace and a large dressing-room. But Chris knew that it had been Anita Horton's room and that it adjoined the chamber where Horton slept. The two rooms had a common bath. When Chris continued to object, Juliet did something she had seldom done before: she reached over, took Chris's hand, and gave it an affectionate squeeze. "Now let's not have any more talk," she said. "I only want you to be comfortable."

Chris moved into the larger bedroom. She did so reluctantly, mainly because she thought the servants would think it strange for her to occupy a room *en suite* with that of the master of the house. She wondered that that phase of the matter had not occurred to Juliet, and she concluded that, never having been married, Juliet's virginal mind was incapable of envisioning such a possibility. She was not permitted to hold that belief long. Evidence accumulated that pointed to but one conclusion: that Juliet knew precisely what was going on, and that she was determined to be helpful. The two had continued their schoolgirl habit of visiting each other's rooms at night for an hour of gossip or discussion of the day's happenings before they went to sleep. Juliet's nocturnal visits ceased. Back in town, she announced one evening that there was no sense in Chris continuing to live in a stuffy rooming-house when there was so much extra space on the hill. Why didn't she come and live with them? Chris refused. When Juliet persisted, Chris decided that the time had come to make a stand.

"I gave her to understand that I wouldn't consider such an idea for a minute," Chris told me. "She said she wanted me to do exactly as I pleased and that she had only made the suggestion because she thought I would be happier with them. We let the matter drop. Then a few weeks later old Horton said he had something he wanted me to see and that he would call for me the next evening at seven. We drove out Sutter Street and up Van Ness and turned west on Sacramento. A few blocks farther on he drew up and pointed out a house across the street. He asked me what I thought of it. I said it was very pretty. I thought it was some place he was thinking about buying and I was pleased because he had asked my opinion of it. Then he drove up the driveway and around to the back and stopped. We got out. I was surprised; there were lights in the house and it seemed strange to be going in the back way. He went in without knocking. There was a Chinese cook in the kitchen. Old Horton spoke to him and we walked through to the dining-room, where there was another Chinese boy wearing a white jacket, and from there we went into the parlor. The servant went ahead and turned up the gas. We went all through the house — the hall, the two bedrooms, the sitting-room and the conservatory in the back. It was very prettily furnished. Everything was brand-new and neat as a pin. We went back to the parlor and sat down.

" Horton said: ' Well, what do you think of it? '

" I said: ' I think it's beautiful. But who does it belong to and why are we here? '

" He smiled and said: ' We won't bother about that now. The main thing is to find out if you like it.'

" I told him again that I thought it was fine. I walked about and looked at the pictures and bric-a-brac, and then the Chinese boy opened the door and said dinner was ready. The table was set for two. I could see that the linen and plates and silverware were all new. When old Horton saw me looking at them, he said:

" ' How do you like them? '

" I said: ' I like them very much. Why do you keep asking me that? '

" He said: ' For a very good reason. I want you to like it here because this is where you're going to live.'

" I just looked at him. I was never so surprised in my life. Before I could say anything the boy came in with the soup. After he had put the dishes down, old Horton said: ' Hoy, this is your mistress, Mrs. Winton. I want you to take good care of her.' Hoy grinned and went out again.

" Old Horton sat watching me while I tried to take it

all in. He looked as pleased as Punch. When I realized
that he had planned it all as a surprise for me, I couldn't
say a word. I got up and went around the table and put
my arms around his neck and kissed him. I never dreamed
he could be so thoughtful. He had the boy open champagne and we drank to the new house. We had a very
jolly dinner. When he told me there was a team of horses
in the stable and a new Brewster carriage, I had to go out
and see them right away. Then I went all through the
house again. The dinner got cold, but I was too excited
to eat anyhow. I told him I couldn't wait to move in.

"He said: 'There's no reason why you should wait.
I think you'll find everything you need right here.' He
was right. There was a toilet set laid out on the bureau and
a robe and slippers and a nightgown in the closet. I even
found a toothbrush and a tin of tooth powder on a shelf
in the bathroom."

"That was very thoughtful of him," I observed.

"Wasn't it?" said Chris, not without irony. "It's hard
to believe, but it never occurred to me that Horton hadn't
done it all himself. I was so excited that for a day or two
I didn't give the matter a thought. Then I began to wonder. I told myself that old Horton might have bought the
horses and carriage and even the furniture. But I couldn't
picture him shopping for sheets and tablecloths, and especially not for the nightgown and slippers. The tooth
powder was the kind I always used. It wasn't like a man
to remember a thing like that. I thought about it all one
day, and when old Horton came to dinner I said:

"'I think I ought to thank Juliet.'

"'Thank Juliet?' he asked. 'What for?'

" ' For furnishing this place so nicely. She thought of everything.'

" He looked embarrassed. He didn't say a word. I said: 'I'll go around tomorrow and tell her how much I appreciate it.'

" Then he said: 'I don't think I'd say anything about it.'

" ' It's only right that I should thank her,' I said. ' She must have worked hard.'

" ' Maybe she did,' he said, ' but just the same I don't know as you'd better mention it. I don't know just what she'd think.'

" I lost my temper. ' I know what I think,' I said. ' I think she's an evil-minded old maid. I never want to lay eyes on her again as long as I live.' I got up and ran out of the room."

I waited for her to go on. All this had happened more than ten years before, but Chris obviously could not recall it without a considerable degree of indignation.

" I made old Horton admit that Juliet had bought everything in the house," continued Chris. " What's more, she'd hired the servants and ordered the supplies and came every day to see that things were unpacked and arranged properly. Can't you see her taking all that on herself? "

" I don't think it was very tactful of her," I admitted.

Chris's lip curled. " If she didn't care how I felt, she might have considered her father's feelings. She might have had the decency to pretend that she didn't know what was going on."

I have never believed that my insight into feminine

psychology is particularly keen, but I could understand that from Chris's standpoint Juliet's behavior left much to be desired.

I tried to smooth her ruffled feathers. " After all, she was only trying to be helpful."

" You'll never make me believe it. She just wanted to get her oar in. She knew it would embarrass me to have her snooping around."

" There's another way of looking at it," I said. " You'll have to admit that she took a broad-minded view of the situation. A lot of people disapproved of you and Horton. I imagine Julie was the only one of your friends who wasn't shocked."

" That's what I'm trying to tell you," snapped Chris. " I could have forgiven her if she'd refused to speak to me. It was her being so helpful and knowing about everything that I found humiliating." She considered this a moment, then she added:

" She always did have a dirty mind."

Chapter 10

O N the day I finished my fourth novel (*Lucy Matt-lock*, Moffat, Yard & Company, New York, 1908) I gave up my Montgomery Street room. During the next few years I was not often in San Francisco. I lived at Berkeley and spent the summers at Carmel. I traveled as often and as far as my limited income permitted. So it came about that when James Horton died, in June of 1912, I was in Mexico City, and it was not until I returned to Berkeley in the fall, and indeed until I had been back several weeks, that I learned the news. One day I chanced to read in a San Francisco paper that the inventory of the estate of the late capitalist had been filed with the probate court and that his entire fortune, estimated at more than five million dollars, had been left to his two children. I sat down and wrote notes of condolence to Juliet and Clifford.

Both replied promptly. Clifford's letter was an admirable document. He appreciated the thoughtfulness that had prompted me to write, and he knew that I, who had known his father's qualities of mind and heart, would realize how keenly he felt his loss and how eager he was to carry on the family name to the best of his ability. It was a model of filial devotion, of courageous determination, and of candid and manly grief. It did him a good deal of credit.

Juliet's note read:

DEAR WALTER: Come and see me on Wednesday or Thursday. I'll be home both days, at four.

It was not altogether convenient for me to answer that summons. But, as my readers may have guessed, I have my share of curiosity and I had besides a genuine liking for Juliet. I was on hand at four o'clock on Wednesday. A full decade had passed since I had last climbed the steep inclines of Russian Hill and I looked about with interest. I could see but few changes. The fire that had completely altered the central part of the town had not reached these upper slopes. The hilltop remained as it had always been, a small isle of the past rising above a transformed sea, and dominated as of old by the baroque and awesome outlines of the Horton mansion.

I climbed the steps and rang the bell, attended by the ghosts of the past. I was expected. The servant who answered the door was a Japanese. I had to smile at that. The Japs were unpopular in California that year and it was not hard to guess that Juliet had hired a Japanese butler for the express purpose of annoying her friends. The Oriental piloted me upstairs, opened the door to the sitting-room, and bade me enter.

Juliet gave me her hand. " I'm glad to see you, Walter," she said. " Here's an old friend of yours."

My eyes traveled past her to a figure in the window. Against the light, I could not distinguish her features clearly, but there was no mistaking that upright carriage, the alert tilt of her head. It was Chris.

We had a very pleasant visit. As everyone knows, unfortunately it is true that when friends who once saw a great deal of one another meet again after a lapse of years, they often find it hard to re-establish the old intimacy. It is seldom easy to turn back the clock. Habits and interests change, new friends take the places vacated by the old, and, try as we will to recapture a vanished mood, it perversely eludes us. The result is that after an hour of forced and hollow enthusiasm, of the exchange of gossip about half-forgotten acquaintances and the bringing to light of happenings of the past that would better have remained buried (we wonder why they had once seemed to us amusing), we end by glancing at our watches, expressing amazement at the way the time has flown, and hurrying off to keep imaginary but pressing engagements.

No such awkwardness marred my reunion with these two friends of my youth. Juliet was never one to sentimentalize over the past (she had greeted me exactly as though we had had lunch together the day before), and I think I have made it clear that Chris found the present far too absorbing to give much thought to what was over and done with.

I was surprised to find them once more on friendly terms, but that was soon explained. It had come about because Chris had answered a classified advertisement in the *Examiner* and because she had discovered when she received a reply that the advertiser was Juliet. The ad was for a forewoman to oversee the workroom of a factory that manufactured women's and children's dresses. Juliet had acquired the property as a by-product of one of her complicated real-estate deals, and she proposed to operate it until such time as a buyer could be found who would pay what she believed it was worth. The two met and talked over the details. The result was that they entered into an agreement to conduct the business in partnership. Juliet put up the capital and Chris contributed her time and experience, and she had the privilege of buying (with her share of the profits) a fifty-per-cent interest in the firm. The factory had been in operation the better part of two years and I was given to understand that business was flourishing. During the busy seasons they hired as many as sixty girls, their salesmen visited the trade as far east as Denver and Cheyenne, and Aunt Ellen (Aunt Ellen was the trade name under which their products were sold) shirtwaists and aprons and sunbonnets were worn by thousands of women all over the West.

They took turns telling me about these achievements, their eyes sparkling with enthusiasm. It was obvious that they were again the best of friends. What resentment Chris had once felt against Juliet had been forgotten in her pleasure over guiding their undertaking to success.

As I listened I found myself reflecting on the devious means by which the human soul weathers the stresses of the years and at last comes safely to port. I saw before me two middle-aged businesswomen. Both were engrossed in the details of an enterprise that, however prosaic it might seem to the world, to them spelt triumph and contentment. Was it for this, then, that these parallel lives had been lived; that two young girls had walked bcneath the eucalyptus groves of Mills Seminary, had gone into the world and faced its problems, coped with its emergencies, met or evaded its challenges, known defeat, triumph, boredom, and ecstasy, had hated, loved, schemed, grown cynical or resigned, and then, as the fires burned lower, had found fulfillment at last — in the ready-made clothing business?

I asked Chris about her husband.

" Foschay? " she repeated. " I left him nearly three years ago. Hadn't you heard? We didn't get along at all."

When it came time for me to go, I suggested that if Chris had finished her visit we might walk down the hill together.

" Christine lives with me now," said Juliet. " Since Father died and Clifford moved into his apartment I've had this great barn to myself. There was no sense in her paying rent downtown. She's putting every cent into the business."

I got up and prepared to leave.

" You'll have to excuse me for not seeing you to the door," said Julie. " We've got some problems on our hands. The girls at the factory are going on strike."

" You wouldn't believe the things these sewing girls demand nowadays," added Chris. " Saturday afternoons off and pay for overtime and summer vacations, and I don't know what else. It's getting so you can't run a business any more. You mark my words, the unions are ruining this town."

I shook hands with my old friends and left.

i i

It is a little difficult to decide at what point this memoir of Jim Horton and his friends should be brought to a close. Should one consider that a man's life ends when he dies and that everything that happens after that date is anticlimactic? Or should one, bearing in mind that some men never attain any real importance until after they are dead, continue to trace their influence as long as it is profitable, or entertaining, to do so, and regard their funeral and the reading of the will as subordinate episodes that belong somewhere about midway in the narrative?

Of one thing only we may be sure: that whatever choice the biographer makes he will have his troubles. For the truth is that a man who undertakes to tell the life story of another is attempting the manifestly impossible; the secret springs that influence human behavior are too obscure to reveal themselves clearly even to the persistent searcher. One can only exercise such judgment as one has and hope that the result will not be too far wide of the mark.

I am only too conscious that the picture of James Horton as I have presented it here is lamentably vague in its outlines. It is like a snapshot made by an amateur; your subject is there, but you do not see him plainly;

the details are blurred instead of distinct, the lights and shadows merge; he is a little out of focus. I am aware of the defect, but I can do nothing about it. The trouble is that Horton lacked those strong, individual qualities that biographers delight to single out as characteristic. There are faces so devoid of noteworthy features that they make no impression whatever; it is as though in them nature had struck an average so deadly that the result is as un-informative as a blank wall. Horton presents a somewhat similar phenomenon. He was neither a good man nor a rascal. He was hard-working and ambitious, but not more so than millions of other Americans of his day and ours. He was ruthless in money matters, and when he got an advantage over a competitor, he pressed it for all it was worth; but so did a very great many others. He quarreled with his wife. He took unto himself a mistress. He tolerated his children and provided for them liberally, without making any attempt to understand them. He liked money and power, and the more he got of both, the more he wanted. He was a typical product of his time and place, and if it had been possible to make him seem what he was not, an interesting or important or signifi-cant figure, I should not have hesitated to try to do so.

The importance of such men, it seems to me, lies not in themselves but in how they influence the lives of those about them. I have sometimes wondered what might have happened to Juliet and Clifford and Christine had Horton, let us say, remained to the end a struggling dealer in scrap iron and old metals. There is no question about Cliff. He would have worked his way through college, where he would have been active in such worthy organizations as the Students' Temperance Society, the Epworth League, and the Y.M.C.A. Later he might have gone into social work and, in a settlement house in some San Francisco slum, have devoted himself to complicating the lives of the uncomplaining poor; he might even have gone the whole hog and entered the ministry. In any case he would have lived his life in dignified poverty, and when he died no one would have had a word to say against him.

As for Juliet, I much fear that without her father's millions to sustain her she would have had a difficult time. Eccentricities, like butlers, are luxuries becoming only to the rich. The imperious manner, the bitter tongue, and the scornful disregard for what others might think of her, all these are picturesque qualities in a lady who has several million dollars at her command; but what if she had been poor? Is it not probable that we should then have regarded her merely as an embittered old maid and taken care to give her a wide berth? In such circumstances Julie might have become the vice-principal of a public school and spent her days striking terror to the hearts of young rebels sent to her for discipline. Or she might have ended as a clerk in one of the departments of our municipal government, facing the public from the authoritative side of a City Hall counter and sourly upholding the letter of the law. Again, I can picture her maintaining an office in a shabby downtown building, holding a notary-public commission and doing on the side a precarious and not too ethical business in real estate.

That Juliet might have joined this bleak sisterhood is

easy to imagine, but what of Chris? In her case one's guess is advanced with less confidence. Who can say with certainty how her life might have unfolded had she never come within the sphere of Jim Horton's influence? Hers was a temperament to which anything might have happened, or nothing. She might have married happily, borne and raised a family, and ended her days in a rocking-chair surrounded by her grandchildren. Or she might have been a very reprehensible woman indeed. Of the little group about Horton, she alone (it seems to me) was unpredictable. Unlike the others, she had no vein of iron in her character that predetermined what course she would follow. The influences that shaped her all came from without. She was ever at the mercy of her friends. What might have happened to her had she never met Horton? My guess is that in whatever role she may have been cast she would have played her part with good humor and a certain dignity, accepting as her right whatever good things were offered and bearing without complaint the blows of adversity, and all the while dispensing happiness and pain with an impartial and liberal hand. I have never pretended that I fully understood her, but I believe there may be something significant in this: She prospered moderately during her last years, while she and Julie were conducting their dress factory. When her will was opened (she died in the summer of 1918, during the height of the flu epidemic), it was found that her estate amounted to about twelve thousand dollars, all in cash and Liberty Bonds; she bequested the entire sum to the S.P.C.A.

There may have been something symbolical about that. Years ago, when she used to visit me at my room on

Montgomery Street, I once asked her what was the secret of her serenity.

She considered gravely for a moment, then she glanced at me and her face broke into a singularly frank and disarming smile.

"That's easy," she announced. "When I'm in doubt I always make it a rule to say yes. You'll never get any fun out of life if you're afraid to take a chance. What I say is, they don't hang people for trying."

The other morning my telephone rang and when I answered it I discovered that the voice was that of Dr. Casebolt.

"Hello," he shouted. "I'm sorry I had to call you so early. I didn't get you out of bed, did I?"

It was past nine o'clock. I assured him that I was up and about.

"Splendid! The early bird catches the worm. I've been up since six myself; I'm not permitted to loll in bed at all hours. The reason I'm calling is that the Literary Foundation is giving a banquet and I want you to be there. I got permission to invite a few friends, and of course I've put you at the top of the list. You won't be asked to make a speech; I'm taking care of the spellbinding chore myself. I just want you there to sustain me."

"I don't know," I hesitated. "I don't much like banquets. What's the occasion?"

"It hasn't been announced yet," said Casebolt, "but I'll let you in on the secret. The Foundation's presenting me with its medal for my biography of Jim Horton.

The jury reached a decision last night; they tell me it was unanimous."

" Congratulations," I said. " They couldn't have made a happier choice."

" Thanks, old man. I know you're sincere. It came as a complete surprise to me, but I won't pretend that I wasn't flattered. After all, there were more than two hundred books submitted, by all sorts of important people. When I reflect that my life of Horton went up against that kind of competition and won out, it makes me feel pretty humble. ' The most distinguished book of the year by a California author ' — that's the way the citation reads. You should see the buttons popping off my vest! "

" When does the shindig come off? "

" On the 24th. At the Fairmont, at seven. You'll be expected to wear a dinner coat. You'll come, won't you? "

" Of course," I said. " I'm always delighted to pay my respects to belles-lettres."

A thought occurred to me. " By the way, have you considered asking Aunt Julie? It would be pleasant to have her on hand when her father's book is honored."

There was a perceptible pause. " I've thought of that," said Casebolt finally. " Frankly, Walter, I've decided against it. Aunt Julie's a very entertaining person; I've always had a high regard for her. But I don't believe she'd feel at home in a crowd of that sort."

" No? "

" I'm sure she wouldn't," continued he. " For one thing, it's going to be a very literary gathering. There'll be some terrific highbrows on hand. I'm afraid she'd feel a bit beyond her depth, and I wouldn't embarrass the dear old lady for the world. After all, you know, I don't think she's got any real appreciation of literature."

I told him that perhaps he was right about that.